PRAISE FOR RACHEL VAN DYKEN

"*The Consequence of Loving Colton* is a must-read friends-to-lovers story that's as passionate and sexy as it is hilarious!"

—Melissa Foster, *New York Times* bestselling author

"Just when you think Van Dyken can't possibly get any better, she goes and delivers *The Consequence of Loving Colton*. Full of longing and breathless moments, this is what romance is about."

—Lauren Layne, *USA Today* bestselling author

"The tension between Milo and Colton made this story impossible to put down. Quick, sexy, witty—easily one of my favorite books from Rachel Van Dyken."

—R.S. Grey, *USA Today* bestselling author

"Hot, funny . . . will leave you wishing you could get marked by one of the immortals!"

—Molly McAdams, *New York Times* bestselling author, on *The Dark Ones*

"Laugh-out-loud fun. Rachel Van Dyken is on my auto-buy list."

—Jill Shalvis, *New York Times* bestselling author, on *The Wager*

"*The Dare* is a laugh-out-loud read that I could not put down. Brilliant. Just brilliant."

—Cathryn Fox, *New York Times* bestselling author

FRATERNIZE

ALSO BY #1 *NEW YORK TIMES* BESTSELLING AUTHOR
RACHEL VAN DYKEN

The Consequence Series

The Consequence of Loving Colton
The Consequence of Revenge
The Consequence of Seduction
The Consequence of Rejection

The Wingmen Inc. Series

The Matchmaker's Playbook
The Matchmaker's Replacement

Curious Liaisons Series

Cheater
Cheater's Regret

The Bet Series

The Bet
The Wager
The Dare

The Ruin Series

Ruin
Toxic

Fearless
Shame

The Eagle Elite Series

Elite
Elect
Enamor
Entice
Elicit
Bang Bang
Enforce
Ember
Elude
Empire

The Seaside Series

Tear
Pull
Shatter
Forever
Fall
Eternal
Strung
Capture

The Renwick House Series

The Ugly Duckling Debutante
The Seduction of Sebastian St. James
The Redemption of Lord Rawlings
An Unlikely Alliance
The Devil Duke Takes a Bride

The London Fairy Tale Series

Upon A Midnight Dream
Whispered Music
The Wolf's Pursuit
When Ash Falls

The Seasons of Paleo Series

Savage Winter
Feral Spring

The Wallflower Series (with Leah Sanders)

Waltzing with the Wallflower
Beguiling Bridget
Taming Wilde

The Dark Ones Saga

The Dark Ones
Untouchable Darkness

Stand-Alones

Hurt: A Collection (with Kristin Vayden and Elyse Faber)
Rip
Compromising Kessen
Every Girl Does It
The Parting Gift (with Leah Sanders)
Divine Uprising

FRATERNIZE

PLAYERS GAME

RACHEL
VAN DYKEN

SKYSCAPE

SKYSCAPE

Published by Skyscape, New York

www.apub.com

Amazon, the Amazon logo, and Skyscape are trademarks of Amazon.com, Inc., or its affiliates.

ISBN-13: 9781477809204
ISBN-10: 1477809201

Cover design by Shasti O'Leary Soudant

Cover photography by Regina Wamba of MaeIDesign.com

Printed in the United States of America

To all the women out there: own your awesome, hold your heads high, and remember how fearfully and wonderfully made YOU are. Grandma always said all you need is a bright lip and heels and you could take over the world. Well, what do you say? #runtheworld

Prologue

EMERSON

Bellevue High School—2007
Senior Year
The Big Game
6:30 p.m.

"Emerson!" Miller slammed his hands against the locker room door at least ten times before he stopped and then started again; this time it sounded like he was using his cleats. "I know you're in there!"

"Emerson!" Miller yelled again. "I will break down this door!"

"Just go away!"

"No!"

"You're a pain in my ass!"

"Well, you have a nice ass," he said, humor lacing his tone.

I smiled.

"You're smiling, aren't you?" he said in a silky voice.

I snorted and tried to wipe the hot tears from my cheeks.

"Don't fight it. You love me."

"I hate you." I was full-on grinning as I stood and shuffled over to unlock the door.

Miller shoved it open.

"You should be warming up with the team," I whispered. "Whatever will our school do without its hero?"

"You tell me. You're the one who's hiding out in the locker room because you let some skinny bitch get to you."

I sighed. "Maybe next time I'll give her a cookie."

As he towered over me, he held his helmet in one hand and placed his other against the doorframe. I'd been bigger than most girls my whole life. Miller was the only person capable of making me feel small. He reached out a massive hand and gripped my chin. "You'd be grumpy too if you referred to bread as Satan."

I forced a watery smile. "You're right. Sorry."

He dropped his hand. "Em . . ."

"Uh-oh, what's that look?" I teased, already feeling slightly better. How could I not when it was Miller Quinton?

The hottest thing to hit Bellevue High since . . . well, ever. With mocha-colored skin and clear blue eyes, he was almost impossible to not stare at without feeling uncomfortable. His Ethiopian mom was drop-dead gorgeous; mix that in with the Spanish heritage from his dad's side and you got model-good looks, giant muscles, and a killer smile that had the power to make even my crappy night look completely blissful.

"I'm your best friend, right?" He stepped closer, reaching for my hand before grasping it and pressing an open kiss to my palm. His lips were warm, his smile gentle.

"Why do I feel like you're about to give me the sex talk right now?"

"You loved that sex talk we had last year. I rocked your world with those pictures." He winked and I felt my cheeks get all hot and splotchy. "But seriously, Em. Have you ever thought that maybe you're perfect just the way you are?"

Air whooshed out of my lungs as tears threatened again. My uniform felt tight and itchy, and the really sick part was that Larissa, my nemesis, was right. Between last year and this year, my boobs had grown, and I'd turned into this curvy woman I didn't recognize. One who would never fit into a size six, or eight, or even a ten.

"Smile, Em."

"Yes, Miller." I forced a smile.

"I'm only friends with the cool kids, right? No losers on this roster." God, he was such an arrogant ass. "Which also means . . ." He grabbed me by the shoulders and turned me toward the field. "I can't win this game unless you cheer really loud for me, boo."

I groaned out loud. "Never say that again. Ever."

"Boo." He burst out laughing. "I think I just lost a brain cell."

"Not to mention all of my respect."

"Well, we had a good run." He gripped my hand in his as we walked back to where the game was about to start. "Cheer loud, cheer girl."

"Don't rip anyone's head off, ya dumb football player." I hugged him tight.

He jerked his head toward Coen. "Except his, right? Because I've been itching to rip his head off since day one."

I followed the direction of his gaze while Coen threw a long pass across the field. "He's your quarterback."

Miller clenched his jaw and pointed at the field with his helmet. "After this season's over, I'm kicking that punk's ass."

"And ruin your chances of going to college because his dad sues you for touching his precious?"

Miller made a face. "What do you see in him anyway?"

"Biceps. Nice mouth. Killer body—"

"Horrible personality . . . cheating tendencies?" Miller finished. "When are you going to finally admit you have feelings for me and throw caution to the wind, hmm?" His dimpled cheeks broke out into a huge smile as he tapped his face with one of his gloved fingers. "Alright, give me some. Platonic. Strictly for good luck."

I tugged his head down, ready to brush a kiss across his cheek, before he turned his mouth and crushed his lips against mine.

I sucked in a breath.

3

Breathing him in.

He broke off the kiss and shrugged. "Whoops." He winked over my head at what I was sure was my furious boyfriend.

"He hates it when you do that." I slapped a hand across Miller's chest.

"Perks of being your best friend. That mouth." He turned and started running away, while yelling back at me. "It's always been mine. I'm just waiting for you to leave the dark side."

Ignoring what he said like I always did, I called after him. "Have a good game."

"Go, Knights, go!" He pumped his fist into the air and then gave me one last cocky grin before pulling his helmet on.

I jolted awake at the sound of my alarm going off. Of course, the night before trying out for the Bellevue Bucks squad, and I dreamed of him. Tears welled in my eyes. I always dreamed of him when I was stressed, and all it did was add fuel to the fire, fanning the flames of my pain until I wanted to scream. I had enough to deal with—why did it always come back to him? He was impossible to escape, all I wanted was a breather. To feel normal. To move past it. To move past *him*. Instead, he was a constant reminder, a constant pain in my ass.

It was still dark out, so I checked my phone. Four more hours of sleep before I had to report to tryouts. I had four more hours to thrust all thoughts and memories of Miller Quinton out of my brain—my heart—expelling even the happiest memories right along with the agony of the bad ones.

He wasn't worth my time.

Or the space in my head and the tiny cracks still infused around my heart.

He may as well be dead . . . just like our friendship was the minute he promised he'd never make me cry—and then walked out of my life forever.

Chapter One

Present Day

Sleep didn't come.

But the memories did.

So while most girls were probably well rested and ready to make the squad, I was stuck with the Ghost of Christmas Past. I checked my reflection in the rearview mirror of my crappy car and willed away the dark circles under my eyes.

I had to make the squad.

I had to.

It was my last shot. Professional cheerleaders didn't get paid much of anything, and with as much time as I spent trying to become one, I was at a crossroads. I just didn't want to give up, I couldn't. My mom had been a professional cheerleader before she died, and I still had her picture under my pillow, the edges torn, the colors faded. Growing up without her had been painful. Not because I remembered much about her, I was too young when she was taken from us. No, it had been hard because my dad hadn't quite got why I was bullied. To him I was perfect. He never saw the flaws everyone else seemed to, and when I grew boobs and hips, and all the other lovely things that girls get when they grow up—he handed me a picture of my mom and said, "You look just like her, and she was perfect." It kept me going.

Until Miller.

God!

I slammed the steering wheel with my palm until my hand went numb. Why? Why did it always have to come back to Miller?

One more.

That's what I told myself.

One more memory surfaced.

And this time, as I pulled out of the apartment complex, I let it.

Because as much as it hurt to admit it, I'd rather have him in my thoughts, where he was safe from hurting me, than lose him forever.

(Then)

The locker room door shut behind the last cheer member, blanketing me in silence. Well, except for the noise coming from the other side of the room.

The walls were thin.

Very thin.

The guys were still shouting and banging hands against lockers.

I grinned and walked over to the door that led into the guys' locker room. A small hallway with two offices divided the space between the girls' and the guys' locker rooms. The athletic director's office was on one side and the football coaches' office on the other. If you wanted to sneak across, you had to get on your hands and knees and crawl.

So I wasn't at all surprised when I opened the door and looked down.

And Miller looked up.

"Fancy meeting you here." I knelt to his level and crossed my arms. "Escaping so soon?"

"You know how I feel about male shower time." His grin was back, but it was shaky. Yeah, I knew all too well how he felt about it.

Both of us had our issues.

I had my weight.

He had the color of his skin.

Stupid.

So damn stupid that tears threatened. Tears for him, not for me.

The white guys made fun of him for being too dark. And the black guys made fun of him for being too white.

He couldn't win.

After a long game, I knew he was exhausted and just wanted to shower and go home.

"Come on." I held out my hand and dragged him into the girls' locker room. "You can shower in here."

"With you?"

"You should be so lucky, Casanova."

"Break my heart, why don't you," he grumbled, placing a hand across his chest, and then grabbed his bag from the floor. He knew I'd let him in. He knew I'd say yes.

We were best friends.

Not that I'd ever admit it out loud since he'd probably want to test me on it—but I'd go to prison for the guy. Cheerfully.

I'd already suffered numerous school detentions in the name of friendship after joining in on several of his harmless pranks.

The principal called us Satan's duo.

I took it as a compliment.

I think Miller did too.

"So . . ." He plopped his bag down on one of the benches and dropped his shorts.

I quickly turned away and stretched my arms over my head.

"What's the plan?" he asked.

"Food. Drive. Maybe stop by the dance?"

"No! Just say no to dances, Em." A rustling sounded, and then the shower turned on. "Besides, last time Coen grabbed your ass."

"He's my boyfriend."

"Don't wanna talk about it," he snapped.

Which wasn't at all like Miller.

"He's cheating again." I figured if I said it like that, like a statement, it wouldn't hurt as bad, but pain still sliced through my gut before nausea made me want to toss up everything I'd eaten that day into the toilet.

Suddenly, huge arms wrapped around me, and I was getting pulled backward.

"No!" I shouted. "MILLLERRRR!"

"Oops, you're wet," he said after I was already underneath the showerhead with him, water pouring over my soon-to-be-mascara-streaked face.

"Why are we best friends again?"

He was quiet and then whispered, "Because I don't make you cry."

"Promise?" I swallowed the thickness in my throat. "Promise you'll never make me cry."

"Promise." He pushed me away a bit. "Now stop hogging the hot water."

Little did I know that his promise would be impossible to keep.

Or that we had precious little time left.

Chapter Two

EMERSON

(Then)

A Week Later

I held his hand as tight as I could.

It didn't take away the pain. Nothing would.

Pulmonary embolism.

His mother died instantly.

I watched my best friend fall apart that day, and I wasn't so sure I would ever have my Miller back.

The funeral sucked.

The pastor tried to make everyone feel better by talking about heaven. It was not what Miller needed to hear.

Because, besides me, his mom had been his best friend, his greatest cheerleader. His Navy dad was hardly home.

They were the dynamic duo, as Miller usually called them.

And now?

Now he just had me.

The shoes were too big to fill.

The task too daunting to even think about.

Encouraging words fell on deaf ears as both Miller and I placed a rose on the casket and walked out into the parking lot.

"Let's get drunk," he announced once we were back in his truck.

I nodded. "Alright."

His gaze sharpened in on me. "Seriously?"

Shrugging, I put on my sunglasses so he wouldn't see my puffy eyes. "I think if anyone deserves some underage drinking, it's you."

We didn't talk again until we were back at his house, in his room, surrounded by liquor he'd taken from his parents' stash.

"This is probably a bad idea," I said.

"Yeah," he agreed, before lying back next to me on his bed and staring up at the ceiling.

The fan whipped around in a comforting rhythm, while I clutched his hand like a lifeline, my own fingers slowly growing numb as he squeezed back.

After a few minutes, he finally spoke again. "I have something to tell you."

"Shit, are you pregnant?" I teased, trying to break the tension.

His laugh was soft and then gone. I hated it. The silence between us. There was usually so much teasing and laughter.

"Miller?" I leaned up on my side and looked down at him. "What is it?"

"Dad—" he choked out. "He was relocated . . ." He gulped. "Down South."

Horror washed over me. "But it's the middle of your senior year!"

"Yup."

"You like it here!"

"Yup."

"Your mom just died!" I was so pissed. So. Pissed.

"And the worst part . . ." Miller finally locked eyes with me. "I don't remember half the funeral—not because I miss her so much, but because I'm going to miss you. It's like I lost you too, and you aren't even gone."

"Miller . . ." I fought to keep my tears at bay, but they started streaming down my face all by themselves. "You have me. You will always have me."

"For now." He sighed. "And next week? When I start at a new school?"

"NEXT WEEK!" I roared, jumping to my feet and nearly kicking him in the junk.

"Damn, you're terrifying when you're angry." He finally smiled a real smile, one without pieces of sadness attached to it.

"Hell yes, I'm angry! He has no right. NO right." I fumed, punching the pillow, my hand dangerously close to taking out Miller's perfect face. "Why don't you just stay here? Live with me!"

"Was that a marriage proposal?"

"Come on, Miller. I wasn't even down on one knee. Don't be dramatic."

"Me? Dramatic?" He shook his head. "Never. You're the cheer-tator, remember?"

"I rue the day I let you watch Bring It On."

"'That's alright! That's okay! You're gonna pump our gas someday!'" He sang in a perfect bravado.

I rolled my eyes. Happy that at least he was acting like himself.

"Did you sleep with him?"

"Well, if that wasn't a complete subject change." I felt my cheeks burn red and suddenly lost the ability to swallow.

"Did you ever . . . sleep with him?" he repeated.

With a deep breath, I whispered out a quiet "No."

He bit back a curse before reaching for me and tugging my shirt over my head, his fingers working the front of my jeans before I could utter my next sentence.

"What are you doing?"

He kissed me long and hard and then whispered against my lips. "Being selfish."

"How?"

"I'm taking a part of you with me."

11

Chapter Three

MILLER

(Then)

Three Days Later
Houma, Louisiana

"I hope you wore a condom" was the first sentence my asshole dad muttered to me once I walked into the plain two-bedroom house on base, after the longest car ride of my life, during which he basically ignored me. I thought at least after the distraction of moving our shit, he'd acknowledge me. Not the case.

"Good to see you too," I grumbled, tossing my duffel bag onto the couch and sitting. I already missed her so much.

Em always said what was on her mind. She'd have given my dad an earful, and it wouldn't have been the first time either. Right after the funeral, she'd marched up to him and told him that he was ruining my life.

I think I fell a little more in love with her that day, if that was even possible.

"*Now listen here.*" *Dad's Southern drawl was thick and irritating as hell.*

I wondered if he'd been drinking. Seemed like he hadn't stopped since the funeral. And he was only too happy to relocate. Like Mom meant nothing to us. Like I meant nothing to him.

"*No son of mine's gonna knock up some white trash and drop out of high school! Not with all your talent!*"

"*Wow. Good talk, Dad.*" *I stood and walked out of the room before I did something stupid, like punch him in the face.*

I had no idea which bedroom was mine.

So, I guessed.

Must have been right, since the first doorway I walked through had my bed, a dresser, and some of my posters scattered around the floor.

I reached into my pocket and pulled out my cell.

I was going to give her shit if she didn't answer.

"*YES!*" *Em shouted into the phone, forcing me to pull it away from my ear.* "*I'm here! I'm here!*"

"*And drunk too, it seems,*" *I joked.*

"*Hah-hah, like I'd ever get wasted without you.*"

I rolled my eyes. "*You're such a good friend.*"

She was quiet.

Damn it. I could sense her sadness, and I hated that I was the cause of it almost as much as I hated my father for having legal custody of me.

If I were eighteen, I probably would have fought to stay in Washington.

Instead, I was in Louisiana.

Freaking Houma, Louisiana.

"*You start school tomorrow?*" *Her cheerful voice was back.*

"*Yup.*" *I looked up at the ceiling.* "*I have a meeting with the football coach too.*"

"*It's going to go great!*" *I could feel her false enthusiasm through the damn phone. She was wrong. Nothing would ever be great again.*

Not without my mom.

Not without my best friend.

And damn if it wasn't painfully true.

I had no idea that when I hung up the phone it would be the last real conversation we would ever have.

Then again, neither did she.

Like death, sometimes life just happens.

Chapter Four

EMERSON

Present Day

My lungs burned as I pumped my legs harder, faster. The tempo of the music was relentless, and my head pounded from the exertion.

"And five, six, seven, eight!" Coach called from the front. "Dip, step, clap, clap—Mary, I saw that. Keep your fingers pointed! And sway right, left—Mary! I said keep your fingers pointed! No sloppy hands!"

I gritted my teeth and finished the routine flawlessly.

Not that it ever mattered.

I'd finished routines flawlessly all throughout college, and even now, two years later.

And I'd still gotten cut.

It didn't mean I'd stopped trying; if anything, it had just pushed me harder. The worst part about trying out for professional cheerleading was the diet restrictions given to the girls, even the girls not yet on the squad. The team dietician often pulled me over and asked why I wasn't following the list of approved foods.

When I told her I was . . .

I'd been accused of lying.

And bless your little heart, her voice had crooned. *The Dallas Cowboys Cheerleaders aren't just America's squad—but the world's! We can't have someone who isn't diligent on the team, no matter how great your splits may be.* Or my personal favorite, *But chin up, you have a really pretty face.*

As if my face existed outside of the rest of my body.

A body I had grown to love.

Even though coaches everywhere saw it as defective.

It was my third time trying out for the Bucks.

I cringed to think what they would say this time.

I had the collegiate experience.

The voice.

The skills.

But I was lacking one thing.

The ability to squeeze my body into a size two, four, six, or eight. Who do we appreciate?

Food, damn it!

I refused to starve myself, especially after everything that had happened. I shuddered and shoved the memory far, far away.

"I promise," he whispered.

He lied.

"You'll be informed if you make the team!" Coach sounded from the front of the studio. "If you aren't contacted, it's safe to assume you haven't made it, though a formal letter will be sent to your residence with your judging sheets and critiques." She nodded. "Thank you, everyone. Good luck!"

I swigged the rest of the water out of my bottle and grabbed my bag.

"Hey, good job." Mary, the one who refused to point her fingers, smiled brightly at me. I remembered her from last year. Neither of us had made it then. She looked like a shell of her former self, like what happens when you diet the wrong way and forget that food is nutrition and necessary to live.

She let out a sigh that I knew too well, because I was just about to utter it.

It seemed history was about to repeat itself.

One of the girls who'd been on the team for the past four years shoved past us in tears, throwing all of her stuff into her bag before glaring at the rest of us and then stumbling toward the door. I frowned after her, then reached for my water bottle just as Mary shared a confused look with me.

"Emerson!" Coach yelled my name. "In my office now!"

"I think," Mary whispered from the side of her mouth, "your luck's just about to change."

Chapter Five

MILLER

"That hurts!" I roared, slamming my hands down on the therapist's table. "Are you trying to kill me? Maim me? Show me how strong you are? Damn it! Stop punishing me!"

Wendy's eyes were steel. Just like her hands. She didn't budge, but continued to roll out my IT band like she was trying to snap the thing in half.

"Breathe." She pushed harder.

I clenched my teeth and tried not to pass out. "I'm trying!"

"You're tense." Her soft voice was the reason I'd always loved working with her. She was four foot ten and ninety pounds of absolute terror.

The first time she offered to work on me, I'd laughed at her.

And left with a slight limp and four ibuprofen.

She claimed her family came from a long line of ninjas, and since she'd been working for the Pittsburgh Pilots, we all believed her. Even our quarterback gave her a wide berth.

"Almost done," Wendy soothed, patting my leg one more time before digging in with her elbow.

Sweat poured down my face as I closed my eyes and tried to go to that empty space in my head.

Only, whenever I closed my eyes . . . I still saw her.

No matter how hard I tried.

I saw curves.

Big blue eyes.

And honeysuckle blonde hair.

I inhaled that hair in my dreams. I let it slip through my fingers.

And then anger spread through my veins.

"Hey," Wendy snapped. "I said to relax!"

"Sorry." I swore and took a deep breath. "Are we almost done?" I didn't want to be around anyone.

Hell. I hated being around anyone when I thought of her.

I needed solitude.

Or maybe just a really great game.

Not that I wasn't known for those. I was the best tight end in the league.

It was my second year in the NFL, and I lived for it.

"Miller." Coach's voice stopped Wendy's torture.

She nodded at him and left the training room.

"We need to talk." His face was pale.

"Everything okay?" I asked.

"I fought it." He slammed his hands down on the table near my legs. "Just know I fought it, but Smith needs to find money, and after last year's loss in the playoffs . . ."

My eyes narrowed. "Smith needs to find money?"

"You're the best tight end in the league."

"Tell me something I don't know."

"You're expensive as hell to keep."

My head snapped in his direction. "Say what?"

"The Bellevue Bucks can afford you. We're trading across, three players for one." He balled both of his hands into fists and let out a violent curse. "You leave tomorrow."

"Coach!" I jumped off the table. "You can't do that!"

"I didn't do it!" He yelled right back at me. "You know we're still building this team. We just . . . we don't have the money. It's the only way to shape up our defense. Contracts have been negotiated. You'll get the rest of your eighteen million for the next three years and get to keep your signing bonus, but they'll take on the rest of your contract starting this season." His look was as sad as it was helpless, and after a few more pats on my back he was gone.

Silence descended as a hollow feeling spread across my chest.

He didn't understand.

Nobody did.

There was a reason I'd stayed on the East Coast.

A very damn good reason, and when the Bucks had tried to draft me out of college, I'd said, *Hell no,* and turned down their offer for twice as much money.

There was a freaking reason!

I kicked the massage table, knocking it onto its side, and threw a chair against the wall.

Chest heaving, I fell to the ground and let memories of her take over. The girl I loved.

The girl who destroyed me.

My best friend.

My enemy.

Because when I needed her the most . . . she'd abandoned me.

When I had nobody . . . she'd walked away.

Hate.

Didn't even begin to describe how I felt about her.

I loathed her.

Even though my body still responded to the memory of her, my mind knew she was trouble. My father had been right.

Which was worse than her abandonment.

I could still see his smug face once I told him that we weren't talking anymore.

"Yo." Devon rapped the door with his knuckles. "Just heard the news. Is Coach for real? Are you leaving?"

"Like I have a choice," I said from my spot on the floor.

"I'm going with you."

I burst out laughing. "They have a quarterback."

"Then I'll play for Seattle, at least we'll be close. Besides, what's Wilson got on me?"

"Oh, I don't know, two championship rings? A yacht? Pop star wife? Want me to keep going? No?"

"Well, at least you aren't crying like some chick."

"I don't cry—" I bit down on my lip. Not since her. What use was it? It didn't bring my mom back, and it didn't bring my best friend back. "Ever."

"Not even last season when Jones snapped his leg in half? Because, no lie, that was some scary shit."

"Watt needs to rein it in," I grumbled. "He's gonna kill someone someday."

"I think he wants to." Devon smirked. "Swear, that man wakes up with a smug-as-hell smile on his face and googles ways to kill men on the field."

"You're full of shit."

"Try not to get a bigger head in Bellevue. You'll always be a Pilot."

"Bleed black and yellow." I took his hand and stood. "Damn Bucks. At least send me somewhere I actually like."

He frowned. "You used to live in Bellevue, right?"

I tensed and locked down the memories.

"Something like that," I finally uttered. "Let's go get drunk."

"You don't drink unless there's a good reason."

"I just got traded to the Bucks, reason enough."

Devon crossed his arms across his bulky chest. "This 'bout getting traded?"

Hell no. This was about going back to the only place I'd ever called home.

"Yeah, it pisses me off." That was at least true.

"Yeah, okay." Devon slapped me on the back. "I could go for some drinks. Besides, you look like shit. Oh, and you're buying."

My smile was forced.

And as luck would have it, when we finally made it outside to the parking lot, a few of the Pilot cheerleaders sashayed past us.

One had blonde hair.

I did a double take.

And then mentally punched myself in the nuts.

She didn't exist.

Not anymore.

Maybe she never did.

Chapter Six

EMERSON

My perfectly rounded nails dug into my palms. I crossed my legs then uncrossed them at least a dozen times before the door opened. Coach Kay strutted in and sat behind a large black desk littered with pictures of athletes, friends, and folks who I assumed were family members.

Awards decorated her white walls.

I was really close to being sick to my stomach when she finally spoke. "You know why you've been asked here."

It wasn't a question. Was it?

I quickly nodded my head and spoke. "I believe you're looking for a new replacement."

"Yes."

Silence stretched between us while her eyes narrowed in on me and very slowly inched down my body. She started at my head until she stood up and leaned over the desk, her gaze never wavering as she inspected me all the way down to my pink-and-black Nike tennis shoes.

"Hmm."

It wasn't a good hmm. Not like *Hmm, that's cute* or *Hmm, that's different.* It was more of a hmm that meant it wouldn't work at all. I'd been on the wrong side of that hmm more than I could count.

Which probably meant she was either stuck with putting me on her roster . . .

Or she needed a towel girl.

My lips ached with the wide smile I kept perfectly pasted on my face. It was a practiced one, one that told her I couldn't be shaken, no matter how rude her perusal of my body had been.

I was awesome.

I just needed to convince her of that.

I refused to accept responsibility for being part of the problem. People tended to think there was something wrong with me, and I had spent a lifetime convincing them that I was just bigger than the other girls, and that it was okay. It was their issue, not mine. I was finally happy with me, and damn her for trying to shake that confidence away.

She could go to hell.

Along with everyone else who'd given me that exact same look and patted my hand as if to say, *But, chin up, you have a really pretty face.*

"It will be hard work," she finally said, leaning back in her chair as her long red fingernails tap-tap-tapped against each other. "Are you up for the challenge?"

"I believe you already know the answer to that question, ma'am."

Finally, she cracked a smile. "You'll need to be strong."

"I can bench over—"

She shook her head, interrupting me by slicing her hand through the air. "Not that kind of strength." A manicured fingernail moved to her temple. "This kind." Her hand lowered to her chest and pressed flat. "And this kind."

"I have those kinds," I said in a clear, confident voice, "in spades."

"Which is why . . ." She stood again and held out her hand. "I'd like to officially welcome you to the Bucks Squad. Practices are at five a.m. every morning and seven p.m. every evening until the first game." She handed me a packet. "Give them hell."

"Them?"

"See you tomorrow morning." She ignored me and sat, then looked up. "Please close the door behind you."

I had reached the door when she called out, "Oh, and Emerson, we have a very strict no-fraternization rule. Remember, the football players are off-limits, even the ones that are dumb as rocks. Got it?"

I snorted back a disbelieving laugh. "Yeah, that won't be a problem. Trust me."

Once I was a healthy distance down the hall, I allowed myself to celebrate by way of jumping into the air and giving a little shout. I made it all the way to my car and burst into tears as I leaned my arms against the driver's side window and full-on sobbed.

My dream.

It had been my only dream since my dad gave me that picture of my mom and told me I was beautiful.

It had been my dream since the only boy to ever tell me that I was pretty left me.

My dream since he took my heart with him.

And never looked back.

Since I was forced to pick up the pieces and glue them all back together.

Some days I still felt broken without Miller, but what do you do when the very person you want is the one who did the breaking in the first place?

"Didn't make the team, huh?" A gravelly voice interrupted my mini sob fest.

Slowly, I turned around and looked up, up, up, and finally met a pair of gorgeous, twinkling green eyes.

Yeah, you'd have to live in a cave not to know who the man was.

Grant Sanchez wasn't just one of the best receivers in the league, he was *the* best receiver in the league. I'd made it my job to know all the players, not because I loved studying football stats, but because they almost always made it a part of our test when we tried out for the team squads.

Lucky for me, I hadn't needed to study much. The Bellevue Bucks were celebrities in our town—and most of them were also notorious man whores with way too much money and privilege. And Grant Sanchez was quite literally—the worst.

"Actually . . ." I finally found my voice. "I made the team."

He held out his hand for a high five. Two of my hands could fit in his palm; it was almost comical. I slapped it and quickly pulled back, nervous that the coach would see me fraternizing, not that it would go anywhere. He was Grant Sanchez, for crying out loud. I might be confident, but I was very aware of my place on the totem pole, and it was midrange, while he only dated the top tier.

His full lips spread into a wide melting smile. "I'm shocked."

"Oh?" I tried not to sound defensive, but it was hard not to as I took a step back and crossed my arms.

He moved in closer to me, nearly pinning me against my own car. "Well, typically they only hire bitchy girls with fake smiles—even faker tits—and celery addictions. God, please tell me you hate celery."

"Celery tastes like water. Who actually likes it?" I countered, and received yet another offer for a high five. Noted. The guy was into high fives.

"I may have a little crush on you, cheer girl." He winked and pulled back then called over his shoulder. "See you around, Curves."

"Curves?"

"I'm big into nicknames, and yours . . ." He turned full around and shook his head. "Damn, they do you justice." He chuckled. "If I hear you celebrated with celery, we can't be friends anymore."

"We aren't friends now!" I called back.

"Yeah we are!" He kept walking.

"No, we aren't!"

He acted like he ignored me and disappeared into the stadium.

Chapter Seven

MILLER

I hated planes.

They reminded me of leaving.

Which in turn reminded me of being left behind.

I always envisioned myself as the one being abandoned. And any sort of travel always reminded me that I basically had been.

I pulled my bag of shit over my right shoulder and took in the expansive practice facility. It was nice.

Nicer than what I'd come from.

Probably because the Bucks bled money, and it showed, from the pristine practice facility to the stadium for games next door. They had lap pools, Jacuzzis, steam rooms, and ice baths. It was like a freaking spa in the locker room. I'd done a double take when I saw my new jersey, my hand trembling when I tugged at the black and white mesh.

For so many years it had been my dream to be a Buck.

Now?

It was a waking nightmare.

(Then)

"You think that was a tackle!" Em yelled. "Come on!" She jumped up to her feet and screamed until she was hoarse, while I sipped on our shared soda and watched with rapt fascination. "What?" She huffed and glared down at me. "Come on! Didn't you see that?"

"Nope." I chewed the end of the straw just because I knew it would piss her off. "I was too busy watching you."

Her cheeks pinkened as she snatched the cup from my hand and rolled her eyes. "If they keep tackling like they're afraid to break a nail, we aren't going to the playoffs this year."

"I love it when you talk football." I grinned up at her.

"You're mocking me."

"If I were mocking you, I'd be smiling."

"You are smiling!" she argued.

"So I am." I stood and joined her and the rest of the row. I had been literally one of the only people not standing and yelling. Then again, I knew the Bucks would pull through. They always did. "They'll win. They just need a field goal."

"I don't care about this game. What about the future! They can't play the Pats with that defense!" Em shoved the soda against my chest and huffed out a breath as pieces of her hair fell from her messy bun and against her face.

"Clearly, they just need to recruit me out of high school. All their problems will be solved."

"And mine," she whispered.

"What was that?" She had my full attention as she finally tore her eyes away from the game long enough to look up at me with a fear-filled gaze. "Em?"

"I don't want you to leave me. Ever."

"Good, because I'm not going to. You're stuck with me like a bad cold." I wrapped an arm around her.

"I hate colds."

"But you love me."

"If you're the cold, then, yes, I love you."

"Atta-girl." I kissed her temple. *"Stop being dramatic."* I paused. *"Aw shit, is it that time of the month again? Is this why we're emotional?"*

"We?"

"We, us—you."

Emerson slapped my chest. *"Stop asking questions you don't want answers to."*

"Does my girl need chocolate?"

"No." She said it too quickly.

"Em . . ."

"I'm totally fine."

"Whatever. I'm feeding you after this."

"I ate dinner!"

"You barely ate anything, and I saw you lusting after that chocolate chip cookie. Don't lie."

"I wasn't lusting!"

"No, but you were drooling."

"Just . . . let's just watch the game." She shivered against me.

I kissed her again and whispered, *"You know I'd do anything for you, right?"*

Her body softened against mine. *"Good. Then this is the plan. Get drafted by the Bucks and I'll cheer for you from the sidelines."*

"As a Bucks Girl," I added.

She blushed. *"Yeah, well . . ."* Her eyes dropped to the cheerleaders bouncing around and yelling. *"I highly doubt they'd let me cheer for them, but I'm going to work my ass off."*

"You're the most talented cheerleader I know."

"And you know so many cheerleaders?"

"I'm a football player. It's kind of my job, Em."

"Ew, gross!" She made a face. "All I'm saying is they're . . . different than me."

"Thank God for that." I cupped her face and forced her to look at me. "I'm glad that you like cookies, Em. I promise I'll play for the Bucks if you promise that one day you'll cheer for them. I can't win without you."

Tears filled her eyes. "I'm not . . . NFL material."

"They'd be lucky to have you," I said above the noise as my hands fell to her full hips. "All of you."

She gulped.

"All of you," I repeated.

"All of me." She sighed and then wrapped her arms around my body. "Thanks, Miller. You're a good friend."

More. I would always want more.

And it was only a matter of time before I took it.

I shook the memory from my head, suddenly in a fouler mood than I should have been, considering how much money I was getting paid. *Look, living the dream, folks.* Only nobody ever told me how much dreams cost.

Or how bad they sucked when you had no one to share them with.

A door to the locker room jerked open.

"Yo." Well, well, well, Grant Sanchez, live and in the flesh. Pretty sure my other dream had involved him suffering a very severe hand injury and being unable to catch anything for the remainder of the season last year.

And now we were on the same team.

FML.

"Miller." He grinned stupidly. "Admit it, you missed me."

"Stole the words right from my mouth." Bullshit. I wanted his head on a stake. How the hell was I supposed to be on his team? The guy was a complete asshole.

A talented one.

But whatever.

"Ah, I know that look." He shrugged his shoulders and kept approaching me.

Damn it.

"Wanna rip my head off?"

"Wow, you're good at this mind reading shit, aren't you?"

"Teammates, amigo." He held out his hand. "So let's put the past behind us, yeah? It's not your fault you were on a losing team with a shitty quarterback . . ." My fists clenched. "And an even shittier coaching staff."

I held out my hand and shook his. "And here I thought you were about ready to throw my welcome party."

"I did. In my head. There were balloons." He gripped my hand hard. "Seriously though, put last year behind you, man. I want another ring." He released my hand and crossed his arms. "Relax. You still look ready to kill someone, and I just got a deal with Armani, so I can't have a black eye ruining that, even if it is warranted."

I rolled my eyes. "I'm just leaving anyway. I wanted to check out the stadium before tomorrow's practice."

"Hah, and I bet the fact that the cheerleaders are practicing out there right now has nothing to do with it?"

"Absolutely nothing," I said in a dead voice.

"He lies." Sanchez was quickly becoming a pain in my ass. "Come on, young friend, let me teach you the ways of the Bucks."

"Did you happen to fail your drug test?"

Sanchez laughed. "Clean, my man. Let's go."

"Where?" He was already shoving me toward another door that led to a dark hallway. Great. If this was a Bucks hazing thing, I was in over my head, jetlagged, and pissed off enough to do some serious harm to my own teammates.

But nobody was on the other side of the hallway.

Just another locker room.

Another two doors.

Three more dark hallways.

And then, one last door that opened up to the top area of the practice facility.

And around twenty of my new teammates.

With binoculars.

And whiskey.

Yeah, I could get on board with this.

"Gentlemen . . ." Sanchez gripped my shoulders with both hands and slowly pushed me toward an empty seat. "Miller has arrived. Now, let's show him a good time and why we're one of the only teams in the league whose cheerleaders have their own bestselling calendar and award-winning documentary."

"God bless cheerleaders," someone piped up.

Sanchez and the rest of the guys mumbled an "Amen."

"No fraternization my ass." Another guy I recognized held up the binoculars and then nodded to Sanchez. "Almost time to make your pick. Remember, one pick, no stealing or trading."

"Stealing or trading what?" I asked.

The guys looked at me with knowing smirks before Sanchez moved around me to sit, patting the seat next to him. Most of the guys were rookies, and the other half were on the practice squad.

"We each—even me—pick a cheerleader during the preseason, pursue her until she gives in, which most of them never do because none of these guys have game, and make bets on how long it takes for her to . . ." He licked his lips and whispered. "B-E A-G-G-R-E-S-S-I-V-E." The idiot actually spelled it out while someone next to him threw his hands into the air like he was doing a cheer.

"We may not haze new players . . . but we still force the rookies to take us out to dinner and leave them with the check." Sanchez pointed out at the field. "We do have one requirement of all newbies, whether you're a rookie or you've been traded."

"Oh?" I wasn't liking the sound of this at all.

"Bang the cheerleader. Save the world," Sanchez said seriously. "Or just pick one to pursue for the season, and we'll see who wins this." He pulled a lame-looking trophy out of one of the duffel bags and tossed it in my direction.

"Player of the Year?" I read aloud. "You're just missing one tiny piece of valuable information. All teams have a no-fraternization policy." I tossed the trophy back at him.

Sanchez caught it then held up his hand. He reached into the same duffel bag and pulled out what looked like a rule book. "It states here that during any NFL season the cheerleaders are not allowed to hang out, date, or enter into a sexual relationship with any of the players. During the off-season, they must use discretion."

"Right." I finally sat down while one of the guys next to me handed me binoculars like I was actually going to go through with their immature plan. Who did that? I was young. Not stupid. "Preseason starts in two weeks."

"Still the off-season . . ." Sanchez shrugged. "Not that it matters. Coach turns a blind eye as long as we win. Come on, have a little fun. It's harmless. Besides, they love the attention. You think they don't know we're up here? Trust me. They know."

"How?"

Sanchez grinned. "Because we tell them. Because they're willing participants. Because we've been doing this for years. It's a Bucks tradition. Wipe that judgmental look from your face, man. The girls love it. Trust me, they get plenty of attention because of it." His smile faded, he gave his head a little jerk. "Those girls down there want one thing from us and one thing only."

"Your tiny dick?" I offered. "Are all Bucks assholes or just you?"

Sanchez threw back his head and laughed. "Yeah we're going to get along just fine. Man, do you really think that any of those girls give a shit about getting married, having kids, buying a dog?" He rolled his eyes. "Hell no, they want attention, and we give it to them, and in response, if they put out, it's a win-win-win, wait how many wins?"

"How do you even know who wins?" I asked.

"Last man standing." Sanchez shrugged. "Last year it was Thomas, he dated one of the girls for a solid year."

A few guys chuckled, one piped up. "Hey, Sanchez, didn't you propose to one of the girls? Oh my bad, that was someone else."

Chuckling followed.

Sanchez didn't join in.

My eyebrows shot up. Grant Sanchez? Down on one knee?

His entire demeanor tensed. "So what do you say, Miller?"

"Pass." I shrugged.

"Miller . . ." Sanchez sneered. "Are you a virgin? Is that what this is about, man? Because if you need to get laid, I can hook you up." Why the hell did it matter so much to him?

"I'd rather not get herpes. Besides, I doubt you could please me, man."

The guys all burst out laughing while he flipped me off with a grin. "Not me, you asshole."

I gritted my teeth and stood. "I'll try not to kick your ass at practice tomorrow. Have fun acting your age, Sanchez."

"Your loss, man." He was already looking back at the field. "They just hired a new one who's actually nice."

"And the rest?"

"Most of them are more interested in their Instagram accounts," another guy said.

"Well, you're welcome to her. I don't date during the season." Or at all, but they didn't need to know that.

"Holy shit, is that her?"

I was ready to leave when a prickling sensation washed over me.

"Hot."

"Big."

"Her tits are huge."

"Those thighs."

"She has a nice smile though."

"Curves for days."

"She should diet."

"She's three times the size of the captain."

"The captain is an evil bitch who likes celery," Sanchez snapped. "Besides, I talked with her earlier. Dibs."

"The captain?"

"No. Curves." Sanchez's voice changed. "She's . . . different." Sanchez seemed to be in some weird trance I wanted no part of, while he watched the girl with an intensity I'd only ever seen from guys on the field.

I glanced over my shoulder. He was staring at the girl. I couldn't see her without binoculars. But it didn't matter. I was done with cheerleaders.

All of them were evil.

Chapter Eight

EMERSON

The cheerleading manual had been brutally . . . honest about what they expected.

They didn't come out and ask the members of the squad to diet, but it was strongly suggested they stay away from anything that could potentially attach itself to the thighs by way of fat.

No sugar. No soda. No fruit! How was fruit bad? What had fruit ever done to a human other than hydrate? By the time I'd finished the first two pages, I was ready to be sick.

Surprise weigh-ins throughout the season?

What was this, Weight Watchers? Hell? Both?

Coach Kay had said nothing about any of this, which meant only one thing. She was either setting me up to fail, or she thought I could handle it.

All talking ceased the minute I walked out onto the field to practice with the other girls.

When I dropped my bag to the ground and started stretching, a few girls eyed me, the bag, and then me again, and started whispering.

One brave one marched over and sat down. "Hey."

"Hey." I swallowed my nervousness and leaned across my right leg. "I'm Emerson."

"Coach and I both made bets about whether you'd show up."

"Oh?"

"Yeah, looks like she won, not that it matters. We need fresh blood anyway."

Her dark hair was pulled back into a tight braid; her makeup looked fresh, and her bright red lipstick stood out against her pale skin like a homing beacon. I had trouble looking away because it was such a stark contrast. The woman was wearing a white crop top and spandex. Shiny diamond earrings caught the light just right, nearly blinding me before she grinned again.

"I'm Kinsey."

"Nice to meet you." Suddenly feeling self-conscious, I started fishing around in my bag for at least some lip gloss. Clearly I hadn't gotten to that part of the manual yet.

The one that said all girls needed to have full makeup for each and every practice.

"You'll love being a Bucks Girl." Kinsey mimicked my stretch. "We get free tanning, free massages, free makeup—" She frowned at me and then cleared her throat. "Not to sound like a bitch, but you should at least get your eyelashes done if you're going to show up with a clean face."

"Oh." I touched my cheeks. They were hot with embarrassment. "I didn't know. I'll make sure to do my makeup tomorrow."

She let out a breath. "Good, that's good. I just . . ." She chewed her lower lip and whispered. "It's going to be hard enough for you as it is . . ."

My heart sank as I tried to suck in my stomach, but it was no use. I was just a bigger girl—bigger than them. I could fit two of those girls in my pants, no joke.

"Because you're so pretty," she finished.

My head jerked to attention. Huh? What did I miss?

Her smile was still in place, and I didn't think it was fake. "You thought I was going to say something else, didn't you?"

I nodded, not trusting my voice. My eyes still searched for any hint of evil bitchiness, only to come up empty. Her smile seemed genuine.

She rolled her eyes. "With an ass like that, I'm surprised Sanchez hasn't already staked a claim."

At the sound of his name, my cheeks burned.

I didn't move.

I was completely terrified I'd give myself away.

Her smile grew. "Ah, so the best receiver in the league has staked a claim?"

"No." I shook my head and then rolled my eyes. "Not precisely." I switched positions and moved to the runners' stretch. She followed. "I was in the parking lot crying—celebrating, actually—and he started talking to me. It was nothing."

Except for the fact that he had one of the sexiest smirks I'd ever seen. But it was a knowing smirk—one that told women just how aware he was of his own sexuality—and that smirk led down a dark and dangerous road I wanted no part of.

Her perfectly matched brown eyebrows bolted upright. "Um, Sanchez doesn't talk just to hear his own voice, trust me. There are girls here he still hasn't even acknowledged, which isn't too hard for him since he's so freaking tall." Her laugh was loud. "Last year, he asked Molly to move out of his way, and she was so stunned that he finally talked to her that she froze. The man had to physically lift her out of the way. I'm pretty sure she suffered a mild stroke."

I frowned and glanced around the field. "Which one's Molly?"

"Oh . . ." She waved me off. "Molly's gone. She slept with one of the players during the season, and he ratted her out because he thought she was cheating on him. The coaching staff found out and fired her ass."

"Whoa." I sucked in a breath. "They mean business about that no-fraternization policy." Not that it mattered since, in my opinion, all football players could burn in hell.

"Eh . . ." Kinsey shrugged and moved to stretch her left leg. "It's a confusing rule. Management turns a blind eye if the guys win games. If not, and they find out, we're the only ones to go, while the players just get more money tossed at them by way of bonuses."

"Isn't that illegal?"

She laughed. "No, honey. It's football."

A loud whistle rang out. Adrenaline surged through me as I quickly stood and waited for Coach's orders. This was it. I was a Bucks Girl.

The excitement was quickly beaten down by the sadness that I refused to acknowledge on a daily basis—sadness and anger that only part of the dream was being realized. Miller Quinton could go to hell. God, I swore I wouldn't utter his name, even in my head, and there I was, standing in the Bucks stadium, thinking about his gorgeous eyes . . . the taste of his mouth . . .

It was hard enough studying football stats without my eyes lingering over his name, his stats, his freakishly amazing ability to intercept every pass that came down the field, threatening his team.

"We'll start with the new routine." Coach Kay's eyes moved across all of the girls and landed on me.

Get it together, Em!

"Emerson, you've got your work cut out for you. The rest of the girls have already been working on it."

"Great." I forced a smile and stood.

Judgmental eyes were all on me.

I felt every stare.

And could have sworn I heard every single thought sent my way.

Too big.

Too fat.

Huge hips.

Her ass.

How did she get on the squad?

I held my head high and let them look their fill.

Whispers grew louder until I finally had to clench my hands into tight fists to keep from throwing punches.

"I'll help her, Coach," Kinsey piped up and then glared at the rest of her teammates before taking a protective step toward me.

Did she just hiss?

Coach Kay smiled at her and then blew her whistle. "Ten laps around the stadium. When you're finished, we'll get started on the routine. Slowest person has to do a hundred burpees before joining the routine."

Everyone took off in a flutter of Nike shoes, pink sports bras, and spandex. I followed close behind a few of the girls, with Kinsey by my side. If there was anything I knew about running, it was never to sprint out of the gate. By the time we were on lap ten, I was ahead of most of the girls and just finding my stride.

I ended right behind Kinsey and felt a surge of pride as one of the skinniest girls on the team heaved out a cough, stumbled to her knees, and started doing burpees.

For being last.

It just went to show that just because I looked bigger didn't mean that I didn't know how to use my legs and brain, even a lot of times at the same time. Imagine that!

"Well done, Emerson." Kinsey raised her hand for a high five. "But I guarantee you'll be last tomorrow if you don't ice after tonight's practice. We have a half hour of grueling conditioning after the dance routine, and last year they lined the field with buckets."

"Buckets?" I repeated. "For the ice?"

Kinsey grinned wide. "Nope. That would be for the puke. Can't be getting the perfect Bucks field all gross with vomit, now can we?"

I groaned. "Great."

"It's worth it." She pointed to the empty seats. "Trust me. Our training is like nothing I've ever experienced. You'll see, and then you'll be thankful that they put you through hell."

"Why are you being so nice to me?"

"Easy." She shrugged. "You own your pretty, and you're probably the only girl on this squad who'd go with me to get a beer, and drinking alone is frowned upon. It's in the manual."

"Is everything in the manual?"

She rolled her eyes just as another whistle sounded. "Don't even get me started."

Chapter Nine

EMERSON

"Are you sure this is okay?" I glanced around the empty locker room and shivered. My body ached in all the wrong places, places I didn't even know existed. Practice had ended a half hour ago, and even though I'd rolled out my muscles and nearly cried from the impact of the foam roller, I still hurt.

"Sure." Kinsey shrugged. "I use it all the time. Just make sure to lock up when you're done. It's one of the perks of being a Bucks Girl." She dumped the last bag of ice in the tub and pointed. "Ten minutes, no complaining. No tears. Buck up, Bucks Girl."

I shivered. "I hate ice baths."

"Everyone hates ice baths, psycho." She patted me on the back and then gave me a friendly shove toward the tin tub. "Keep your sports bra and underwear on just in case one of the night janitors walks by or, you know, a player."

I glared. "A football player?"

"No worries. It's preseason, and practice is at the ass-crack of dawn tomorrow. It's too late for them to be out, the big babies."

"Okay." I sighed, buying myself more time before Kinsey crossed her arms and waited. "You're not leaving until I'm in the tub, huh?"

"I'm not leaving until your ass is in that tub."

"I take back what I said about you being nice."

Laughter burst out of her. "I don't give a rat's ass. Now get in the tub, Em."

With jerky movements, I pulled my tank over my head, tossed it on the floor, and jerked down my black leggings.

"Get in." Kinsey pointed.

"I am!" I snapped. "I just . . . was thinking."

"You were stalling."

"You're a bitch."

"Name calling? Really?"

I gripped the sides of the tub and slowly lowered my sore body. A rush of cold stole the breath from my lungs as tiny needles started jamming into my skin.

"S-so cold." I hated Kinsey. "I hate you, I hate you."

Her answer was to shrug then grab a red kitchen timer and crank it up to ten. "Alright, see you tomorrow morning, friend!"

"I have no friends!!" I yelled back at her. I heard her laugh as the locker room door closed.

Teeth chattering, I tried to think of something to distract myself with while I was blanketed by chilly silence and an insane amount of pain. But the agony was intense, and my muscles seized with every breath I tried to suck in.

The locker room door opened again.

"We still aren't friends!" I yelled as my body convulsed beneath the icy water.

"Well, that's disappointing," came a dark, sexy voice. "I could have sworn we made a pact of sorts this morning."

I glanced up through frozen eyelashes to see Sanchez towering over my icy hell with a grin on his smug face.

"Why are you here?"

"Forgot my cell." He grinned wider. "How was the first day, Curves?"

"Frigid," I answered in a bored tone.

"Doubtful." He dipped a finger in the water, flicked some in my face, then gripped either side of the tub. His large body loomed over me, casting a near shadow in the dark. "Even the word sounds awkward coming from your mouth."

"You're in my space."

"I'm big. I'm in everyone's space."

"You're not making the next few minutes easy. I can't exactly escape. Is this how you trap all your friends?"

"Only the ones I really like." He winked, leaned back and pulled out a chair, then propped his feet up on the rim of the tub. "Tell me you're naked under all that ice."

"Sorry to disappoint." My teeth chattered again as I rested my head back and cursed. "How many more minutes?"

Sanchez whistled, his green eyes flashing to the timer. "Four."

"It's only been six minutes!" I didn't mean to yell.

He burst out laughing. "Let me help you take your mind off things."

"No."

"Yes."

"Sanchez!"

"Wow, you screamed my name, and it's only our first date."

"We aren't dating!" I was yelling at the best receiver in the league, a gorgeous celebrity. He was talking about distracting me, and I was yelling. Maybe because my heart didn't flop.

It didn't flip.

Nothing moved.

No butterflies.

Just awareness that he was hot.

And I was freezing my ass off.

"Three minutes." He knelt by my head. His hands cupped either side of my face like he was inspecting me. "What do you say, Curves?"

"To what?" My icy tomb was starting to numb my brain because I seriously had no idea what he was talking about.

"To warming you up a bit," he said before silencing my protests with a searing kiss that did wonders for my current state of terror.

I kissed him back.

Because his kiss was the type you had no choice but to respond to, it didn't ask permission, it made you curious, and it promised to give you answers if you kissed back.

So I did.

Our tongues met with a frenzy of heat that I was seriously not prepared for, and when his hand slid behind my neck, pulling me closer, I went with it.

Because it had been six years since I'd been kissed like that.

Almost that long since I'd let myself feel.

And I realized it felt good, so good to be wanted, even if it was by a stupid playboy football player who probably had enough notches in his bedpost to make it look like Swiss cheese.

He pulled away; his lips slid down my freezing neck, and then his mouth was back on mine.

The timer went off.

I tried to move.

He wouldn't let me.

"Warm?" He tilted his head, his smirk gone, replaced with something I would probably question later while trying to find sleep.

"Hot." I swallowed the nervousness I suddenly felt in his arms.

His green eyes fell to my mouth one more time like he wanted to kiss me again, and then he did something that I could only assume was completely out of character. He stood up, grabbed a towel and handed it to me, then turned around.

"Thank you." I shivered one last time, my entire body numb as I shakily got out of the tub and wrapped the towel around myself.

Was he secretly a gentleman? Or perhaps . . . just that insanely smart that he knew the only way to get in a girl's pants was to play the nice guy and then pounce?

"I can hear you thinking from over here, Curves."

"Sorry." I was gaping at him. I gave my head a little shake, then quickly stripped out of my wet clothes and pulled on my sweatshirt and sweats I always kept in my duffel bag. "Okay, I'm . . . uh, no longer naked."

"Fuck." He hung his head and then glanced over his shoulder. "You lied about being naked?"

"Gotcha."

He swallowed, his eyes slowly glazed over as he looked his fill. "Damn shame."

"Excuse me?"

"That you have to wear clothes." He winked. "You ready to go?"

"Sure." I grabbed my bag while he walked over to one of the separate rooms and returned holding his phone in his hand.

The late summer air warmed me just as much as his kiss. We walked side by side, silent, into the parking lot.

"You need a ride?" he asked.

I glanced at my junky Honda and shrugged. "Nah, she'll make it."

"You sure?" He pointed. "Shocker she hasn't been stolen."

"Very funny."

He shoved his hands in his pockets. "I have to be at practice early tomorrow to go over some stuff with our new teammate. I'll drop you off, then pick you up in the morning. How's that sound?"

"It sounds"—I unlocked my door and got in—"like you're trying to find out where I live."

He braced himself between the small space of the car door and the rest of the car. "It's more of a professional interest in making sure our new cheerleader makes it home safely."

"Yeah, I call bullshit."

He grinned. "Total bullshit. I really just want to fuck you."

"Well . . ." I tried not to look too offended. "At least you're honest."

"It usually works better than flowers."

"I'm not really a flowers kinda girl."

"Somehow, that makes sense." He exhaled and then ran a hand through his hair. "I'm kind of . . . not used to getting rejected."

"Take an ibuprofen and have a nice glass of wine tonight, Sanchez. Things will look so much better in the morning after a good night's sleep."

"Sarcastic little shit." His grin widened. "Tell me it wouldn't be good between us."

I couldn't. I knew it. He knew it. Because it would probably be explosive and then based on his track record I'd end up punching him for some asinine comment, and he'd apologize and round two would only get better. Only to end.

But I didn't want better.

I tried to choke back the tears.

"Whoa, whoa." He knelt to my level. "Curves, what the hell? Where did that expression come from? Because it sure as hell wasn't from me."

"Nothing." I shook my head. "Seriously. Nothing."

"I'm not leaving until you tell me why you lost your smile."

"Wow." I gripped my steering wheel and shook my head. "You know, if you used your powers for good, you might actually find yourself in a stable relationship, with kids, a dog, maybe even a parrot. Dream big, Sanchez."

"I do like birds." He didn't take his eyes from mine. "Now, what has my curvy, one-night stand so sad?"

"We aren't sleeping together."

"Who sleeps? I meant sex. I'm sorry. Was that confusing?"

"Sanchez."

"God, I love it when you say my name." His sexy grin fell. "So really, what's wrong?"

"Nothing. I'm fine."

He gripped the door. "I have all night."

He wasn't going to go away. He was like a really hot case of the flu or a lingering cough. The point? I needed sleep, and I was already losing the battle of wits with the guy. Honestly, he was exhausting, and I was semi-pissed at myself that I couldn't be that girl, the girl that just jumped into his waiting arms and agreed to a no-strings-attached good time.

"I love football. I hate the players. Let's just say I had a really, really, really bad experience."

"Clearly, since you said three *reallys*."

"Really bad."

"That was four."

"May I leave now?"

"Yup." He tilted my chin toward him. "You know we could have fun . . . forget all the drama."

"You are the drama." I shoved him away with a laugh. "Go fraternize with another cheerleader. This one's on lockdown."

"We'll see." He shut my door and waved me off.

Thank God, my car started.

Because I wasn't sure I had the willpower to say no to his easy smile again. The fun banter in the parking lot of the Bucks' stadium reminded me so much of Miller that it made my stomach hurt—that and my heart; the stupid muscle kept jolting at the thought.

Miller and I could have had that.

And sadly, a part of me still wanted it.

I wanted Miller.

Not Sanchez.

I wished attraction to a football player was easier.

But it wasn't.

I pulled into my apartment complex and rested my head against the steering wheel, then slowly made my way up the three flights of stairs. Home.

"Hi, Dad!" I tried to keep the happy in my voice.

"Baby." His tired eyes drank me in. "How was practice?"

"Good." I swallowed the thick tears in my throat.

I hadn't been lying about not having friends. Between working my ass off to make the squad and helping take care of Dad, I was exhausted most days. Luckily my job allowed me to work from home.

Home.

The apartment was small. More of just a roof over our heads, since all of our money went toward medical bills, medicine, and his home care.

"Great. You always were such a wonderful student." His empty eyes blinked before he started to break down. "I can't believe you're graduating in a few weeks!"

"Yeah." I looked past him to Connie, the live-in nurse. She had her dark hair pulled into a low ponytail, her black-rimmed glasses sliding down to the middle of her nose as she put her hands on her narrow hips. "Me either."

"It was a good day," she said, her kind eyes always a welcome sight. "How was yours?"

She'd been in our lives for two years. It allowed me the reprieve I needed, especially when he had hard days. It was devastating to see someone crumble, a bright mind just . . . gone.

"Emerson? Your day?" She repeated.

"Um, very uneventful." Except for a scorching kiss from one of the most famous NFL players in the world and a lingering suspicion that, had I said yes, my night would have ended with multiple smiles rather than the choking sadness and emptiness I felt in my own home. "I should go to bed."

Chapter Ten

MILLER

Sanchez was waiting for me in the parking lot with the dopiest smile I had ever seen on any human's face.

"Why do you always look like you're high?" I asked, once I got out of my Mercedes and grabbed my duffel from the trunk.

"High on life, my man." He shrugged, the grin back full force. "I just had a good night. Can't a man smile about a good night?"

"I don't want to know." His reputation was legendary. It wouldn't surprise me at all if the little shit took home four cheerleaders last night and let them take turns doing cartwheels on his dick.

"I wouldn't tell you anyway." He grabbed his bag and walked with me toward the practice facility. "You ever been in a relationship?"

I stopped walking.

"Miller?"

"We're not friends."

"Why the fuck do people keep rejecting my friendship? First Curves and now you. Damn, it's like some sick joke."

"Curves?"

"Hottest cheerleader ever. Rejected me. Twice. But I did get in a nice kiss. Then again, she was trapped. Never mind."

"You trapped a cheerleader and forced yourself on her?"

Sanchez gave me a pissed-off look. "Do I look like the kind of guy who has to force anything?"

"Chill." I held up my hands. "I spent the last two years of my life hating you. Cut me some slack, teammate."

"Everyone hates me." He grinned. "I take it as a compliment. If you liked me, it would probably be because I wasn't as dirty as I am on the field. We only hate the good players. We like the shitty ones. It's how football works."

"Except for Russell."

He nodded. "Damn Wilson. Unicorn, that's what that dude is."

I reached for the door, but Sanchez slammed his hand against it, keeping it shut. "Really, man?"

"Listen . . ." He looked uncomfortable, his green eyes darting everywhere before finally settling on me. "I don't want trouble. I want another ring. They're good guys, all of them. So the minute you walk in, I need to know you're in, that you're not still pissed about getting traded. It's a big-ass compliment, alright? So leave the baggage at the door. Losing isn't an option."

I had to respect him for being protective of his team. And I knew that had some punk been traded to my old team, I would have given him the same talk.

"Losing sucks ass," I countered, holding out my hand in a peace offering. "And I'm in. I swear."

He studied me for a few minutes before finally clasping my hand, then nodding his head and opening the door. "Then welcome to the Bucks, officially."

I grinned. "So, last night, not so official?"

"Last night was . . ." His face did that shit-eating-grin-thing again. "Interesting."

"No details." I held out my hands.

Laughter and shouting greeted me as I made my way into the large locker room; the damn thing looked like it belonged in a spa magazine, with its huge tubs, tiled showers, and steam rooms. I wasn't sure I would ever get used to it.

"Miller Quinton." Sanchez said my name with authority. "Best tight end in the league. With over a thousand yards, and six touchdowns last year, we're lucky to have him on our team." My new teammates nodded in my direction; a few of the looks were stern, but for the most part, my reputation preceded itself; thus, the eighteen-million-dollar addition to my contract that my old team still had to cough up. "Now that the introductions have been made . . ." He paused. "Let's go win that championship."

Cheers erupted.

Adrenaline spiked through my system as I joined the rest of the guys in a huddle.

"Bucks, Bucks, Bucks!" I'd only ever seen their team cheer as an opponent, but now I was a part of it, a part of the team that six years ago I would have sold my soul to be a part of.

"Who are we?" Sanchez yelled.

"Bucks!" I joined in, feeling oddly at home with my new team.

"What do we do?"

"Buck them up!" we shouted.

"What say you?" Sanchez roared.

"Buck you!"

Sanchez and I locked eyes at the end, and I knew I wasn't just looking at a future teammate; I was looking at a brother, a soldier, a possible friend.

We'd war together.

And we sure as hell were going to win a championship. I could feel it in my bones.

"Let's do some work." I nodded to him.

"You heard the man." Sanchez returned my intense stare. "Let's kick some ass."

Practice was a blur.

A blur of searing pain.

Mixed with running drills.

And another heavy dose of pain as Thomas, one of the defensive ends, decided it would be a good idea to nearly remove my head from my body.

I spit out blood and wiped my face. "Again."

Sanchez burst out laughing. "You heard the man!"

Jax, our quarterback, the quietest football player I'd ever met, threw a spiral. I ran my route, doubled back, and caught the ball for the touchdown.

"Hot damn!" Sanchez roared. "I can already see that ring. I need to buy a new case."

"A ring case?" I teased. "Really?"

"I like nice things." He flipped me off.

My old team had been my only friends. But with a lingering glance at the practice field, the sweat, dirt, and constant shouting, I knew I was finally home.

I was just missing the most important part of the dream.

The girl.

"Whoa." Sanchez punched me in the arm. "Wipe that sadness off your face and turn it into anger. We still got two hours left of practice."

"Anger . . ." I nodded. "I can do."

Jax threw several more passes in my direction; I caught all of them. It was important to be on point with your QB and, although he was deathly quiet, there was a strength about him that commanded not only respect but also your full attention.

When practice finally ended, I was more exhausted than I'd been during the last few years of football put together.

And that, folks, is why the Bucks are the best.

Because they nearly killed their players during practice and played like they never lost a game in their lives.

"Good job, man." Jax tossed his helmet and held out his gloved hand. His hair was cropped short to his head, jaw clenched, and brown eyes were locked onto mine. He looked like he belonged on the cover of *GQ* more than he did on the football field.

"Uh . . ." I shook his hand. "Thanks."

"God, you're pretty, Jax." Sanchez came up behind me and fluttered his eyelashes.

"Hey, pain in my ass . . ." Jax was clearly talking to Sanchez as he released my hand. "Try catching the ball next time."

Sanchez pointed to himself. "Best receiver in the league." He pointed to Jax. "Second best QB. Sorry, man. Can't win them all."

"Bite me."

"It's good you guys get along so well," I interrupted. "Solid."

Jax smirked. "It's more like I put up with his shit so we win."

"We win because he puts up with my shit, and I catch his balls." Sanchez shrugged. "And I mean the leather ones, not the tiny things you swear up and down that you actually have, even though none of us has ever seen you with any chick other than your mom."

Jax narrowed him with a glare. "She makes good soup, so drop it."

I burst out laughing.

"She does make good soup," Sanchez agreed.

"Jax's mom's making soup again?" Thomas asked. "The taco kind?"

Jax cursed and then yelled, "My mom's not making soup!"

Thomas threw his helmet down. "Damn it. I love that woman's taco—"

"Thomas . . ." Jax threatened. "Leave it. Don't pounce on the taco comment. I'd hate to punch you in the face."

"You always need to worry about the quiet ones, Miller . . ." Sanchez slapped me on the back. "Always."

"Ouch." I winced and then followed the rest of the guys off the field and down the hall, only to wonder why the hell whistles and catcalls were permeating the air.

And then I saw a flash of black and white.

Cheerleaders.

My lip curled with disgust.

Evil, all of them.

Several eyed me up and down as they shimmied by; a few tried to touch me, and I jerked back as if they were diseased.

Sanchez moved to stand in front of me.

"Dude," I groaned. "I'm tired, sweaty, and sore. Stop blocking the way so I can get a shower."

"I'm busy," he called over his shoulder.

"Staring at the wall?" I shoved him away and stopped, paralyzed. Unable to breathe.

Emerson.

She was busy pulling her hair into a ponytail. Hell, how many times had I pulled that long blonde hair? Visions of us in bed, of her laughter, of me chasing her so damn hard I swore up and down it was impossible to catch my breath.

She was all curves.

Ass.

Hips.

Muscle.

Perfection.

Irrational anger surged through me. My body shouldn't still respond to the way her dimples lit up the room or her light-blue eyes that always seemed to look right through my shit.

"Curves!" Sanchez yelled. "I see you read your manual."

"Full makeup!"

She held up her hand for a high five.

My brain did the mental calculations.

From last night.

To his morning.

She'd kissed Sanchez.

The guys had all taken bets.

He'd called dibs.

My vision turned red; my eyes burned.

My heart cracked a little bit more as she tucked the rest of her sweats into her duffel bag and tied her shoes.

She still hadn't seen me.

A huge part of me wanted to run.

But the other sick part wanted her to see me, wanted her to see my pain, my anger, my fucking broken heart.

So I stood there.

And waited.

Finally, she was walking in my direction, Sanchez hot on her heels. I swear time stood still, paralyzed just like I was.

Two steps.

Three.

And then, a glance.

A gasp.

The duffel bag dropped right along with her water bottle.

I continued to glare in complete and utter disgust. What fucking right did she have to look so hurt when she'd abandoned me when I needed her the most.

"M-Miller?"

Sanchez looked between us, his eyes searching mine before he wrapped a possessive arm around her and tugged her away from my space.

"Sorry." I licked my lips and offered her an angry smirk. "Do we know each other?" I nodded to Sanchez. "See ya, man." One last look, one last, obsessive look. "Have fun."

You'd think I'd slapped her.

She jerked away from Sanchez, her eyes glassy as if she was ready to burst into tears.

But the joke was on her. Her tears would never be a match for mine—for the days spent in agony that my best friend, the love of my life, my soul mate had abandoned me without warning, without good-bye.

Chapter Eleven

EMERSON

Just like that, I remembered. All it took was one lingering look from the guy who broke my heart, and it was there. All of it. I fought to keep the tears in. I failed.

(Then)

"You have to let go, boo."

"What did I tell you about using that word?" I sobbed against his chest and refused to untangle my arms from his body.

"A lot of things that I can't really remember, since all my focus is on the fact that I totally saw you naked."

"More than once."

"Twice. I counted." Miller's smug response had my face burning red all the way to the tips of my ears.

"Thank God, you can count that high," I countered.

Miller kissed the top of my head. "Hey, I get good grades. I'm smart and shit."

I rolled my eyes even though he couldn't see me and finally, finally pried myself free.

His clear gaze was locked onto me.

"Don't go," I begged.

"Trust me." Voice gruff, he brushed a kiss across my mouth. "The last thing I want to do is leave my partner behind."

"This sucks." I huffed, wiping at a few stray tears.

"Man up, Emerson. It's not like you don't have a cell phone."

"You hate talking on the phone," I pointed out. "Last time I called you, you fell asleep."

He grinned.

"While I was still talking."

"You were talking about a dance routine. Forgive me if I dozed off a bit, but damn, girl, I don't know what the hell a pike is or why it's important. And I'm the last guy who'd be able to tell you if your legs were straight."

"They were." I sighed. "For the record. I'm awesome at pikes."

"You're also super awesome in bed, but you don't see me calling to tell you something you already know."

I tried not to blush for a second time.

"There it is." He cupped my face, his thumbs grazing my bottom lip. "Don't forget me."

"Like I could ever forget such a thorn in my side, a pain in my ass, a—"

He crushed his mouth to mine then jerked away, his eyes pleading. "We'll make this work, yeah?"

"Absolutely." Doubt washed over me. He was moving across the country. Literally.

And he was Miller Quinton.

Sexy.

Charismatic.

My best friend.

But not my boyfriend.

I told him it would be too hard with us living separate lives so far away from each other.

It was a painful decision for both of us. What if he fell for someone else? What if he replaced me? What if I did the same? Was I even capable of that? How was it even possible to move on from your first love? Your best friend?

"You look pale." Miller tugged my ponytail. "We'll talk, alright? Just think, in ten months we'll be out of high school and starting college. I'll apply to UDub, and you'll cheer for them. That was always the plan."

I chewed my lower lip. He was going to be far away now. Before it wasn't a big deal if he didn't get the scholarship because the plan was to stay close to one another, but now, he was moving across the country. "What if they don't offer a full ride for football?"

"They will," he said in a confident voice. "Has my sexual prowess ruined all thoughts in that pretty little head?" He leaned down and whispered. "I'm Miller Quinton."

I exhaled and crossed my arms while he cupped his ear and grinned.

"I'm waiting."

"Nope. I'm not doing it. I won't do it."

"I could always make you." He eyed my mouth with a hungry gaze. "Now, who am I?"

"Miller Quinton," I grumbled.

"Who's going to give me a full ride?"

"UDub," I said a bit louder.

"Right on." He held out his hand for a fist bump. "No more tears. I've got this shit on lockdown."

"Promise?"

"When it comes to you," he whispered, "I will never ever break a promise."

"You'll always be my best friend."

"And you'll always be the girl I tripped in sixth grade."

"Wow, solid emotional moment. You lasted five minutes."

"That's what she said."

"Miller . . ." I fought back more tears.

"I promised never to make you cry." He pulled me in for one last hug. *"So let me keep that promise and suck those back in, yeah?"*

I nodded.

"Love you."

"I love you too." My voice was wobbly, and I couldn't feel my legs. *Miller turned on his heel and got in his truck.*

I stood in the street as he pulled away, my mind going back to all of our stolen moments . . . his hands on my hips, his lips on my neck. I already missed his touch and it had been seconds. My body jolted at the memory of his tongue as it slid against my lower lip, all before we made a decision that would change our lives forever. It was our first time but little did we know that eventually—we'd have to pay the emotional price.

It was going to be fine, I reminded myself.

And then again:

Everything would be fine.

I sniffled and then nearly ran into a wall.

Until Sanchez jerked me into the hall bathroom between the two locker rooms and crossed his arms. "That's the guy."

"What?" I tried looking at the sweat and dirt on his practice jersey, but he gripped my chin in his hand and forced me to look him in the eyes.

"Curves," he whispered.

And I lost it.

Just completely and utterly lost my mind and started sobbing against the guy who, last night, had said he only wanted to have sex with me.

Had I fallen that low?

Or did I really just have no friends?

"You loved him."

I didn't say anything. Maybe I didn't have to.

"You know, this could all be avoided if you'd just let me fuck him out of your system," he said softly. "But part of me thinks that wouldn't work, would it, Curves? You'd just imagine his hands on you and not mine, and that pisses me the hell off."

"It's nothing." I wiped the mascara from under my eyes. "I mean it was a silly high school crush on my best friend."

"You went to high school together!" His voice rose an octave. "Best friends?"

"I need to get to practice." I tried moving past him, but he was a very solid wall of muscle and determination.

"I'll write you a note."

"Sanchez . . ." I shoved his chest. "I need this. I've always wanted to be a Bucks Girl. I can't be late."

"This isn't over." His look held promise of hunting me down if I didn't agree.

"Fine." I crossed my arms. "We'll talk . . . later."

"Later when?"

"Just . . . later."

"Dinner."

"What?" My head whipped around so fast I got dizzy. "Why would you want to have dinner with me? I've already established I'm not sleeping with you."

"First, you've only rejected me twice, or was it three times? I have a way of wearing people down. Second, you need to eat. Humans need food. And third, you'll be starving after day two. Trust me, most girls puke."

"Well, thanks!" I threw my hands in the air. "That was the worst pep talk ever! I don't want to puke up cornflakes and eggs!"

He made a face. "Shit, you're fucked. Neither would I."

"Sanchez!"

"Do you mix them together, or is this more of a separate meals thing?"

"Move!"

"Dinner."

"FINE!"

He moved out of the way but not before calling after me. "Wear something sexy!"

I hated him.

And adored him at the same time.

In an *I kind of want to punch him in the face while simultaneously call him when I get a flat tire* kind of way.

"Get over here!" Kinsey hissed, once I jogged onto the field. Thankfully, the girls were still stretching.

Coach Kay blew her whistle and grinned; it was evil, that grin. Goose bumps erupted all over my skin. "Welcome to day two. Known as hell day." Amidst moans of protest, the coaching staff started unstacking buckets and placing them around the stadium.

"They're trying to kill us," I muttered.

"All men must die." Kinsey winked.

"*Game of Thrones* reference. I knew I liked you."

"I'm so marrying Jon Snow if this whole cheerleading thing doesn't work out."

"Well, good thing he's still alive!"

"Ugh, hopefully that's our future too." She puffed out her chest and put her hands on her hips.

"Twenty laps." Coach Kay grinned. "And then line up for push-ups, sit-ups, and army crawls. I need your cardio in pristine shape. If you complain, you run an extra lap, and if you're last . . ." Kinsey tensed next to me. "You owe me burpees. And if you fail, you're off the squad."

"What constitutes as failing?" I whispered out of the side of my mouth.

"That's easy." Kinsey smiled. "Giving up is failing. If you keep going, then you stay on the squad."

"And if I puke?"

"Be quick about it."

"Great."

The whistle blew again.

"Run!" Coach Kay yelled.

It was going to be a really long morning.

Eight hours later, and I was ready to crawl into a dark hole and die, let someone find my body, bury me in white satin and all that crap.

Seriously. I ached everywhere.

I didn't throw up.

In fact, I learned early on to just take my time doing everything; so I set a manageable pace and was able to power through, while a lot of the girls looked ready to die. Half of us were smart about pacing ourselves and drinking protein shakes and water when we were given breaks. Part of me wondered if the reasoning behind this was more strategic than anything. The strongest girls would survive.

And while I felt like hell, I also felt strong after the morning practice and even earned a few *Good jobs* and high fives from some of the snottier girls.

Things were looking up.

But I had to know the universe wasn't going to be in my corner for much longer. You can only steal all the luck for so long.

I stopped at the store to grab a bottle of wine to say thank you to Sanchez for letting me use him as a giant tissue when I felt it—the prickling sensation hit the back of my neck and slithered down my spine until, finally, I gave up and turned around.

Miller.

Why? Why out of all the Whole Foods in Bellevue was he at this one? Did that mean he lived close? Where was he staying? Why was I so curious in the first place?

No good would come from interacting with him.

Only pain.

Hadn't I learned that the hard way?

When I'd called him for help?

When I'd needed him the most in my life, and he'd been too busy with other girls? Too busy with his new life to even call me back?

Bitterness won out over sadness.

And for a minute, I contemplated throwing the wine bottle at his head. In fact, I was having an intense stare down with the bottle, wondering if it was worth wasting on his body, when a shadow cast over me.

Slowly, I looked up.

He'd gotten hotter.

It shouldn't be possible.

The universe shouldn't allow things like that to happen, for already good-looking guys to grow more muscle in all the right places . . . for his eyes to turn electric blue . . . for his lips to somehow tease and invite more than they used to.

Thickly corded muscles lined his neck, stretching down his biceps, wrapping around his triceps, forcing his T-shirt to strain across his huge chest.

"Drinking alone?" he finally said.

"No," I answered, quickly dropping the wine into my basket. "It's a gift."

"For Sanchez?"

"Why? Does Sanchez like wine?"

"You tell me. You're the one fucking him."

I flinched. He may as well have driven a stake through my heart.

I glared. "You pretended not to know me."

His icy-blue eyes raked over me with disgust. "It's not really pretend when it's true, is it, Em?"

My hands shook. He called me Em. But he wasn't the same Miller. All traces of teasing were lacking, as was his normally bright smile and happy demeanor.

"What happened to you?" I whispered.

He shook his head. "An evil cheerleader happened."

"Who was she?"

"Shit, you really are clueless, aren't you?"

Tears burned my eyes. "Was she some—"

"Look in the mirror. Have fun with Sanchez tonight." He walked off, his posture rigid.

Me? He was pissed at me?

When he was the one who abandoned me!

What the hell!

I wanted to run after him and beat him over the head with my shopping basket! At the same time, I was so confused I stood there for a few seconds trying to figure out what the hell he was talking about.

My brain hurt.

My body hurt worse.

I quickly paid for my cheap wine and stomped out of the store, pissed off that he thought he even had a right to be angry with me in the first place when he was the one who'd left me—left us.

I briefly allowed myself a few seconds of pity, for the lives he left behind—mine included—then started the car.

Only it wouldn't start.

It wouldn't even budge.

"Come on!" I tried again, hitting the accelerator a bit.

Nothing. Completely dead.

I couldn't call my dad; our roles had switched. I was the caretaker now, the breadwinner, the girl trying to balance cheerleading with everything else, including bills and now, apparently, finding a car that worked.

A soft tap on my windshield had me nearly jumping out of my own skin, and then my door was pulled open.

Miller.

Of course, and my shame was complete.

"Let me try." He held out his hand.

"Okay, stalker." It slipped.

"You wish."

I stuck out my tongue.

I'd been in his presence a grand total of five minutes, and I was already itching to tackle him to the ground and lick the side of his face. He had a thing about getting licked, but I never found out why.

I slammed the key onto his hand and waited while he tried to start the car in the same way I had, only to get out of the car and declare, "It's dead."

"No shit."

"Come on." He reached for my grocery bag. "Grab your shit."

"I can Uber it."

"Imagine that. A blonde cheerleader who knows how to download an app. Color me impressed."

"Miller." I stood my ground. "Seriously. I'm fine." I wasn't fine. I wouldn't ever be fine, not with this chasm of pain separating us, making me lash out, making him do the same.

"No." His blue eyes searched mine. "I'm not sure it will ever be okay, but I'm sure as hell not going to let you wait here while some stranger from God-knows-where picks you up . . ." He swore. "Looking like that . . ." He kicked the curb. "And promises to drop you off at an unknown location."

"Sanchez," I whispered. "I could call Sanchez."

"Great, call Sanchez," he challenged.

"I don't . . ."

"Don't have his number?" he offered, with a knowing smirk that made me feel dirty and cheap and used.

"No." It burned to have to admit it out loud.

"Grab your stuff. I won't ask again."

I opened the trunk, seized my duffel and purse, then slammed it down and hit lock on my key fob. "Happy?"

"Overjoyed," he said dryly.

When did he get so sarcastic? Hadn't that been my job in our friendship? He was easygoing. I was sarcastic.

My mumbled thoughts clouded even further when we walked fifty feet to his car.

A Mercedes-AMG.

Of course.

Gone was the blue truck he used to drive, the one that had the rust near the hubcaps and made a funny screeching noise every time it pulled up to a stoplight.

My throat felt like it was going to close.

Maybe I should just go home.

But the thought of him seeing where I lived, not the pretty house on the lake I used to live in, but the apartment building I shared with my dad and our live-in nurse, made me want to puke all over his fancy car.

My stomach revolted as he jerked open the door and basically shoved me inside. Everything smelled new, and the leather creaked under my weight. Of course it did.

Shame heated my cheeks until I thought for sure he could see the red from his spot in the driver's seat.

He turned the key. "Where's home?"

I didn't answer.

My tongue was glued to the roof of my mouth. Why? Why did he have to come back to Washington after all this time? And why did his clear blue eyes have to look straight through me? As if the past didn't exist between us. As if it never would.

He shook his head, and his jaw clicked before he pulled out into traffic and made his way downtown.

To exactly where I'd been heading before he'd found me, ready to cry into my purse over the fact that my cheap-ass car wouldn't start.

It was hard to breathe. The air was thick with tension swirling between us, the smell of his cologne hard to ignore, as was the way his massive size seemed to make me feel like if I didn't press my body closer to the door, our arms were going to touch.

And if they touched.

It would hurt.

Physically.

Emotionally.

I kept the walls up, just like I knew he did, because what choice did we have? Talk? About the past? About why he abandoned me?

More shame washed over me until I was sick with it, choking on its essence.

We pulled into a large car garage.

He didn't stop the car until it got to the top floor.

It was connected to Sanchez's apartment building, which I knew because he'd scribbled out instructions and left them in my bag shortly after our little run-in.

The only reason I'd even seen the note was because it had been stuck in my bra.

That was Sanchez for you.

Miller parked the car and stared straight ahead, then pulled the keys out and grabbed my stuff.

A protest died on my lips as he gathered his too.

What? Was there a team sleepover that I didn't know about?

"Miller—"

"Don't," he snapped. "Not right now. Just please . . ." His eyes pleaded. "Please don't talk to me."

The rejection hurt more than I thought it would, especially since I'd convinced myself on the entire car ride over that my walls were back up, only to realize that the minute he locked eyes with me, those same walls were more than willing to crumble to the ground for one look at him.

At my best friend.

Imagine what those walls would do if he gave me a hug?

I shivered and crossed my arms over my chest.

I was wearing black leggings and a long Victoria's Secret sweatshirt with Nike shoes. It's not like I was exactly dressed up for a date or anything, but he didn't seem to care. As far as he was concerned I was off to seduce Sanchez with my sweats and wine!

The elevator was just as silent as the car. With his free hand, Miller punched the penthouse floor.

Confusion washed over me, but I kept silent.

What game was he playing?

The doors opened to a long marble hallway with two doors on either side of the hall.

Penthouse A.

And Penthouse B.

Miller marched over to the one that said A and knocked on the door so hard I thought that the door was going to come off.

Someone jerked it open.

Sanchez.

His grin faded and then grew as he looked behind Miller and gave me a smirk. "You do deliveries now?"

With a flourish, Miller dropped my stuff at Sanchez's feet, including the wine now snugly sitting inside my duffel bag, and stomped over to Penthouse B and let himself in, slamming the door behind him.

"Neighbors?" My voice was completely unsteady, hoarse like I'd been smoking a pack on the way over. I couldn't handle it anymore.

I wanted to launch myself into Sanchez's arms and pretend they were Miller's.

It was unfair.

But pain had a way of not caring what was fair or not. It just was.

Sanchez took another look at me then wrapped me in a hug and said way too loud, "Guess that means no sex, huh?"

I shoved his chest and laughed.

"Cock blocked by a dude who doesn't even like you. I'm wounded," he teased, pulling my crap into his apartment and opening the door wide.

I nearly swallowed my tongue.

It was massive.

Gorgeous.

My entire apartment could fit in his gourmet kitchen.

"You have two ovens," I pointed out lamely.

"Yeah, well, a guy's gotta eat." He leisurely walked into the kitchen. I didn't know what else to do, so I followed him.

He had a bottle of wine on the bar, two glasses, and loads of fruits and cheeses.

"Hungry?" He didn't turn around.

"Not really," I answered honestly. "A certain jackass stole my appetite."

"About that." His shoulders tensed as he poured a glass of wine, still not looking at me. "Is there a reason my teammate and your ex-best-friend just dropped you off at my apartment like we were about to engage in a fucking playdate?"

I looked down at the shiny white floor. "I was buying wine, we fought in the grocery store, my car wouldn't start, and he wouldn't let me call an Uber."

"Good," Sanchez barked.

I glanced up to see him towering over me. How did he move so fast? And so quietly? He was at least six four!

"Now . . ." I could smell the rich wine on his breath. "Tell me what you want."

It was on the tip of my tongue to say *You.* To beg him to make me forget, but I wasn't that girl. I wouldn't ever be that girl.

"I should go." I slowly backed away from him.

His eyes narrowed as he reached out and grabbed my arm and gently pulled me toward one of the walls on the other side of the kitchen; then with a flourish, he slammed his hand against the wall by my head.

My jaw dropped, probably creating an awesome triple chin, as he slapped the wall again and then with a smirk, yelled out, "God, you feel so good, baby!"

"Sanchez," I hissed, covering my mouth with my hands. "What are you doing?"

"I'm giving you what you want, baby!" He basically screamed it in my face, trapping me once again before sliding his cheek down the front of my sweatshirt until he was at eye level with my hips. "I'm going to make you drive him crazy—help you forget all about Miller—and then, if you want to stay, I'll even give you the guest room."

"Why?" I had a hard time finding my voice as he slowly moved his head back up. It was impossible not to feel the heat from his body.

He stopped, looking me in the eye. "Because one day, he's going to regret walking away from you. And I want to be there when it's too late—when you're in my arms, my bed instead."

"You seem so sure of yourself," I said, finally finding my voice as his smile turned deadly, his lips grazing my ear. I was ready to shove him away when I heard a crash from the apartment next door and the sound of glass breaking.

I sucked in a breath.

"Bingo." Sanchez's deep voice rumbled near my neck; his lips were hot on my pulse. "So, guest bedroom?"

"I should . . ." I shook the haze from my thoughts. "Probably go home."

"Nah." Sanchez pulled away and went back into the kitchen, leaving me a complete mess as my ears strained to hear anything else that would give me a clue about Miller. "Stay and spy. I'll even give you a nice glass cup to put against the wall." He winked, peeking his head around the corner.

"Hilarious." I rolled my eyes and followed his voice.

"He hates you," he said cheerfully. "Care to tell me why, Curves?"

"He . . ." I jerked the wine from his hand; screw the cheer manual. "Took my virginity before leaving for Louisiana my senior year of high school."

"Fuck." Sanchez lifted the empty glass from the table and filled it. "Cheers, then?"

"He . . ." I was on a roll. "Didn't bother calling me back when—" I shook my head "Never mind. It doesn't matter."

"When . . ." Sanchez prompted again.

"Seriously." I plopped down on his couch. "Is this real leather?"

"No, it's fake, because I only make fifteen million a year compared to Miller's eighteen."

I felt my cheeks heat.

"It's real, Curves, just like my cock."

"Yeah, I should have seen that coming."

"I would love to co—"

I glared.

He didn't say anything more, just held up one hand and the empty wineglass.

"You know . . ." He moved to sit next to me. "I'm a really good friend."

"Weird, because most of my friends aren't always trying to have sex with me?"

"What if I told you I just wanted to win a bet?"

I eyed him with disbelief. "A bet."

"Bang the cheerleader. Save the damn world," he whispered, an edge of irritation lacing his normally raspy voice. "Alright, enough of this shit. We need to sleep. We both have practice and, as much as I'd love to stay up and talk about my feelings, I'm pretty sure I don't have any anymore . . ."

"And yet you're still trying to convince me to sleep with you?"

"I'd fully allow you to leave your heart at the door right along with your clothes. I'm a gentleman like that." He shrugged as if it wasn't a big deal.

But to me it was.

Because the last guy to touch me had just broken what sounded like at least three glass objects against the wall next door and, as mean as he was, as cruel . . .

I wanted him still.

"Hell, I know that look." Sanchez yawned. "Off to bed, Curves. Sleep well knowing that Miller's going to wonder for the next twelve hours if I've tasted all of your crevices. Let him suffer. By the sound of it, he deserves it."

My shoulders slumped.

"Posture." He jerked my shoulders back then tapped his temple with his finger. "That's in the manual too."

"Please tell me you didn't memorize the cheerleading manual so you could hit on all of us?"

"I've slept with half your squad." He shrugged, and then raw pain flashed across his face before he smiled. "Trust me, I know the rules. Most of them don't even eat around me because they're afraid I'll tattle."

"Do you?"

"Do I what, Curves?"

"Tattle?"

"Only on your bitchy friend," he said in a singsong voice. "But look at that. Storytime's over. Get some shut-eye, and we can make Miller miserable over some eggs."

"You make eggs?"

"I make everything." He grinned. "How else am I supposed to get my dick in all the right places?"

"You disgust me."

"Bullshit." Sanchez was touching my face again, his lips too close. "I fascinate you."

"Dinosaurs fascinate me." I tried to keep my voice bored.

"I used to have a T. rex collection."

I pressed my lips together in a smile to keep from laughing out loud. "Why does that feel like a lie?"

"Because I still have it." He shrugged. "Guest bedrooms are down the hall to the right. New toothbrushes, and anything else you may need. Oh, and, Curves?"

"Yeah?"

"Lock your door."

"So you don't accidently stumble in?" I asked in a deadpan voice.

"Nah, so you don't accidently stumble out." He winked and swaggered away from me like he owned the world and knew it.

And maybe guys like him did.

I was in over my head.

I was screwed.

And for some reason . . .

I was smiling.

Chapter Twelve

MILLER

I wasn't sure how long I'd stared at the blank wall.

The paint was a muted tan that only seemed to remind me of my own emptiness—and of the need to fill the wall with something that felt like home.

I'd never put up pictures.

It had seemed pointless.

The only ones that had ever meant anything to me were of Emerson and my mom.

My dad only wanted me for my money and, ever since my mom's death, had found most of his answers at the bottom of a bottle.

Unpacked boxes littered the apartment. I'd taken the first available penthouse apartment in Bellevue, with hopes that the security would be enough to give me privacy.

And if I was being completely honest, it was also far enough away from my childhood home, from her, from the McDonald's we used to go to, from the high school we'd both attended. I sure as hell shouldn't let my brain go there but it did, and just like that one of my last memories with Em pushed through the surface, begging to be remembered.

(Then)

"Eat." I slid my fries across the table. When she didn't reach for them, I opened up some ranch dipping sauce and sniffed it. "God, that smells good. Don't you think this smells good, Em?" I held it right underneath her cute-as-hell nose. She flinched before casting a murderous glance in my direction.

"I think I'll dip my fries in this."

I knew what I was doing.

Stomping all over her weaknesses. The girls on the squad were mean to her because she was a threat—Emerson always saw it the other way around—she was bigger, curvier, ergo their words must be right. No matter how many times I tried to convince her that any guy would give his left nut for a chance to even hold her hand—she still thought she was the one lacking, and unfortunately that even trickled into food.

"Mmm." I shoved five french fries in my mouth as ranch sauce fell in a gooey blob onto the table. "That's the spot, baby." I grinned over another huge mouthful. "I'm so close!" I slammed a hand onto the table. Everyone at the burger joint turned to stare at us.

Her lips twitched while her eyes snapped to my fries with longing, damn french fry, making me want to trade places. "You're not funny."

"Eat the fries before I orgasm in front of the entire restaurant, Em."

"We'll get blacklisted . . ." She sighed. "Again."

"The first time was bullshit, and you know it," I said defensively.

"Miller."

I wasn't going to take no for an answer, French orgasm here I come, I snickered at my own word play. "OH, OH, OH—"

She quickly shoved two fries in her mouth and glared at me. "You're a pain in my ass, you know that?"

I glanced under the table and then moaned. "But your ass is second only to your face. And that comes from the heart, Em."

"I think that was a compliment."

"You're welcome." Satisfied, I spread my arms wide and chuckled while she swallowed and drank me in with her eyes. I knew what she saw. My Bellevue Football team T-shirt was stretched tightly across my lean muscles. She looked away and shivered. Nobody would have noticed the effect I had on her—I noticed. I always had.

Fucking memories.

A chill ran down my spine as my ears strained to hear anything else on the other side of the wall, aside from Sanchez's moaning. Why? Why did it have to be her? Why. Why. What the ever-loving-F why!

I wanted to believe the Em I used to know had grown into a mature adult who wouldn't just jump in bed with a guy like Sanchez because he smiled in her direction.

Then again, I didn't really know her anymore, did I?

And I blamed her for that more than I would ever blame myself.

I clenched my hands so tight my palms burned. I wanted to seriously take an axe to that bare wall and chop until I made my way through.

The whole scenario was straight out of *The Shining*. I seriously needed to get my shit together if I was going to be able to focus on our first preseason game in two weeks.

Focus, Miller.

Not on the noises next door.

If I closed my eyes, I swore I could still feel the way her body felt beneath my fingertips . . . the buzzing awareness of her mouth as it drew each kiss, sucked the life out of me.

I kicked one of the ugly brown boxes full of shit I didn't need and heard the sound of glass breaking.

I was ready to throw the box across the large living room when a knock sounded at the door. I tripped over four more boxes in an effort to answer it.

I jerked the knob and swore. "Sanchez."

"Miller." I hated that I was inspecting him for any hint that she'd been kissing him, tugging at his clothes, sucking his—

Yeah, I needed to stop.

He sidestepped me, breezing right into my apartment like he owned it.

"Did you need something?" Hadn't he already done enough?

"Nice place." He did a slow circle where he stood and then crossed his bulky arms over his chest. "If you need the name of a decorator I can—"

"Cut the shit," I interrupted. "It's late, and we both have practice in the morning. What do you need?"

His green eyes flashed. "I called dibs."

Not what I expected him to say.

It felt like someone had punched me in the face and then shoved me off the nearest cliff. "You can't just call dibs on a person, Sanchez. Besides, I'm sure if she knew about your little bet with the rest of the guys, she'd feed you your own heart."

His lips twitched. "I can see my girl being violent like that, kinda kinky. I think I like it."

My gut twisted. The metallic taste of blood filled my mouth as I bit my tongue in an effort to not rip his face off. I had no right to be possessive. No right to be upset. No damn right.

"Was that all? I'm tired."

His eyes narrowed. "So, you're cool with this? With me dating Emerson?"

It was the first time he'd said her name, which was my first clue. He wasn't kidding. He was serious as hell.

"I don't even know her anymore." I shrugged like it wasn't a big deal and immediately felt like I was going to throw up. "You can screw who-ever and whatever you want, man. I'm sorry if I gave you the impression you needed permission."

"Good." His smile grew. "Because this girl's different."

I know she is, my heart screamed.

"Sure she is." I snorted. "Just wait."

"You sure sound bitter for someone who stole her virginity then left her all alone." His gaze met mine. "Something you're not telling me before I go back into my apartment and strip her naked?"

Red. I saw fucking red. "Nah, man, have at it. Just make sure to wear a condom."

I sounded like my father.

My drunk, bitter father.

I'd never hated myself more than I did in that moment.

"I always protect those I'm with, even if it's from themselves," he finally said as he walked by me. I could smell her on his skin, and I hated them both. I couldn't afford to hate him if I wanted to win games, but damn, I'd never wanted to inflict physical harm more than I did in that minute.

All I needed him to do was trip over at least five boxes, the heavy ones, snap his leg in two, and then he'd be out of the picture, and I could go back to being lonely.

And angry.

Why the hell had I been traded now?

I ran my hands over my buzzed hair and swore again.

"Hey, Miller?"

"Yeah?" I tried to sound casual. I failed.

I knew he could see right through me. My posture was rigid, my voice hoarse, and my eyes probably looked as wild as my heartbeat.

"Never say I didn't warn you."

He nodded. "Game on."

"Game?"

"May the best man win." He winked and shut the door quietly behind him, leaving me blanketed in silence, until of course, his own apartment door opened and footsteps sounded.

Followed by female laughter.

I couldn't tell if it was the TV or if it was Emerson.

And then I was irrationally angry that I'd forgotten the way her laugh sounded, and that if she was laughing, it was because of him.

Sleep.

I needed to go to sleep.

Or I was going to lose my mind.

And be complete shit at practice.

But when I slid into my sheets a few hours later, my head resting against the pillow, the only vision that would come was that of Emerson crying and clinging to me, her nails digging into my biceps.

"Promise me."

"I promise."

Chapter Thirteen

EMERSON

It was quickly turning out to be the worst morning of my life. I woke up to Sanchez hovering over me with a mirror under my nose.

He was afraid I wasn't breathing.

Good to know that his first response wasn't to call an ambulance or even feel for a pulse, but to grab a freaking bathroom mirror and shove it underneath my nostrils.

Things just got worse from there.

I'd been trying to do the whole protein shake thing as per the manual's instructions, only to wake up to sausage, bacon, toast, and eggs.

He'd made it all.

And while that would normally be the sweetest thing ever, he refused to let me leave until I ate everything on my plate.

Because, didn't you know? Kids are starving all over the US, going hungry. Plus, he wanted me to keep my curves.

Okay, so maybe that was the good part of my morning.

But it quickly went to hell after I grabbed my bag and moved to the elevator.

Either Miller was literally stalking us through the peephole, or I had the worst luck in the world.

I heard the door open first.

Smelled his cologne second.

It was different than what he'd worn in high school, but somehow it still made my legs liquid and my heart pound a little harder.

Sanchez wrapped a possessive arm around me and tugged me into the elevator, but at least held it open for Miller.

"This is fun," Miller said, seemingly to himself.

My lips twitched and then, maybe it was the breakfast, or the fact that I'd had a horrible night, but my heart hurt.

And I laughed. Hard.

Both guys looked at me like I'd just grown two heads.

"Don't mind me." I wiped tears from under my eyes. "I laugh when I get uncomfortable."

"The hell?" Sanchez shook his head. "That can't be convenient."

"She laughed at her grandpa's funeral," Miller apparently felt the need to add.

Sanchez grinned. "No shit?"

"I had to keep handing her tissues so people would assume she was just sobbing really hard. And not heartless." Miller sounded pissed, but I knew that if he remembered that memory correctly, we were also holding hands underneath the hymnal, and he'd inched my skirt at least halfway up my thigh in order to distract me from laughing.

(Then)

Forgive me, Father, for I have sinned.

I could still feel his lips whispering against the outside of my ear as he confessed to wanting nothing more than to make out with me.

I was still dating someone else.

It felt so . . . forbidden.

The elevator dinged.

I gave a little jolt and glanced up at both of them, fully aware that my cheeks were pink and my breathing was a bit labored at the memory.

Miller's expression changed from angry to . . . perceptive. Something shifted between the guys. I had no idea what.

When the elevator doors opened, Sanchez let me go first and then Miller. I could have sworn I heard Miller mutter, "First point goes to me," as he strode to his Mercedes.

Sanchez rubbed his jaw like he'd just taken a hit.

"Everything okay?" I asked. It took a lot of concentration to not look behind me as Miller started his car.

"Yeah." Sanchez grabbed my free hand and brought it to his lips. "How many years were you guys friends? Just high school, yeah?"

I gulped. "Since we were seven."

"Shit."

"What?"

"Nothing." His grin was sexy, but it looked forced. "Now, get that nice ass in my car so I can take you to practice. And if your coach sees you, just tell her that your car wouldn't start, and I was the only knight in shining armor available."

I rolled my eyes. "You're more like the guy that kills the knight in shining armor then puts on said armor and steals all the maidens."

He threw his head back and laughed. "See? We're already best friends, and it's been two days."

I glanced away. "And here I thought you just wanted sex."

"Best friends who have sex. That's what makes the best part . . . best." He pulled out of the parking garage and turned up the music. "Now, promise me we can go out this week."

"No."

"Please?"

"It's weirder when you're polite."

Another laugh. "Would you rather I say something like 'Bitch, you're coming with me!'?"

Laughter erupted between us. "Please don't ever say that again." I checked my cell and panicked. "Crap!"

"What?" His expression paled.

"If I'm not at practice in five minutes, I'm going to have to run."

"Hell no." He slammed his foot on the accelerator, making it feel like my body was still five miles behind us as we careened toward the stadium. "I'm not letting them take away that ass."

So, my morning had started off bad.

But after that comment?

Things were looking up.

♥ ♥ ♥

"You're flushed," Kinsey commented after practice.

I gulped the rest of my water and wiped my mouth with the back of my hand. "I think, after that practice, everyone is flushed."

Her eyes narrowed. "Hmm, I'm not buying it."

I rolled my eyes.

"Curves!" Sanchez yelled at the top of his lungs, gaining the attention of every single person in the parking lot.

Great.

"Hold up." He called again, his voice closing in.

Kinsey gave me a knowing look and crossed her arms. "Looks like someone has a crush."

"I don't," I said quickly.

"Wasn't talking about you, Em," she said in a singsong voice and then, "Hey, Sanchez. Quick, what's two plus two?"

His icy glare was so ridiculously out of character for him that I didn't know what to say to cut the obvious tension between them.

"I don't know, Kinsey. Say, how do you drown a cheerleader?"

"If you say 'Put a mirror at the bottom of a pool,' I'm going to give your balls a little tug and show Emerson how small they really are."

"Time out!" I stepped between them. "Something I should know?"

"She wouldn't sleep with me." Sanchez shrugged just as Kinsey rolled her eyes.

"I wouldn't sleep with him."

"So, the hostility comes from lack of sex?" I offered.

Kinsey's lips pressed together in an amused smile. "What can I say? I think Grant"—it was the first time she'd said his name—"is still under the impression that if you don't use it, you'll lose it. I think his biggest fear is waking up without an erection."

"That . . ." Sanchez nodded seriously. "And waking up with you naked."

She flipped him off.

"Miller!" Lily, one of my teammates, called out his name and basically hung on his bicep like a cheap Christmas ornament. Her sports bra covered huge boobs, and her tiny shorts could double as underwear. "I'm having a preseason party. You should come."

Kinsey and Sanchez both laughed.

What was I missing?

"Um . . ." Miller politely removed her hand from his body. "Yeah, I'll think about it. Thanks."

Lily walked off, her hair bouncing across her shoulders like she was on the catwalk instead of at practice.

"Ask me how many NFL stars she's been with," Kinsey said with a laugh. "It's almost comical how fast she launches those talons. Last year after stalking Thomas during the entire preseason he finally fell for her charms. The poor guy ended up buying her diamond earrings and a trip to Mexico before he realized she'd already slept with half the team."

Wow. Alrighty then.

"I think every new guy falls for it at some point," Sanchez said, his eyes darkened before he looked right at me and shrugged. "It's the tits."

I smacked him on the arm.

"What?" he roared, rubbing the spot that I knew wasn't even sore from my lame hit. "She's got a nice rack, and sometimes it's nice to just rest your face on the pillows for a minute . . . get some shut-eye . . . rub a little—"

I threw my hands in the air. "I seriously don't know why I talk to you."

"Best friends." He nodded confidently. "But only if you say no to celery."

"Gag." Kinsey made a face.

Sanchez moved away from us and nodded to Miller.

I didn't hear their conversation.

But any time they talked it made me nervous.

And then I felt stupid with that same thought because, how arrogant did I have to be to assume they were discussing me?

Miller looked over Sanchez's shoulder when Sanchez was busy on his phone. Our eyes locked.

His had always been so blue.

So clear and pretty.

In perfect contrast to his mocha-tanned skin.

Full lips.

Lips that knew how to do things that no high school boy should ever know how to do.

And a mouth to match.

A shiver racked through my body before I could stop it.

"That." Kinsey pointed to the two guys. "I'd be the cheese in that meat sandwich." She sighed. "I'd just have to make sure I faced Miller instead of Sanchez, you know, because . . . Grant." The way she said his name had me wondering if she really hated him or just hated that she and every other female was attracted to him and couldn't help it—and that he knew we couldn't help it.

"Miller had your car towed last night." Sanchez tossed me his cell phone. "Give me your number, and I'll call the tow truck company and have them deliver it to your house."

"Convenient way to get someone's number," I grumbled. My fingers felt huge as I tried to type in the number as fast as possible. For some reason, giving him my number in front of Miller felt wrong. Like I was cheating.

"Well, Miller tried to have it delivered to your old house and found out the hard way that you no longer live there. There was no forwarding address so, yeah."

Kinsey shook her head slowly at him. "What are you? A spy?"

"I ask the right questions in order to get the right answers." He caught his phone as I tossed it back at him. "And I'm the one with the girl's number even though last night that prick was doing all the work. See? Point, me."

I looked between them.

Point?

Hadn't Miller said something like that this morning?

I shook off the bad feeling and then realized that I didn't have a ride back to my apartment.

"Shit." Sanchez checked his expensive Rolex and popped on a pair of probably equally expensive dark sunglasses. "I have the Armani shoot in an hour." He pulled me in for a quick hug then brushed his lips across mine before I could protest. "You need anything?"

I shook my head, momentarily stunned by the way my lips still buzzed from his touch.

"I'll call you later, Curves."

He got in his car and left.

By the time I turned around, Kinsey was talking to another one of our teammates, Cassie, who was really tall and smiled a lot. I actually liked when she hung around to chat, but she had a little girl so she was usually rushing back and forth between her house and practices. They were lost in conversation.

Which left me and Miller.

Alone.

His expression didn't give anything away, but if the tension between us was any indicator, we were in unfamiliar territory—something I'd never experienced with him.

I'd been his biggest cheerleader, literally.

And he'd been mine.

My heart cracked a bit as he blankly stared, as if he didn't recognize me. I wanted to yell at him. To tell him he could go to hell, that his judgment meant nothing, that he couldn't hurt me anymore.

But it would all be a lie.

The pain of being told you were already forgotten—being told you were annoying—that the person you loved most in the world was avoiding you so he could let you down easy . . .

He's destined for bigger and better things.

The words still burned.

Hung over my head like a blazing neon sign.

Miller turned and opened the door to his SUV then turned back toward me. "Need a ride?"

I shook my head no.

"So, let me get this straight. Sanchez can drive you anywhere, but I've got the plague?"

"You hate me."

"I don't know you." He shrugged his shoulders. "Can't hate someone you don't really know. Can you, Em?"

I held up my phone. "I'll call an Uber."

"At eight in the morning." He crossed his arms. "When everyone else is doing the same thing in order to get to work on time? Downtown Bellevue?" He took another step toward me. "I'm taking you."

"You're bossier than I remember," I grumbled.

"You're prettier," he whispered and then, as if realizing he'd said it out loud, he shook his head. "Sorry, it slipped. Old habits."

I smiled. "You never did have a censor."

"Censors are for—"

"Sissies," we said in unison.

He smiled briefly and looked away. "Get in the car, Em."

He was right. But I still didn't want him to see where I lived.

I still had my pride.

And my really crappy online teaching job that I needed to log into in about an hour.

"Okay," I said quickly. "Thank you."

I'd just have him drop me off on the side street.

He didn't need to know that I lived in the apartment building.

Or that my dad was sick.

Or that my world had crumbled the minute he walked out of it.

"So . . ." He slammed the door shut. "Where to?"

I fired off instructions and tried to glue myself to the door so that I wouldn't have to smell his cologne or, like a psycho, lean over the console and take a giant whiff.

He had no right to smell so good this early in the morning!

Traffic wasn't too bad, which meant I'd at least get to grab something to eat before I logged in and started my day.

Neither of us spoke, but we'd never been those types of friends, the ones that had to fill the air with needless words.

Our words, even in teasing, had always held a purpose.

For some reason, just thinking about how we used to be had tears burning in the back of my eyes.

And then, of course, we had to roll to a stop in front of the McDonald's where Miller and I'd had our first kiss.

I sucked in a breath.

The air stilled in the car.

Like someone had pressed pause on our lives and simultaneously shown us a preview of the past.

(Then)

I stood by his giant blue truck.
   I felt his hands in my hair.
   His tongue in my mouth.

The SUV jerked to the right so abruptly that my cheek nearly collided with the glass window.

And then we were parked in the exact same spot.

The lines of paint in the parking lot were faded.

The smell was the same.

Somehow it was the same.

"When you left . . ." I swallowed past the lump in my throat. His hand was tense on the steering wheel and the car still on, as if he was trying to figure out if he should ram it through the building or turn it off and park. "I used to grab a small order of fries and sit here . . . and pretend you were with me. Stupid." What was I doing? "I know."

I glanced at him out of the corner of my eye.

Both hands still gripped the steering wheel.

His jaw flexed.

Miller's eyes closed briefly, then flashed open before he jerked the key from the ignition and barked out, "Breakfast."

It was like slow motion, jumping out of his SUV in my sweats, walking behind him as he led the way to the doors.

He let me go first.

My legs felt like lead, and my skin erupted in a million tiny goose bumps as I tried to find my voice, to decline food right along with the trip down memory lane.

"What can I get for you?" The teen didn't look up from his fry-caged prison behind the cash register.

"Five sausage and cheddar McMuffins, two orange juices, and . . ." He paused. "Water."

The guy repeated the order.

Miller didn't ask if I was hungry or thirsty or anything.

I assumed I at least got an orange juice.

Then again, I never ordered at fast food restaurants. I'd always felt like I was getting judged, even if I made healthy choices; it was as if I couldn't be free to eat what other people did because I somehow didn't deserve it, even though I was healthy. I was over it—but I still hated dealing with the looks so I avoided them at all costs.

We waited for our food.

I tried to look at anything and everything but Miller, but everywhere I looked was filled with the past.

Even the stupid red and yellow straws reminded me of when we used to steal them and use them at school in our sodas. How he used to toy with them between his teeth, making my stomach flutter and my legs clench.

"Holy shit, you're Miller Quinton!" a pubescent voice screeched. The guy who was helping us finally looked up. I blamed technology for people's inability to look others in the eye.

"Yeah." Miller's entire demeanor changed from kicked, pissed-off bulldog to suave, confident, and sexy, and in front of my eyes, he became exactly everything I'd been haunted by during every stupid ESPN interview he'd ever done.

"What's up, man?" Miller shook his hand.

And he then signed enough autographs to make my fingers hurt.

We walked in silence back to the SUV.

And I was tossed a McMuffin.

"What's this?" I held the greasy thing in the air, and the paper crinkled as my fingers dug into the heated goodness. Saliva was already pooling in my mouth, damn him.

"Food."

"I know what it is. I just thought you ordered for you?"

"Eat."

"Are we resorting to one-word conversations now?"

He grunted and took a giant bite, his perfect teeth ripping at least half of the sandwich into his mouth.

The smell was killing me. I wanted to eat the damn thing so bad that my stomach growled, totally betraying me to Miller, who was already finishing off his last McMuffin and sipping his orange juice with a knowing smirk.

"It's not in the manual." I tried to hand it back to him, even though I wanted to eat it. It wasn't even hunger that was winning, just some sick, misplaced nostalgia that if I did, things would be back to normal again.

He didn't budge.

"Miller." I groaned to myself. "I have to do weigh-ins every week."

He sipped the orange juice louder, the straw coming up semi-empty with every draw. Miller shoved the empty cup into the cup holder, grabbed the sandwich, slowly unwrapped it, took one bite, and then handed it to me again.

"It won't work." I breathed out the lie even as I licked my lips. Yeah, it was already working.

The sandwich touched my lips. He grinned and then tilted his head in a very taunting, sexy-as-hell way.

He couldn't get any sexier in that moment.

Holding a sandwich against my lips like it was better than sex. *Which, let's be honest . . . close tie.*

"I won't tell," he whispered.

And suddenly, my brain wasn't just lusting after the sandwich.

I took one bite.

A huge bite.

Too big for my mouth.

Miller's eyes heated.

It was dirty McDonald's foreplay.

I chewed.

He made a noise in his chest before visibly adjusting himself and letting out a curse.

I took the sandwich from him and neatly wrapped it back up, then tucked it into the bag and wiped my mouth with a napkin.

His breathing was heavy as he shoved the orange juice into my empty hand, then turned on the car again. He drove toward my apartment.

"Take a right," I whispered, my chest heavy. "And then another left. I live just up the road so I can walk from there."

Miller's eyes gazed over the part of town I was embarrassed to be living in. He was in a penthouse, and I was living in the cheapest part of Bellevue, which wasn't really even Bellevue anymore. The gas station across from the apartment had bars over the windows and a bail bonds company was attached to it.

"No." He bit out the word like he was pissed again. "I'm not letting you walk. I don't care that it's daylight. Now, where do you live?"

My eyes watered.

They weren't tears, right? Because that wouldn't be fair. That he'd take me on a trip down memory lane and then remind me once again how far I'd fallen without him.

"Em." His eyes pleaded.

"Go another half mile," I whispered.

When he was close to the apartment building, I closed my eyes and said, "We're here, on the right."

Luxury Apartments.

That's what the sign said.

But anyone with two working eyes could see that the paint was chipping off the walls, the grass hadn't been mowed in weeks, and the sign still had rates from three years ago.

A few people had Christmas lights on from the previous year, and trash was littered around the four-level building.

"Do you live here by yourself?" he asked.

"No." I breathed a sigh of relief that I didn't. "My dad and I live here."

"What happened to your house?"

"That's enough questions for today." I swallowed the harsh pain swelling in my throat, making it hard to breathe.

"Em—"

"Drop it." I opened the door and grabbed my duffel bag. "It's not your problem, alright? I'm not your problem, remember? You don't even know me."

I threw his words back at him, hoping to inflict pain, even if it was minute compared to the emptiness I felt every day.

My phone rang, and the screen flashed Sanchez's name.

He nodded slowly, eyes flashing. "You're right. I don't."

"Thanks for the ride." I tripped over the words and slammed the door so fast I was surprised I didn't stumble backward. I let the call go to voice mail.

And let a few tears slip onto my cheeks before putting my armor back in place and walking into my apartment, head held high.

"Hi, baby!" Dad grinned from the couch. "Hope you listened well in school today!"

"Yeah." I forced a smile and lied. "I, um, have homework. So, I should get on that."

"I'm so proud of you." He looked down at the book in his hands and frowned. I knew before he said anything that he hadn't remembered reading it, even though it was his favorite. Some days it brought him out of his fog; other days it just made him angry and confused him more.

The good days were happening less and less.

And I knew it was only a matter of time before I had to figure out another plan for him. The state only paid for so much, and putting him in a home cost more than an Ivy League school.

My only hope was getting a better job.

But getting a better job also meant I couldn't cheer.

I couldn't follow my dreams.

Before my dad got this bad, he'd made me swear I would never give up my dreams for him.

It was unfair of him to ask at the time, without knowing how fast the disease would wreck his mind. We'd thought we had years before he lost his job, before he lost his sanity.

We'd been wrong.

Chapter Fourteen

Miller

I don't know how long I drove around—a few hours, at least. Finally, I made my way back to my empty apartment, my duffel bag in one hand and an empty McDonald's bag in the other.

I could have thrown it away in the parking garage trash.

But for some reason, my fingers were having a hard time parting with just one more memory that I knew would be soon forgotten.

Nothing made sense.

Why would Emerson and her father have to move out of their house?

He'd had a really good teaching job at Shoreline College. The man had a PhD.

The more I thought about it the more curious I felt. The more sick that she'd been living like that—and that maybe I'd been wrong about her.

Until the elevator door opened to my penthouse, and loud music greeted me.

Damn Sanchez.

I went to his door first and banged my fist against the wood grain so hard I was surprised it didn't splinter.

He jerked it open and turned toward the living room.

Was that an open invitation?

With a curse, I dropped my duffel outside the door and entered. "Can you keep it down?"

"Nope." A few of my teammates, Jax included, waved from their spot on the couch. Naturally, they were playing *Madden* because we didn't get enough football every day of our lives.

"I've got Brady!" someone yelled.

"Beer?" Sanchez tossed me a Sam Adams before I could protest. I didn't want beer. I needed something a bit stronger if I was going to have to look at that guy's ugly mug for the entire season, especially if he was going to keep kissing Emerson in front of me.

With a sigh, I sat down, knowing that if I went back to my apartment, I'd just mope around or study playbooks, and that sounded depressing and boring as hell.

It just proved the point. Money doesn't buy happiness.

I hadn't been happy, truly happy, since Emerson.

Football. College. I'd smiled at the cameras. I'd dated here and there, but there was always this emptiness, like she'd dug out my heart and left an empty hole in my chest.

"Chug it." Sanchez slapped a hand on my shoulder. "And then get another. You're way too tense, man, it's probably why I'm winning."

I scowled. "I never agreed to a pissing match."

"And yet, who's keeping score?"

I flicked off the cap and drank.

"I'm loaning her a car."

The beer shot out of my mouth, nailing Jax in the back of the head and dripping down the nice, white leather couch.

"Thanks, man!" Jax called over, while Thomas grabbed a towel from the kitchen and tossed it at Jax's head.

"The hell you are!"

Sanchez's grin was pure evil. My fingers itched to punch him, maim him, throw him out his own window, and run him over with my car!

"Why?" He frowned. "When I called the mechanic—thanks for that info, by the way." He took a long draw of his beer. "They said it would cost more to fix the car than it was worth. So, she sells the car for parts, saves up a nice little nest egg, buys a new car, and in between, I let her use one of mine."

My eyes narrowed. "How many do you have?"

Sanchez didn't say anything before looking away. "Well, yesterday I had one."

I ran a hand over my buzzed head. "And today?"

"Two," he said slowly. "Sorry. It's hard counting that high."

"So basically . . . you bought her a car that you're going to loan her, all because you want to have sex with her? Does that sound about right?"

"Who?" Jax called out.

"No one," Sanchez and I said in unison.

I nodded toward the kitchen.

He followed.

"She won't take it, trust me. This is Em we're talking about. Plus, she's going to see right through you. It's like a sex gift. You can't give her a sex gift if—" I stopped talking. What the hell was I doing? Helping him date her? I stared inside the beer bottle and then peered at Sanchez. "Did you drug me?"

He burst out laughing. "Actually, I was wondering the same thing. It's not like you to spill secrets, especially about a girl you want as bad as Em."

"I don't," I lied.

"Alright." He licked his lips. "So you really don't mind then? If I just fill those giant shoes you left behind and step in as boyfriend, best friend, bed buddy, and all-around best sexual partner she's ever had?"

"Do whatever you want, man." I tried to keep my voice even. "Just don't hurt her."

"Something tells me she's been taking care of herself for a while, no thanks to you." He tossed his empty beer bottle in the trash. "It's not like I bought a brand-new Maserati."

I frowned harder. "What did you get then?"

He grinned like he'd just won the presidency. "Brand-new Honda."

Yeah. I was going to kill him.

Any other car would have embarrassed her.

And Sanchez had to get noble and buy her a newer version of the car she already has? So she doesn't feel weird?

"Bastard," I mumbled under my breath.

"Hey, at least I warned you."

The fact that he was taking care of her, that the team whore was willing to do anything to sleep with her was making me dizzy. But he hadn't proven that he wasn't the better man. And I knew just like everyone else, the guy was a freaking serial dater, he went from woman to woman, and the fact that he'd been engaged before made absolutely no sense.

Because when I was driving around feeling sorry for myself and pissed at her for abandoning me, it hadn't even occurred to me that she'd need transportation if she wanted to stay on the squad or what it would cost to take an Uber every day, four times a day.

I'd been selfish and pissed.

And once again allowed Sanchez to swoop in and play the part of the hero, which just proved I really didn't know her at all.

And in three days . . .

He'd already figured out things that had taken me years to pull out of her.

The insecurity . . . the need for a low profile with a car that didn't cost more than most people's houses . . .

He'd done the impossible, earned her friendship.

Which meant all he had to do was earn her trust and her loyalty. And then, her heart.

The beer went sour in my stomach.

"Two choices." Was Sanchez seriously still standing there? Watching my mental breakdown? Great. "You can let her be happy, let her try with someone like me . . . someone who doesn't come with baggage from the past . . . or you can fight me, hurting her in the process."

"Why does it matter? When it's just about sex?" I countered.

"Girls like Em don't sleep with guys like me," he admitted. "So, what's it going to be? You going to be my friend and hers? You going to be a good teammate and help us win the championship? Or will we war?"

"Who talks like that?" My head was starting to pound from all the stress.

Sanchez shrugged and then let out a grin as his phone buzzed on the counter; he swiped it and eyed me before saying, "Hey, Curves, I was just talking about you."

His demeanor changed around her.

And even though she would die before admitting it, hers changed around him. She was less guarded—and she smiled.

She fucking smiled.

I swallowed my hurt.

My pride.

And the breaking in my heart as I nodded toward him and mouthed, *"Friends."*

Chapter Fifteen

I'd said yes.

But it was only out of desperation, and when Sanchez said he had a spare car, the way some people talk about having spare toothbrushes or toilet paper, I'd caved. Maybe it was because I hadn't slept all night, between my dad having nightmares and roaming around the house asking for my mom, to the fact that when I logged in to my bank account I nearly burst into tears, who knew? I finally had my dream, but now that it was in my hands, I could see it so easily slipping away. Everything I promised my dad, everything I'd worked for, and for what? So I could put on a uniform and yell?

I felt so selfish.

And on top of that, I was playing with fire, the very fire that would burn me from the inside out if I even thought about stepping outside the lines. Sanchez made it clear he only wanted sex, and Miller wanted nothing to do with me. But the fact was I wanted both of them, and all it would take was a misstep on my part—or Sanchez finally getting what he wanted and then kicking me to the curb—to lose everything.

And now a car.

It went against every fiber of my being.

Taking charity.

Since I'd basically been up all night anyway, I crunched the numbers trying to figure out how to make it work financially, and the only thing I could come up with was that I either needed transportation to practices and home games, or I had to quit.

The cost of a shared Uber every day was still more than I could afford, and on top of that, my hours with cheerleading weren't exactly normal hours; plus, I didn't have time to spare, and the more I stressed over it the more I wished I had kept that bottle of wine I'd left at Sanchez's apartment, so I could drink my troubles away.

He'd said the car would be waiting for me at the stadium.

It took a good fifteen minutes in traffic. Yeah, I couldn't do this every day, especially if every Uber driver liked their music that loud.

I hopped out of the Uber and looked around. I didn't see anything.

His car wasn't there either.

A loud honk sounded as a brand-new red Honda sped into the parking lot and did a little donut before stopping a few feet away.

It was gorgeous.

It wasn't cheap.

Then again, this was Grant Sanchez. Did he ever do anything without flair or style?

He shoved open the door. He was wearing tight black football pants and a practice jersey, the keys dangled from his giant hand, and he was wearing the biggest grin I'd ever seen. I swallowed the dryness in my throat. His smile did funny things to my stomach and made me want things I had no business wanting—especially since he'd made it painfully clear in the beginning that he wanted sex. And me? Well maybe that was the cruelest joke of all, because my entire life, all I'd ever wanted . . . was love.

He stalked toward me in that predatory, larger-than-life way.

I swallowed again.

"I know that look." He stood, towering over me, and then his hands were on my hips, pulling me against his body. "It's one that says, 'Please kiss me, Sanchez. I want you. I need you. You're . . .'" He blinked his eyes. "'Amazing.'"

"I don't say *amazing* in a high-pitched voice like that," I said, a little breathless, as he started wrapping pieces of my blonde hair around his finger.

"All white girls say *amazing* like that."

"I'm not all girls."

"No . . ." His green eyes heated as he dipped his head. "You're not."

We kissed.

In the parking lot.

In front of whoever pulled into practice a half hour early. And I wanted to kiss him more. He tasted amazing, like warm cinnamon gum . . . and spice.

I laughed against his mouth.

"Never laugh at a man mid-kiss, Curves."

"This kiss is amazing." I said it in the high-pitched voice, causing a rumbling laugh to burst out of him before he pressed his mouth to mine again, forcing me to forget my own name.

Six years ago, I'd kissed a football player and lost my heart.

Five seconds ago, it felt like, maybe, I had been given a part of that heart back, and it felt good, really good.

Keys were pressed against my hand before he pulled back and kissed my nose. "It's important that all Bucks cheerleaders get to practice on time, and I've always had a hell of a lot of team spirit." He glanced down at the front of his pants. "As evidenced . . . here."

I covered my face with my hands. "Oh—kay."

"Are you blushing?" He pulled my hands away, his grin huge, and those dimples . . .

He needed to stop being so sexy, before I did something stupid like kiss him again where my coach and anyone else on the team could see us.

"You are blushing! I like it," he whispered, still gripping my hands as he kissed my nose again. "I like that I'm responsible for it."

"You would."

"Well, I am amaazzzzing." He drew out the word and winked. "Try not to get any scratches on her, Curves." His grin grew as he eyed me up and down, licking his lips like he was seconds away from devouring me. "She's delicate."

"She?"

"All red cars are girls. What? They don't teach you that shit in school?"

I rolled my eyes. "You're impossible."

"And amazing . . . say it."

"You don't need me to say it. You know it." I crossed my arms and tried to think about anything but the fact that his ass looked rock hard in those tight football pants. What the heck was I doing? This wasn't me.

Flirting with a football player that could get me fired from my dream job?

In the parking lot?

Taking a car from him?

Was I that desperate?

Or was that part of his charm? He made girls feel so good about themselves, so desirable and wanted, that once he got what he wanted, he dropped them and everything to do with them.

I wasn't sure I could trust him.

But I hated that I wanted to.

I hated that he reminded me that I had this big gaping hole in my heart that Miller used to fill—and a part of me mourned that it was Grant Sanchez doing the filling.

And not my best friend.

"Hey . . ." Sanchez winked. "Don't make me kiss that frown off your lips, Curves."

I smiled just as Miller's SUV pulled into the parking lot right next to my new cherry-red Honda. Not mine. Sanchez's. Loan, it was a loan.

I had nothing to feel guilty about.

He already had a car.

Right?

It's not like he could drive two cars at the same time.

So why did I feel ashamed?

Why did my face no doubt match the exact color of the car when Miller turned off the ignition and approached us, wearing the same mouthwatering practice uniform?

Could a person die if they experience too much sexy in one minute?

He pulled off his sunglasses and tucked them into his duffel bag, his grin huge. "Red, of course. It suits her."

Wait, what just happened?

He was smiling at me.

Miller.

My ex-best-friend who hated me.

Who force-fed me McDonald's and dropped me off at my apartment last night and fled like I had the plague.

"I'm flashy like that," I countered back with a smile of my own.

Miller's eyes held mine for a few seconds, apparently searching, darting back and forth as he licked his full lips and then held out a hand to Sanchez. They bumped fists.

"Sanchez!" Another voice sounded.

I turned around. Jax and Thomas were approaching. Sanchez gave me one last smile and walked to meet them.

Leaving me alone with Miller.

"So . . ." He nodded to the car. "You okay with this?"

I snorted. "What do you think?"

"I think the old Emerson would have felt like a prostitute, but the good kind like in *Pretty Woman*." He grinned. "And the Em now?" He eyed me up and down, scrunching up his nose. "I'm assuming you're just desperate enough to take him up on the offer but probably won't sleep until you can figure out something on your own."

"Damn it." I looked away. "And you say you don't know me anymore."

He laughed.

I held on to that laugh.

I breathed it in.

I memorized the way it made my body shiver in response.

I missed it so much that tears quickly replaced my excitement at hearing it.

Miller took one look at me, and then I was in his arms.

In.

His.

Arms.

"I'm still pissed," he whispered gruffly. "Livid, actually."

I stiffened.

He held on to me tighter.

"But . . ." He cleared his throat. "Sanchez helped me remember something last night."

"He did?" The jersey on his chest muffled my voice. I was having a hard time breathing. Did he really have no idea how strong he was? His biceps were attempting to break through the jersey!

"Yeah." He sighed, his heart was racing, so naturally mine decided to match its cadence. Stupid heart. "Remember when I stuck gum in your hair in sixth grade, so you told all my friends that I wet the bed?"

I burst out laughing. "How could I forget? I also told them you had Donald Duck sheets because you were afraid of Batman."

His laughter joined in. "We've had our share of fights, Em. I guess what I'm saying is . . . if I can get over that, I mean it was middle school, basically the most traumatic years of our lives, then I'll try to get over this. I just need time."

"That's the problem," I whispered, all humor suddenly gone. "The last time I gave you what you wanted, I never heard from you again."

He pulled back and frowned. "What are you talking about?"

I shook my head. "You're right. It doesn't matter anymore. Let's just . . . try to start over."

"Bury the hatchet," he agreed.

"Make peace." I nodded.

He frowned. "Start fresh."

We began walking side by side toward the stadium. "Come to terms?"

"Mend the fence!" he yelled in triumph.

I opened my mouth, my mind reeling. "I have nothing."

"Winner." He held up his hand for a high five.

I rolled my eyes. "It's like your eighteen-year-old self is stuck in your twenty-four-year-old body!"

And just like that . . .

I had a part of him back.

So why did I still feel guilty?

Why was I confused when Sanchez greeted me at the entrance of the stadium with a satisfied grin? And why did I feel empty when Miller took the high road and, with a quick wave, stepped off to join the other guys?

"Have fun at practice, Curves!" Sanchez grinned.

Miller turned around and added, "Two, four, six, eight, who do we appreciate?!"

"Jax!" Thomas shouted while the quarterback rolled his eyes and continued walking past everyone.

I laughed.

Maybe I was overthinking things.

I brushed by everyone in an effort to make it into the girls' locker room and felt someone staring at me.

I quickly glanced over my shoulder.

While the guys were wrestling, laughing, and being immature asshats, Miller stood there, his heated eyes focusing on nothing but me.

I shivered.

His lips pressed into a knowing grin.

Well, crap.

I felt that grin all the way to my toes, and scolded myself for allowing one simple grin to affect me more than Sanchez's heated kiss.

Chapter Sixteen

MILLER

Friends stared at each other's asses all the time. That's at least what I told myself when I watched her hips sway back and forth, her heart-shaped ass making my mouth water, and, since nobody was looking at me . . .

No harm, right?

Until she turned and locked eyes with me.

Because it was Em we were talking about.

She *knew*.

She could feel my stare.

And maybe a part of me wanted her to turn around, wanted her to see the look on my face, the hunger I still had despite my anger toward her.

"Yo." Sanchez slapped me on the back. "You in?"

"In," I repeated, wracking my brain for what they could possibly be talking about.

"Rookie dinner." Jax grabbed his helmet. "We're not as bad as some teams. It's not like we always leave the bill for them to take care of, sometimes we help them out."

Sanchez and Thomas high fived, and then Thomas snickered. "Last year it was over seven grand."

"How do you spend that much on dinner?" I wondered out loud.

"Dude, I heard New England left a forty-eight-thousand-dollar bill for their rookies last year," Thomas said seriously, his eyes wide.

I shook my head while Sanchez let out a low whistle.

"Jax has delicate tastes," Thomas said with a straight face as our quarterback approached, obviously lost on our conversation.

"Screw you." Jax gave him a shove. "It's a preseason tradition. The rookies take us out, and we get to pick, so what do you say?"

"I say . . ." I cringed, trying to think of the first restaurant that came to mind. "Cheesecake Factory?"

The guys groaned.

"What?" I laughed. "It won't be expensive, we can be as loud as we want, their servings are huge, and they serve alcohol."

"He had me at alcohol." Thomas sighed. "Alright, seven tonight, guys."

Coach chose that moment to walk into the locker room. "I don't pay you ladies to make dinner plans."

"Actually, you don't pay us at all," Sanchez pointed out.

Coach Mike glared. "You're right." His glare turned into an evil grin. "And thank you so much for volunteering to lead us through conditioning this morning, Grant."

"Fucking hell," Sanchez groaned. "Tell me we don't have the tires today."

"Good news!" Coach shouted. "We have tire flips today!"

I smacked Sanchez on the back as we all filed out of the locker room and onto the field.

The cheerleaders were almost always in the other practice field whenever we had the same practice times. The music to one of their dance routines floated through the air.

I ran out onto the fifty-yard line and put on my helmet.

And the thought hit me.

Emerson was on the other field practicing.

And I was a starting tight end for the Bucks.

The dream we'd had so many years ago had happened—just not the way we'd planned.

Because in every single one of those plans, I'd always seen her by my side.

As if Sanchez was reading my damn thoughts, the shit turned around and howled as he ran toward the first tire.

Our conditioning coach, Rob, hated us.

Or life.

Breathing.

It was rare to walk out of the stadium without praying for a wheelchair or at least a stretcher.

I'd had only a few days of practice and I'd never been so sore in my entire existence. Most football teams stuck with pretty strategic weight lifting programs and fundamentals, not the Bucks. No, the Bucks liked to use large objects, body-weight exercises, sprints, and a hell of a lot of agility training, the kind of training that appears easy but ends up kicking you in the ass.

"Let's go, Miller!"

I took a deep breath and charged after the next tire.

"Miller!" Rob yelled my name so loud my ears hurt. "You can do more flips than that; when you're done you hit the ground, chest touches the ground, then you're on your feet with high knees for fifty meters, then you touch the ground again, got it?"

I wanted to ask when I could stop.

But I knew if I did he'd just give me more.

With a grunt I flipped the tire five more times, then hit the ground, jumped to my feet, did my high knees, then hit the ground again. When he didn't say anything I repeated the process until my legs ached.

He blew the damn whistle fifteen minutes later.

Fifteen. Minutes.

People could get rhabdo from that shit.

But that's why the Bucks were the best. The agility training itself, the yoga stretches, the stretching in general is what made them fast as hell on the field, and tough. Gone were the days of three-hundred-pound offensive linemen, now we had guys who were six six, two fifty, and could run just as fast as some of the running backs.

Athletes. I was with true athletes. And it felt good.

"Again!" Rob yelled.

Sanchez gave me a look of pure irritation, then made a gun motion and pointed to his head before he grabbed the tire and went at it. I had to hand it to him, he joked a lot, he teased, but one thing about the guy was always true: he always worked his ass off and he expected everyone else to as well. The man was hard to respect off the field—but on the field? I could get in line with that type of leadership. Loath as I was to admit it.

"Water!" Rob called. "Sanchez, two more flips then you can break."

He grunted.

"Hey." Jax tossed a water bottle at me. "How are you liking things so far?"

"Is this the QB leadership talk or are you being serious?"

Jax cracked a smile. "This is the *hey kid you're doing really good don't fuck things up talk*, how am I doing?"

"Great." I smirked and then watched Sanchez literally do tire flips down the rest of the field. "What the hell is he doing?"

"Leading." Jax shrugged. "My guess is Rob had a number of flips he wanted everyone to do and we were short a few, and rather than have someone else jump on the field midbreak—Sanchez did it himself. He's like that."

"Sanchez." I repeated his name. "Really?"

"I know." Jax's tone turned serious. "It's hard to believe but, as much as I put up with his shit—it's not because he's so good that I have to—it's that the guys respect him, other teams fear him, and well, he finally dumped the ex-fiancé that nearly destroyed his life by way of cheating on him with good ol' Thomas."

"Whoa, back up." I held up my hand. "Thomas?"

"It's a rumor. Neither of them will confirm it. Hell, I don't even know how the guys are still friends let alone teammates, there was a huge fight in the locker room. Accusations thrown around, it was in the middle of playoffs last year. Thought Sanchez was going to take Thomas's head off—I told him to leave it on the field and he did, though it didn't keep him from giving Thomas a black eye. The guy apologized, said she came on to him or whatever, which was probably true, the girl was poison."

"You girls done gossiping?" Sanchez's voice interrupted our conversation. "Besides, my past isn't all that interesting." He chugged some water then tossed the cup into the trash.

"How many more flips?" I asked.

He locked eyes with me. "Ten. Why?"

"Next time I'll do them."

He pressed his lips together in a firm line and then gave me a nod. "Yeah, thanks, you know you don't have to though."

"Right." I slapped him on the back and grabbed my helmet. "But neither do you."

Jax watched the exchange with interest and then followed us onto the field.

Rob took one look at us and shouted, "Run!"

It was going to be a long ass day.

"I can't feel my legs." I groaned from my spot in the ice tub, next to Sanchez's ice tub. He was setting a record for the amount of times to say "Fuck" in under a minute.

"Miller!" Jax's voice interrupted my pain session as a million little needles attacked my body all at once. "You did good today." He stopped in front of the tub and gave me the look.

It was the look that all quarterbacks give when they don't want to use words to say that your shit didn't stink. I'd always respected Jax as a quarterback. He'd been drafted ten years ago, and at thirty-two, he was still just as good as he'd been when he started for the Bucks, and he was a franchise quarterback, the type who started with one team and would retire with them too.

He rarely spoke, but when he did, my ears always strained to listen because, for whatever reason, I liked him. I barely knew the guy, and I wanted to go to war with him.

Football.

"Thanks, man," I finally said. "I'm still getting used to some of the plays. I know a few of my progressions were shit today, but I've got you."

"I know," he said quickly. "Just make sure that none of your old teammates take off my head when we play the Pilots in twelve days, and we'll be good."

I nodded. "That's what I'm here for, to keep you alive."

"And to keep your dick working, even though we all know how rarely it gets used," Sanchez chimed in, earning an eye roll from Jax before he walked off.

"You keep giving him shit, and he's not going to throw to you." I'd seen it before, quarterbacks that got pissed at their wide receivers and were willing to throw to anyone, even their own center, to keep from adding good stats.

"Jax?" Sanchez cursed again and checked the timer. "Could have sworn it's been longer than five minutes." He leaned his head back against the silver tin tub; it was uncomfortable as hell. "He and I go way back. I give him shit. He ignores it, passes me the ball anyway, and I make big plays. The only thing that could ever come between us would be his sister, and believe me, I want none of that."

"His sister? I'm not following."

"Hah!" Sanchez grinned up at the ceiling. "Kinsey. Your ex-best-friend's new best friend, my soon-to-be girlfriend's best friend—the cheerleader—that's his baby sister."

"Kinsey?" I repeated. The little brunette spitfire who looked ready to shank Sanchez for even breathing in her direction. "She's—"

"Jax's total opposite, believe me. Where he calms the room with a freaking stare, she brings down the house with her voice. A shame really, since she's so hot—but that voice. It's like nails on a chalkboard. My dick trembles, man, and not in a good way."

My body was numb.

My brain was going a million miles a minute. He'd said *girlfriend*. He was going to make Emerson his girlfriend, and the sick part, that was his right. He didn't pretend not to know her; he didn't ignore her. He didn't force her to eat McDonald's then demand she spill about the last six years.

She left me.

I clenched the edge of the tub and tried to get my breathing under control as memories snaked around my chest, making it hard to breathe.

(Then)

"You were out late," Dad slurred. "You sleeping around?"

"No." I hated him. I hated him so much that it was all I felt when I looked at his glassy eyes and messy hair. He'd been drinking. Again. I prepared for the worst.

Instead, he started mumbling about taking care of "that disaster, Emerson." My heart clenched in my chest.

Our calls had gotten less frequent, and last week when we had our Friday night chat, she'd said she needed to talk to me about something important, and then she'd cried. I'd pressed her for info but she said it had to wait . . .

"I'm going to bed." *I shoved past my dad.*

"Pathetic. You gonna call that white trash again?" *An evil laugh accompanied his swaying.* "I got news for you. She won't be bothering you again."

I ignored him.

And went into my room in search of my phone.

Only to come up empty.

I stomped up to my dad. "Where the hell is my phone?"

"It broke." *He shrugged.* "Get you a new one in the morning."

I had her number memorized; it would be totally fine.

But it wasn't.

Because that very next day, with my new phone in hand, I called her.

The number had been disconnected.

"Get your ass out." Sanchez splashed cold water onto my face. "I'm hungry and I need a ride back to our place."

I groaned. "Please don't call it *our* place. We don't live together."

"You'd be a shit roommate anyway," he grumbled. "Do you even know how to smile? Have a good time?"

I grabbed my towel and stepped out of the tub. "Yes. I just prefer to keep my good times to myself." I winced.

Sanchez's eyebrows shot up. "Please tell me that came out wrong."

"Completely." I burst out laughing.

He joined in.

And suddenly I realized the impossible had happened. The guy who was going after the love of my life—who dreamt about seeing her naked—was becoming my friend.

Here I'd been so worried about them . . .

That I hadn't even thought about myself.

Or how lonely I'd been.

Maybe that was his superpower; Grant Sanchez was able to weasel his way into any situation and come out on top.

I just hoped, for Em's sake, that he really liked her.

And not just because she had a nice ass.

"Did you just groan?" Sanchez asked.

"No." Shit.

"Yeah, you did."

"You're imagining things because your dick nearly froze off." I started walking toward my locker.

"Uh-huh, and how is it that yours doesn't seem to be suffering from any sort of . . . shrinkage." He pointed.

I quickly covered up with my towel. "Are you seriously staring at my cock right now?"

"Who were you thinking about?" He grinned. "Come on, tell me. We're friends, right?"

"We will never be good enough friends where cock-staring is acceptable, man." I tossed a towel at his head and finished dressing to Sanchez's laughter.

A few minutes later, and I was driving us to our home.

Shit.

I said *our* home.

As if he and I had one together.

"Did you just sigh really loud?" Sanchez asked.

"Do you EVER just keep things to yourself?" I asked.

He hesitated and then said, "No, I don't like silence."

"Shocker."

"See ya in a few hours." He unlocked his door.

"Huh?"

"Team dinner. Rookies paying. I'm getting steak. Salads are for bitches."

"Jax eats salad," I pointed out, since I'd seen him chow down on more than one occasion.

"He says if he puts steak on it, it doesn't count. Trust me, I've had this argument numerous times. I always let him win. See? I can play nice."

"When it benefits you." I unlocked my own door and pushed it open.

He threw his head back and laughed. "That's true. Just don't cross me, and all is well, yeah?"

His laughter was gone.

Leaving a challenging glint in his eyes.

And I suddenly felt like shit.

He'd done nothing but help me.

And I'd been thinking about a certain girl's ass.

"Heard ya loud and clear, man," I said. "I'm going to take a quick nap before tonight."

He saluted me and went into his own apartment.

Chapter Seventeen

MILLER

The team dinner went about as good as any team dinner could go. We ordered an insane amount of alcohol—and didn't even drink most of it since we had a grueling practice the next day, and the same went for food.

All in all, the final bill was around eight grand, small by most standards for the rookie meal.

Justin Ranz, our newest rookie, offensive line, took one look at it and paled.

"Chill, man." Sanchez hit him in the back. "You get your bonus in, what, a few days?"

"A week." His voice was disgusted.

"Right." Sanchez nodded. "And you got a three-million signing bonus. This is chump change." He frowned. "Well, I mean technically, after taxes you only get, what, that would be around half, considering you're in a whole new bracket, and then you're going to want to buy a car, because who doesn't need a nice vehicle to transport them in?"

"Don't forget a house," I piped up, knowing exactly what he was doing.

I'd heard of it before, the mentors making sure the rookies didn't shit away all their money just because they were suddenly professional athletes. I snapped my fingers.

"And all those family members. Friends. Cousins that come out of the woodwork and need a favor." I whistled. "Wow, guys, what does that really leave our rookies with?"

The game was simple. Make the rookies think twice before they start swiping their credit cards. The rookie dinners sucked for a lot of reasons, and mine last year had been pure hell since I hadn't gotten my bonus yet. I'd had to fucking beg the owner of the restaurant to let me hit him up once I had my money. I even went as far as to write a check for the money I didn't even have yet, with my agent's number on it so the owner knew I was good for it.

Hell, it had been demeaning, especially since I thought I was the shit. I mean I'd gotten over eighteen million for five years. As a rookie. That didn't happen to tight ends, even the good ones. It had been a humbling experience, and one that I'd never forget. I hoped to do the same thing to the guys on our team, the ones who were currently looking at us like we were complete monsters.

"To answer your question, that leaves you with jack shit." Jax grinned, his voice commanding as ever. I wouldn't put it past the guy to have the majority of his money in investments and Roth IRAs. He just screamed responsibility.

Justin looked ready to puke. "I don't have this kind of money now."

We all stood.

Except for the rookies.

There were around seventeen of them and not all of them would even make it past the first game.

"Well . . ." I shrugged. "That's not really our problem, is it?"

"Let's go." Sanchez chuckled as we all walked out of The Cheesecake Factory into the brisk Bellevue air.

I took a deep inhale while Sanchez slapped me on the back. "What was the damage for you last year?"

I shrugged. "Over three grand. You?"

"Seven."

"Please tell me you mean hugs," I joked.

"Hah!" he barked. "Bullshit. I would have hugged every damn person in the restaurant if that were the case. Those little shits got off lucky, and you know it. If they split between the seventeen of them, they'll still be skipping through rainbows and screwing unicorns come tomorrow morning."

"Does one actually screw a unicorn?" Jax wondered aloud.

"I'd do one," Thomas offered.

"On that note . . ." I shook my head at the guys as a sense of belonging washed over me. My last team had been friends. These guys were quickly turning into brothers.

Something I'd always wanted.

But never had.

Sanchez had been the only guy to give me shit, and the more I got to know him, the more I wondered if he'd done it to see if I would flip my shit or ignore him.

He seemed like that kind of guy. Always gauging other people's reactions to see if they could control themselves. Clearly, there was more than met the eye with that guy.

Damn it.

And now I was thinking about Emerson again.

The legitimate like I felt for Sanchez pissed me off because the guy was already texting on his phone, his grin huge like he was about ready to get laid.

Meanwhile, I wanted to punch a brick wall and imagined his face.

And he hadn't done a damn thing wrong.

"Practice!" Jax called out to everyone as he opened the door to his sleek Mercedes. His green eyes flashed. "You guys all need to head to bed. I heard conditioning's going to be complete hell tomorrow, just a heads up."

We all groaned.

All of us but Sanchez.

Who was still grinning at his phone like an idiot.

"Sanchez," Jax barked. "You hear me?"

"Yeah, yeah." He waved him off without once looking up from his screen. "Practice, hell, early, bed."

"Sometimes I wonder if he just remembers keywords and repeats them back to me." Jax rolled his eyes. "Later." With a wave, he was in his car, and I was still staring at Sanchez, my body tense with that creepy stalker feeling you get when you know you shouldn't be eavesdropping but wonder if it's totally inappropriate to ask to see his phone and lie about forgetting yours.

"So, I'll just see you later then." Maybe my voice was a little too loud, my stance rigid as hell. "Yeah, Sanchez?"

He finally glanced up, a smirk marring his features. "Don't worry, Mom. I'll be in bed on time. I just have something I gotta do first."

Please let that something not be Emerson.

"Right." I scratched my head as fury pumped through my veins. "Have a good night."

"You too, brother." He waved me off with his phone and kept texting.

My legs may as well have been filled with cement as I made my way back to my car and numbly opened the door. What the hell was I doing?

Nothing.

I was doing nothing.

Because I didn't know what to do.

And a part of me was still angry.

Hurt.

Pissed.

And the other part?

Was longing for the same relationship that had slipped through my fingers so many years ago.

The one that Sanchez and Emerson now had.

Bastard.

I had a bad feeling that he was texting her.

And an even worse feeling that she was texting him back.

Texting should burn in hell.

And I probably should too, since during Sanchez's bathroom break, I had taken full opportunity to find her number on his phone.

And store it in mine.

Chapter Eighteen

EMERSON

Sanchez: Quick, take a picture of your panty drawer. I want to win a bet.

I rolled my eyes and yawned as I swiped away from the book I was reading and started typing in messages.

Me: Don't have one.
Sanchez: "Dead" Where the hell is that emoji?

I couldn't suppress my laugh.

Me: How much have you had to drink?

Sanchez: Clearly not enough if the thought of you not wearing panties is giving me a boner the size of Texas. I would send a picture, but I'm afraid it won't fully fit in the screen, and that wouldn't be fair to you.

The guy was insane! Like a psychotic, wiggly hot worm that worked its way into your life and refused to let go. I relived his stupid kiss about as many times as I relived Miller's heated look.

I was in deep.

And the worst part was that I didn't remember how I ever got there. What had I done to gain Sanchez's unwanted attention? And why was Miller so pissed at me? Especially when he seemed to think I was the one who put him on a friendship time-out? I wanted to ask him, but I was afraid that the more I dug into his past . . .

The more he would dig into mine.

And I wasn't quite ready for that conversation. I wasn't sure I would ever be ready for that conversation or for the emotional wreckage that came with it.

Me: How sad for me. I'll draw a stick figure and use my imagination. Happy?
Sanchez: STICK FIGURE?

I yawned again. I was exhausted.

Me: What? Is that not the same thing?

Sanchez: Let me come over.
Me: No.
Sanchez: I'm sorry. That's one of the 5 words I don't recognize in the English language.

Me: And the other 4?

Who was this guy? Seriously? My stomach flipped a bit as I waited for him to respond back.

Sanchez: Go on a date with me this week and maybe I'll tell you.

I groaned out loud.

Me: I see what you did there. Hook, line, and sinker, yeah?
Sanchez: This isn't my first rodeo.

I grinned.

Sanchez: Say yes.

Honestly, he didn't need to bribe me; I'd already decided to give him a chance. I needed to put all thoughts of Miller as far away from me as possible and actually come to terms with the fact that whatever we'd had in the past was over.

And it was time to stop living in the broken pieces of what was left of us.

Me: Yes.
Sanchez: I just screamed in the parking lot. I think I scared a lady. Don't worry though. I told her I was just really excited that the prettiest girl in the world said she'd have sex with me.
Me: I didn't say sex.
Sanchez: I'm very optimistic.
Me: Tone it down or I'll say no.
Sanchez: Deal. So . . . Saturday night?

I chewed my lower lip. It was the last Saturday before preseason games started, so if I wanted to go on a date with him, that would be the best time. Especially with both of our grueling schedules. Besides, the guy was letting me use his car. It was the least I could do, right?

My stomach did that little flip thing again at the thought and then dropped when my eyes fell to the manual on the floor. The one that included a solid chapter about not fraternizing with the players. But that same manual also talked about how long my fingernails should be, maybe they just liked to cover all their bases? The more I thought about it the more I tried to justify the fact that I was texting him back my answer and risking everything for a guy who said he just wanted sex—but pursued me like he actually cared about me.

Me: Deal.
Sanchez: See you soon, Curves.

I fell back on my bed, my phone somewhere near my fingertips as I stared up at the cheap ceiling. It had stains from water damage. My room really wasn't any bigger than most people's closets, modestly decorated with a desk, a nightstand, and a cute pink chair that Miller had gotten me for my sixteenth birthday after he saw me lusting after it at Target.

I winced at the thought of that stupid chair.

And the fact that he used to sit in it because it made me laugh to see his giant body in such a tiny spot.

Memories had such a painful and annoying way of popping up when least expected, especially when I was trying my hardest to focus on Sanchez.

On the good.

On my future.

Groaning, I slammed my fists against the mattress a few times then grabbed my phone, only to see the screen light up with an unknown number and a text.

The message was long—longer than most text messages should be.

Unknown caller: Do you remember State finals our junior

year?

My heart froze in my chest.
I quickly typed back.

Me: Who is this?
Unknown caller: Who do you think? Miller.

I had a choice. Text him back or tell him it was late and I needed to go to bed. Somehow it felt wrong, finishing a text with Sanchez only to start texting Miller. His teammate. Building mate.

My ex-best-friend.

Suddenly hot, I threw the covers off and texted back.

Me: How did you get my number?
Miller: I stole it.
Me: From?
Miller: Doesn't matter. It's mine now.

I knew he was a possessive guy, but he had rarely shown me that side, maybe because he didn't really have a reason to in high school, until he finally admitted he had feelings. A chill erupted down my spine.

Me: Of course I remember State. You caught for a touchdown, defense held their offense at the 40-yard line with 8 seconds left, and they couldn't get close enough for a field goal. We went to IHOP to celebrate. And you ate two orders of pancakes.
Miller: With whipped cream.

I licked my lips as my stomach clenched.

Me: And strawberries.
Miller: Good memory.
Me: Yeah, well, I like pancakes.
Miller: Want to know what else I remember?

I was afraid this was going someplace we couldn't return from, but I was stupid enough to fall for it, stupid enough to still care.

Me: What?

My throat was dry as I waited for him to respond. I could see he was typing, but beyond that, nothing.

Miller: You dipped your finger in my whipped cream—and I sucked it off.

My jaw nearly dropped to the floor. Was he flirting with me? After he'd agreed to be my friend? And had basically given his blessing for me and Sanchez?

Me: You bit me too.
Miller: On purpose.
Me: Because you wanted to draw blood?
Miller: Let's just call it accidental over-aggression because of the fact that I had you in my mouth.

Okay, and we just jumped over that line and pounced.

Me: Oh?

Seriously, what was I supposed to say to that?

Miller: You busy tonight?
Me: Yup, sleeping.
Miller: Not hanging out with your new boyfriend?
Me: Not my boyfriend, and no, we're going to go on a date
later this week though.

I don't know why I said it. I wasn't trying to make him jealous; maybe I was just desperate to lay down the boundaries of our relationship again—because Miller had way too much power over me. A simple conversation had me holding my breath . . . a heated look had me clenching my thighs . . . and it wasn't fair.

Not to me or to Sanchez.

Not even to Miller.

Miller: Have fun.

He didn't text again.

I tossed and turned for the next two hours until finally giving up and padding over to my pink chair with my blanket. I imagined the chair was Miller's arms.

I hated myself for needing the comfort that fantasy brought.

Almost as much as I hated the fact that when I needed his arms the most, he'd all but dropped me from a cliff.

Chapter Nineteen

MILLER

I felt guilty.

I'd slept like shit, and it showed during practice. I was caught unaware by both Xander and Elliot, two rookie defensive ends, and it was more than embarrassing when Xander took my helmet off.

"Miller!" Sanchez yelled. "What gives?"

I shook my head. "Nothing. Tired. No excuses." I eyed Jax. "Can we go again?"

He nodded, and I ran my route, this time blocking and turning for a catch. I was the last option—a good one—but typically my job was to make sure that Jax had enough time to get shit done.

I caught it.

Our offensive coach, Merill, motioned me forward. Great. I wasn't ready to get my ass chewed out because I'd been texting Emerson for ten minutes, only to stare at my own ceiling for three hours unable to sleep because I kept imagining Sanchez kissing her. Not that he'd know that. I only had myself to blame, right? I was flirting with danger.

And I couldn't stop.

I'd texted her a few more times this morning, asking her about practice and her day. Shit. I was an idiot.

"What's up?" I pulled off my helmet.

Merill tapped me on the temple. "Everything okay up here?"

"Yeah, Coach." I shook him off. "You know how it goes. Jet lag."
Really? Still? It was bullshit and he probably knew it.

He nodded knowingly. "I want your head in this, alright? You're
a leader. People look up to you. Between you, Sanchez, and Jax, I
have some of the best players in the league, but even the best players
have shit for brains when it comes to their mental and emotional
health. I need you okay here . . ." He pointed to my head again. "So
you can be the greatest out there." He jabbed his finger at the field.
"Now, tell Jax we're running the play again, and this time, block like
you mean it, son."

"Yes, sir." I jogged off and threw my helmet on.

We ran that same play until I could do it in my sleep.

I was so sore from blocking that I was actually looking forward to
the ice bath that usually came after practice. I could even get on board
with the trainer massaging my legs out.

Coach was right.

My head needed to be in the game.

And that shit started now.

I needed to unpack.

This was my home now.

And even though I was still exhausted from practice, I knew if I
didn't stay busy, I'd just text Emerson again.

And if just texting her was distracting enough to throw me off my
game, then I knew if I kept doing that and going any further, stepping
over any more lines, who knew what that would do to me during the
season. Maybe the coaches were right about that whole no-fraternization policy.

A loud knock sounded on my door, and I nearly tripped over a box to get there before the pounding fist took down the entire structure. "What?" I jerked open the door; Sanchez was just about to knock again, his grin huge. It was hard to stay pissed at him when he looked so . . . friendly. The guy had killed it out on the field today again too, and encouraged me to shake it off when I wanted to slam my hand into Xander's face after getting hit again.

"Well, good evening to you too!" he shouted. Why was he shouting?

"Huh?"

"Let's go." He tugged my arm. "I decided to have a party. And I invited women. You do know what those are, right? Curves in all the right places, gorgeous bodies you can't wait to sink your . . ." He stopped talking and winked. "You know."

"I'm exhausted," I said honestly as he continued pulling me toward his door. "And I played like shit."

"Your shit is another man's best game of his life, just sayin'." Sanchez shrugged. "Now, go drink and try not to bark at the girls. Biting, however, is completely allowed."

He pulled me through my door and pushed me toward his.

Soft music bumped from his surround sound system, and every food imaginable was on his main dining room table, along with enough alcohol to get our entire building drunk.

Most of my teammates were there. Jax was in the corner looking pissed as hell, and Thomas was taking shots.

Yeah, tomorrow was going to be a rough one for Thomas.

I didn't recognize the girls surrounding a few of the rookies, but I did recognize Kinsey as she approached her brother and started throwing her hands in the air like she was ready to slap him across the face.

I didn't know her well. But I did know Jax, and I'd never seen him look so pissed in my entire life. Who knew the guy even got angry?

I grabbed two beers from the cooler and made my way over to them before she took his head off.

She stormed away just as I made it to him.

Wordlessly, I handed him the beer.

He took it without looking at me then gulped half of it down before saying, "She's making me lose my hair."

I almost spit out my own drink, barely managing to swallow before I laughed. "What?"

"My hair." Jax didn't take his eyes from her. "I think I found a bald spot. I blame her." He took another drink. "I also never drink during the season."

"Still technically preseason."

"And now she's turning me into an alcoholic."

"It's half a beer."

"Right, and it's going to take at least another six in order for me to forget the fact that about five minutes ago she was dancing on one of the tables because Sanchez made a bet with her and she lost."

"What kind of bet?"

"Oh, Sanchez bet that he could get Emerson to kiss him in front of everyone, and she did. Loser had to dance on the table. Kinsey was the loser. She could have said no. Sanchez and I have an understanding, you know?"

My body buzzed with anger and awareness as Emerson's laugh rang out. She launched her fist into the air in triumph and started doing a little dance while Sanchez pretended to pout next to her.

"Again!" she shouted, grabbing a deck of cards.

"What are they playing?"

"Indian poker." Jax sighed, "I've never seen Sanchez so obsessed. I'd say it was pathetic, but it's kind of nice to see a side of him that isn't constantly screwing anything with a pulse, especially after everything with his ex."

I needed a subject change, and fast. I didn't want to like Sanchez, and yet I was viewing him as a friend and not a potential enemy for chasing the one girl I could never forget.

"Holy shit, is that the bald spot?" I pointed to Jax's ear.

He spit out a mouthful of beer and touched his head. "Seriously?"

I grinned. "Sorry, I had to."

"Jackass. See if I pass to you ever again." He smirked.

"You need me." I folded my arms and laughed. "Admit it."

"You're still a jackass."

Kinsey glanced over at us, then smiled at me before glaring at her brother again.

"I hate that she hangs out with the players." He downed the rest of his beer. "But the more I argue the worse she gets. It's almost better not to say anything, you know?"

"Yeah." I eyed a laughing Emerson. "I do."

Jax elbowed me. "Lusting after another teammate's girl?"

I knew he said it in teasing.

And I had a hell of a time not confessing everything right there, so instead I shrugged. "We went to high school together."

"Was she that hot in high school?"

"She's hotter now. All woman," I admitted.

Emerson threw her head back and laughed as blonde hair whipped down her back. Her black leggings were paired with a gray beanie and an off-the-shoulder T-shirt that made my mouth water. Her shoulders had always been one of my favorite things, and like a freak I was staring at them as if she'd actually let me lick them . . . touch them . . .

I swallowed the dryness in my throat and looked away, but not before catching her gaze. It said all the things that she never said out loud.

And it killed me.

Yeah, I needed another beer—now.

I made my way back over to the drinks. Kinsey was pouring herself a glass of wine and still glaring at her brother from across the room.

"If looks could kill." I smiled.

"Sorry." Her face fell. "He's just so . . ." She made a fist. "Overprotective."

"Sorry to break it to you, but he's your big brother. He'd probably lock you in a closet if it was legal."

Her lips twitched. "You think he hasn't tried it?"

"Let me guess. You escaped with nothing but a bobby pin and feminine wiles?"

"How'd you know!" Her eyes widened in shock, her words dripping with sarcasm. "Seriously, I think my only hope is to get him laid."

I tilted my head. "And how are you going to manage that?"

"Well, I was going to force Emerson into slave labor, not that it would be a hardship. Jax has an eight-pack and would worship her, but it seems Sanchez already peed all over her, so . . ." She shrugged. "I need to find fresh meat."

I gripped my beer bottle so hard my fingers ached. "Sanchez and Emerson." Why? Why was I setting myself up like this? Again? "Did they hit it off right away or what?"

Her eyes narrowed. "Why don't you ask her?"

"It's not my business."

"And it's not mine either." She smiled sweetly.

"Well-played." I knocked my drink against hers, but not before she sent a fleeting look toward Sanchez. I would have missed it had I not recognized it right away because it was the same damn look I wore every freaking day. "How long?"

"What?" Her head whipped around so fast I was surprised it didn't come clean off and land in the chip bowl. "How long what?"

"Have you been in love with him?" I sighed knowingly while she started gulping down more wine than I'd seen a cheerleader gulp, ever.

When she came up for air, I grabbed the glass out of her hand and set it on the table, then replaced it with a water bottle.

"Thanks," she mumbled. "And it doesn't matter. My brother would kill him, literally. I'm not talking kill, as in he'd have a talk with him then punch him in the face. I'm ninety-nine percent sure that Jax would rip his head off and feed it to his iguana."

"Jax has an iguana?"

"That's what you take from this conversation?"

"But it's an iguana," I pointed out.

"It's Sanchez's head."

Point, Kinsey.

"I hate to admit it, but you're right. I'd never seen Jax angry until tonight, watching you flirt."

"Right." She grinned. "So, flirt with me and piss him off more."

"No deal." I took a step back and held up my hands. "As much as I like iguanas—favorite pet in the third grade, by the way—I don't really feel like getting fed to one, head or no head. You understand, right?"

"Where's your sense of adventure!"

"Adventures are for people who don't play football. I got all I need here, and, oh look, I even get to keep my head. Amazing, right?"

"Boo." She gave me a thumbs-down and then tilted her head. "Okay, I have another idea."

"Wow and so soon. Imagine that."

She burst out laughing and took a step toward me. "Whisper in my ear something stupid, at least give me that much to go off. If he storms over here, I win two of your tickets to the first game to sell online. If you win, I'll help you find a girlfriend who doesn't just want a free NFL ride, and believe me, the world is full of bitches like that. Just ask Sanchez."

"I'm not interested." I shrugged. "Sorry."

"Fine, then what do you want?"

Emerson.

My eyes betrayed me.

And hers widened a bit before she let out a sigh. "Wow, we're a pathetic duo, aren't we? Maybe we should just get together."

"Something tells me our hearts wouldn't be in it. No offense, because you're gorgeous, and I'm pretty sure even prettier naked."

She put a hand to her chest. "Sweetest thing a football player's ever said to me."

"You're welcome."

"Fine." She looked over her shoulder. "So just do it for me, for your new friend?"

"Is that what this is? The start of a new friendship? I didn't know you were in the market."

"I know you are."

Yeah, she had me there.

"Fine." I took a step toward her and whispered in her ear. "Friends."

Jax came stomping over two seconds later, his face red as a beet.

"Brother . . ." Kinsey looped her arm in his. "Miller here just agreed to be my friend in a platonic non-sexual way that guarantees I won't be having any one-night stands in the near future. Wasn't that sweet of him?"

Jax visibly relaxed. "I did it again, didn't I?"

"You're too easy, man." I smacked him on the shoulder. "Lighten up, or you're going to be bald and on heart medication before forty."

"Yeah, bro." She patted his cheek. "Lighten up. Now, why aren't we taking shots?"

She bounced off.

Jax groaned.

"Better follow her." I laughed at his horrified face and then locked eyes with Emerson.

She'd been watching us.

And because I knew her, knew her inside and out, I knew that look.

She was pissed.

And she was jealous.

Point, Miller.

Chapter Twenty

I had no right to be jealous. But I was. So jealous I was ready to lose my mind. I'd had too much to drink, that much I knew. Typically, I only allowed myself a maximum of two, but I'd had a third after Sanchez kept beating me at stupid Indian poker.

Kinsey and Miller were talking in the corner again, and it took everything in me not to eavesdrop. He wasn't mine. I had no claim on him. And it wasn't fair that I wanted both him and Sanchez.

What type of person did that make me anyway?

Disgusted with myself, I quickly started tossing red plastic cups in the trash and cleaning up the best I could.

My hands were shaking by the time I got close enough to hear them exchange phone numbers. When I looked up, they were saying good-bye to the rest of us.

Were they leaving together?

Was it my business?

A few of Sanchez's teammates followed them into the hall, talking loud enough to make my ears ring.

Leaving just Sanchez and me.

"You're staying, right?" He came up behind me, wrapping his arms around my stomach.

I wish I could say it made me shiver, that his touch did things to me—and it did, to an extent—but the feelings he evoked were nothing compared to the ones I was always comparing them to. Just another thing that made me a horrible person. Sanchez was in a contest he would never win, and he literally had no idea.

"You tense when I do that," he whispered in my ear. "I hug you, and you tense. I kiss you, and I can almost hear the wheels turning in your head."

Maybe it was because I'd been drinking, but I hung my head and whispered, "Sometimes it's hard to forget the past."

Sanchez tightened his hold on me. "You can't move on if you keep holding on, Curves."

I leaned back against him. "I know. I just . . . A part of me misses him."

"You never had closure?"

"No." I wasn't sure how much to tell him. "I called and was told he'd moved on. I mean what else do you do, right? When I tried calling him again, the number had been disconnected."

He hissed out a curse.

"We were kids," I said in defense of both of us.

"Age doesn't make pain any less traumatic."

I turned around and wrapped my arms around his neck. "For a football player, you're pretty smart."

His forehead touched mine. "I went to Stanford and graduated with honors, Curves. I'm a fucking genius."

"And so humble too," I teased.

"You humble me," he fired back just as fast. "Care to change that no to a yes?"

"Nope."

"Can I at least kiss you then?"

I didn't answer.

"You know." Sanchez's eyes sparked with intensity, and they were focused solely on me. It was enough for my stomach to erupt with butterflies. Guys like him were dangerous to girls like me, girls who desperately wanted to give their heart to someone who promised to take good care of it. "I wasn't always this suave playboy with a heart of gold."

I couldn't suppress my smile. "Oh? Do tell."

He wrapped his arms around me, my heart thudded in my chest while he slowly licked his lips. "At the risk of being completely transparent with the girl who won't let me see her naked." He sighed heavily. "I used to believe in monogamous relationships. Ones where the guy fell for the girl, the girl fell for the guy, they bought a house together, a dog, two fighting beta fish, no goldfish in my fantasy." The corners of his mouth dipped into a smile. "The point is, I believed in it, because I had no reason not to."

"And now?" I asked my voice shaky.

"Now." He sighed. "You make me want to, which makes me want to fuck you and send you on your way, because I know you're the type of girl who will always demand more for yourself, and hell if I don't respect that. But the past has a weird way of defining us, yeah?"

I nodded. "Who was she?"

"She belongs in the past."

With Miller.

He didn't say it.

He didn't have to.

"You're confusing when you're honest," I whispered.

"I've been honest since day one. Just because I've never been painted as the good guy, doesn't mean I don't want to be. Some people are worth taking risks for, and others . . ." He shrugged, his voice trailed off, and he was already pulling away.

I didn't want him to.

There were so many layers to him and I wanted to know them all, and at the same time I felt selfish for putting him in a position where I was the villain, not him.

Because in that moment, I wanted him.

Even though, I still felt like I wanted Miller.

I reacted.

I stopped thinking.

I stood on my tiptoes and kissed him as hard as I could; my body wrapped around his, fitting perfectly. He groaned against my mouth, his hands sliding down to cup my ass and pull me against him.

"Sorry, left my—" Miller's voice sounded. "Jacket."

I pulled away from Sanchez, but he refused to let me go.

"I think it's on the couch, man."

"Great." Miller jogged over to the couch, grabbed his jacket and then glanced at both of us, a genuine smile on his face. "Thanks for the invite, man."

"Anytime."

It felt wrong.

I wanted it to feel right. It didn't.

"And you . . ." Miller eyed me, his eyes were indifferent. I hated it. "Better get to bed. I heard that your coach is making you do a burpee day."

"WHY!" I whined. Yeah, I'd had way too much to drink.

Miller and Sanchez both burst out laughing.

"It's just too easy," Miller called over his shoulder before waving good-bye and going into his apartment. Alone.

I exhaled in relief.

"You pull away when you see him." Sanchez finally released me.

"You don't let me."

"I never will." His smile fell as he grabbed the trash bag by my feet and continued cleaning up. "Why don't you go take a shower. We both have early days tomorrow."

"Sanchez—"

"Grant." He sighed. "Call me Grant."

"Grant." His first name felt funny on my lips. "I like you. You know that, right?"

He looked like he wanted to say something; instead, he bit down on his lip and dropped the bag, then walked over to me and cupped my face with both of his hands. He slammed his mouth against mine, making it impossible to think or breathe. His hands were everywhere, the heat of his mouth addicting as his tongue fought for dominance. The man kissed like he played—without apology and without fear.

He jerked away. "Sleep."

"What?" My voice was breathless. "You're not going to ask me to have sex with you?"

"Nope." He went back to tossing things in the trash. "Because when you actually like a girl, you're willing to wait until she's ready."

"Ready?" I repeated.

"You're not ready. Go. Shower. Bed. Before I kiss you again."

"I kind of like that threat," I mumbled, then let out a little gasp at his laughter. "I said that out loud, didn't I?"

His laugh turned into a groan. "There's only so much I can take of this . . ." His gaze was liquid fire as it roamed over my body from head to toe and back again. "Leave before I go back on my word and ask you for sex, because for some reason, I think you'd say yes, and then you'd hate me after, and I'd hate myself and—I can't believe these words are coming out of my mouth right now. GO!"

With a laugh, I skipped down the hall toward the shower.

It wasn't until I grabbed my phone and saw a text from Miller that my grin fell and my heart started pounding against my chest. It made me feel horrible, that the slight buzz from Sanchez's lips didn't even begin to match the burn in my fingertips as I gripped my phone like a lifeline and read.

Miller: I'm sorry. I didn't know.
Me: Know?

Steam filled the bathroom, and my hands shook as I waited for his response.

Miller: I didn't know you tried calling. Your number was disconnected too. I had no idea. I came home one day, and my dad said my phone was broken. He threw it away. I had to get a new number. I didn't know.
Me: I changed my number after what he said.
Miller: What the fuck did he say?
Me: Does it matter?

"Hey!" Sanchez called. "You fall down in there? And are you naked?"

"Stop!" I laughed. "I'm a girl. We take long showers."

"No, guys take long showers for obvious reasons, and I have the need for a very long shower after that kiss, so hurry it up, Curves!"

"Sorry!"

Miller's text popped up.

Miller: You know it does.
Me: He said you were with your new girlfriend, that you'd moved on, that you wanted nothing to do with me. He said you felt sorry for me, and that you had a new life. It was bad. I cried.
Miller: You don't want to know how angry I am right now. How much I want to fucking kill him for that shit. I spent my senior year of high school sitting by myself at lunch, doing extra homework so I didn't have to go home to my abusive alcoholic father, and praying a college would pick me up

so I could leave. I had one friend. And that friend was you.

Tears ran down my face as I quickly jumped into the shower and thought about what he'd said.

Why? Why would his dad do that to us?

It was almost like he'd known the reason I'd called.

But that would be impossible.

Right?

I dried off as fast as possible, grabbed my phone, and slid it into my sweatshirt before opening the door to a glaring Sanchez.

"You crying?"

"No," I lied, and flashed him a smile. "Eyes bloodshot from booze. It's what happens to me when I drink more than one drink."

"That's sad, Curves. Now I want to cry."

"Hah!" I snuck past him. "Have fun in your long shower!"

"Give me some material, and we'll see!" He crossed his arms. "Come on, just a little boob. Do me a solid?"

"Use your imagination!"

"I failed that class in school!" he yelled after me. "Come on, Curves!"

With a sigh, I walked back to him and kissed him softly on the mouth, tugging his lower lip between my teeth. "Fantasize about that."

He let out a groan and reached for me, but I jumped back just in time. "Play fair!"

"Hey, at least you're in the game."

His eyes narrowed. "I'm not just in it. I'm going to win it."

Something about his gaze told me that he wasn't just talking about a figurative game, but something much more serious.

My cell phone burned in my front pocket.

"Good night." I didn't know what else to say. I made a beeline toward his guest bedroom and locked the door—I always locked the door. He said it was for me, but tonight, it was for him.

Because something in his gaze told me things were shifting.
And I was either going to get caught up in the crossfire or burn alive.
I quickly grabbed my phone and texted back.

Me: I'm so sorry. I had no idea. I was too hurt. I thought
you wanted to end things. I thought—I don't know. I was
emotional and stupid. I'm so sorry.

Miller: I promised you.
Me: You did.
Miller: And you clearly didn't believe me.
Me: I was . . . hurt.

God, I wanted to tell him. But I knew it wasn't the time; plus, it
was the past. It wouldn't fix anything now.

Miller: We really do need to start over, put this shit behind
us. I want to be your friend again. I want us back. The us
without kissing, I guess, since Sanchez cock blocked me
before I even got a shot.

I burst out laughing, even though tears still ran down my face from
our conversation.

Me: It's one of his finer attributes.
Miller: Tell me about it . . .
Me: Yes.
Miller: Yes???? Did you just say yes to my offer of
friendship? Should I make bracelets?
Me: No need. I still have our necklaces.
Miller: Tell anyone we had friendship necklaces, and I'll
deny it till I die.

Me: Your half was pink!

Miller: I hate you.

Me: And when we put them together, they made a heart!

Miller: I'm deleting all of these texts, just so you know.

Me: Remember our handshake?

Miller: It had snaps.

Me: Your favorite part!

Miller: I take back the friendship offer.

Me: No you don't. You know you're laughing right now and trying to get the stupid handshake out of your mind.

Miller: Damn it.

Me: If you remember it tomorrow AND do it, I'll bake you cookies.

Miller: You're on.

Me: I missed you.

Miller: That's in the past.

Me: Deal.

Miller: And Em?

Me: Yeah?

Miller: I'm pretty sure, I missed you more . . .

Chapter Twenty-One

MILLER

I gripped the necklace in my fist and walked toward the locker rooms. I knew Sanchez was already there. His car was in the parking lot right along with Em's.

After last night, I didn't know what to think. But I did know that I couldn't go on like this, constantly lusting after her, breaking rules of friendship and every other guy code out there just because I was still in love with her.

And that was the part that killed me.

It twisted inside my chest until I wanted to scream.

She never left me.

I believed her.

Which meant, had I just tried harder, had I not let my grief and anger overtake common sense, we would have been more than friends.

More than these strangers who used to hang out on the weekends and binge watch movies until four a.m.

We used to fall asleep under the stars; she'd shiver in my arms and promise me we'd be friends forever. It was where our friendship necklaces came in. I'd bought them as a joke.

But the minute I clasped the chain around her neck, she'd burst into tears and thrown her arms around me, squeezing my body so tight it hurt to breathe. I knew in that moment that our friendship wasn't normal. The bond we felt for each other was extraordinary.

I'd sworn to never take it off.

And besides for games, I didn't.

The night she left me, I'd thrown it in my dresser and yelled.

But I'd never had the heart to throw it away.

A few strides later, I was in the noisy locker room, the smell of equipment and Icy Hot filling my nostrils as I made my way down the hall.

Sanchez had his helmet in his right hand and was leaning against the wall, talking to Emerson, but not touching her.

Touching would definitely get him a talking-to by Coach.

I'd already started to notice the practices getting more intense, and the last thing any of us needed was a distraction. I'd expected the coaching staff to say something about us partying with the cheerleaders, but they really had turned a blind eye.

I guess that was what happened when you earned two championship rings in the past three years.

You got away with all kinds of shit as long as you won.

"My man!" Sanchez nodded toward me. "Did my girl tell you she pleasures herself in the shower?"

Emerson's face flushed bright red. "You ass! I do not!" She smacked him in the chest.

Sanchez's laugh was infectious. "Then why else were you in there last night for over a half hour? Damn woman. Wouldn't even let me join you."

I tried to keep my smile in place.

I'd been texting her.

Shit, I needed to stop.

But even as my brain logically explained in vivid detail all the reasons it was a bad idea to stay friends with her, to keep my distance, my heart freaking jumped for joy when I saw her.

Damn it.

"Seems like you still ended the night on a good note, Sanchez." I fought like hell to keep smiling. "You did end up with the girl, no?"

"This is why I keep you around. You're smart." Sanchez winked at Em and gave me a nod of approval.

"Sanchez!" Coach yelled. "Get your ass over here. Don't make me ask you twice."

"This would be three times, Coach." Sanchez grinned. "Not that I was counting."

"Now!"

"Movie night." He stole a kiss from her lips—my lips—and then glanced over his shoulder. "You should come too. It may help keep my manhood intact since I'm letting her pick."

It wasn't my place to tell him she hated romantic comedies and favored action, so I simply shrugged and said, "Yeah, maybe."

His back was to me and Em while he chatted with Coach.

Em's blue eyes snapped to mine.

They were bright.

But a bit bloodshot.

She'd been crying last night.

I'd bet money on it.

"You gonna make it?" I whispered.

Her eyes widened briefly before she blinked and nodded, unfolding her arms and letting them hang at her sides. "Yup."

"Good." We locked eyes, and then I was reaching for her hand. I took a step toward her, grabbed that hand and hid it behind her back, then placed my necklace against her palm. "I think you owe me cookies."

"You really kept it." Our hands pressed against each other so intensely that I felt the imprint of the heart on my palm—the sting of the edges of the metal digging into my skin.

Just like that, and things shifted back into a place I never imagined when I got traded.

Her breathing went from calm to ragged as she backed up against her hand until her ass was touching her hand, and her other hand was touching my thigh. If anyone was watching, it would look like we were simply having a conversation.

But my body was on fire.

"I guess I do."

"I like chocolate chip," I whispered.

"I remember." She sighed.

I released her hand. "Have a good practice." I felt the loss so violently that I had to flex and reflex my fingers.

Her eyes searched mine. "Friends, right?"

"Friends," I lied.

She knew it.

I knew it.

"Yo, Miller!" Sanchez called for me. I was already a safe distance from his girl, but it didn't matter if I was a foot away from her or five hundred miles. I felt her.

And maybe that was the problem.

I would always feel her.

Even when I'd thought she'd rejected me, I'd felt her every breath, every heartbeat, and let it fuel the hate I had for her.

But now? Now she was so close and still not mine.

"Whatever that expression means." Sanchez glared. "Leave it on the field, got me?"

"Always," I barked, shoving on my helmet and running after him.

I never knew that I'd become the type of man who wouldn't just lie to my best friend, but also to my teammates, and worse of all, to myself.

Lust was an ugly, terrible, unbeatable thing.

And I was drowning in it.

Chapter Twenty-Two

EMERSON

I was a nervous wreck.

On top of feeling guilty about texting Miller yesterday and my heart warring with my mind over the fact that I was kissing Sanchez, we had a weigh-in.

The manual said that every weigh-in would be a surprise.

Thank goodness last night I hadn't eaten anything; that was part of the eating plan for the Bucks Girls.

"You're making me nervous. Stop twitching," Kinsey said behind me. "It's going to be fine. The worst that can happen is you gain a few pounds, you get a warning, and they make you lose it before the next game, which just means a lot of protein shakes and dehydration. You aren't going to get kicked off."

"Wow, only? That sounds awesome!" I said with fake enthusiasm. I knew the drill. And dehydration was basically the only way for a woman to lose weight that fast without starving herself. It would be a week and a half of broccoli and chicken with no salt, and small amounts of water.

After the last failed tryout, I swore to myself I wouldn't do that to my body again.

But now, the temptation was there, to be that girl who freaked out over every single morsel of food that passed her lips.

"Seriously," Kinsey hissed. "If you don't stop bouncing around, I'm going to lose my mind! I had beer last night!"

"You're like a size half-zero!"

"That's a total exaggeration, and you know it. I'm a six."

"I'm literally more than double that, so, sorry for being a bit freaked out!" I said through clenched teeth.

"You're strong," Kinsey pointed out. "You have muscle, you have curves, and you look gorgeous, alright? I would kill to have your ass and hips!"

My shoulders sagged.

"Stand straight." She kicked me in the ass.

"Hey!"

Coach Kay eyed her clipboard. "Emerson Rodner."

I felt sick to my stomach as I slowly walked to the sidelines where the coaches had two scales. Actual scales for us to stand on. We went two at a time, which just made it that much worse. I was going to weigh in at around a hundred and ninety pounds, and the chick next to me was going to be like half my size plus an apple.

I cringed as I stepped up on the scale and waited for my coach to shake her head, or at least for someone to make a snide comment about how the scale creaked under my pressure.

"Thank you." Coach Kay flashed me a smile and called out the next name.

That was it?

I'd freaked out for nothing?

"Emerson," Coach called my name, "a minute?"

I stopped walking, nearly puked out my cereal on the grass, and waited.

"Turn around," she said softly.

I met Kinsey's panicked look as she stepped forward and onto the scale, only to have the coach record her weight and motion for her to come over too.

Oh great, now I was getting her in trouble.

"Emerson." Coach let out a frustrated sigh. "You haven't gained weight, but the look on your face tells me you were worried you had. Can you tell me why?"

Shit. I didn't want to exactly tell her it was because the guy I was seeing forced me to eat chocolate or that the other guy—you know, the one that I wasn't seeing but texting at night—made me eat McDonald's. I opened my mouth and shut it.

"It's that time of the month," Kinsey said smoothly. "You know how we tend to bloat and I, uh, may have given her chocolate, so she didn't kill anyone at practice today."

"Okay." Coach eyed the two of us. "I want you girls to be healthy, but you do need to abide by the rules, eating at least six small healthy meals and drinking at least a gallon of water a day, got it?"

"Yes," we said in unison.

"Good." Coach gave me one last look before nodding to Kinsey. "You gained a few pounds, but it looks good on you."

She walked off.

Kinsey's jaw nearly came unhinged. "Did she just say I gained a few pounds?"

"You forget that she also said they looked good on you."

Kinsey glanced behind her then did a little circle.

"Whoa, what are you doing?"

It seriously looked like she was a dog chasing her tail. "Trying to see if I finally have an ass!"

I burst out laughing then covered my face as a few girls gave us nasty glares. "You almost have an ass, Kinsey."

"Yes!" She jumped up and down and then stuck her tongue out at one of our teammates who rolled her eyes at us.

"Don't take it personally," I whispered. "I saw her staring at a cookie the other day before throwing it in the trash."

"No!" Kinsey stomped her foot. "How wasteful! You think it's still there?"

"You're not digging through the trash can."

"Not now I'm not, but I could. Later. After practice. I like hanging out with you, you know." Her voice softened. "I'd rather have an ass than throw away junk food. Last year I was too worried about what people would think. None of the girls would go to the guys' parties with us, then the new girls finally warmed up, until Lily and a few of the others got their talons in them and now they're just as grumpy and boring as everyone else."

I wrapped my arm around her. "Good thing you have me."

"Yup." She grinned. "Good thing."

"Death by . . ." Coach yelled. "Push-ups. GO!"

We groaned and dropped to the ground.

The victory was short-lived, but the good news was that I had been so preoccupied with the weigh-in and then enough push-ups to kill a person that I wasn't focused on Miller or the fact that I felt like I was emotionally cheating on Sanchez, even though we hadn't slept together or even said we *were* together.

Imagine that. Push-ups and weigh-ins were the only way to distract me from my daytime television life.

"Hit the showers!" Coach yelled. "And we're cancelling practice tonight. Good job, ladies. Remember, you only have one full week before the first game against the Pilots!"

Miller's old team.

My body ached as I followed Kinsey into the locker room and started stripping; normally I hated showering in front of the other girls, but today I was too sweaty to care.

All talking stopped the minute I dropped my clothes to the ground.

Awareness prickled down my spine as I slowly turned to see girls whispering and pointing.

Kinsey growled in their direction then nodded to me. "Own it. Not everyone can have hips like that. Besides, you have Sanchez. They're just pissed because nobody's been able to land him since Jacki."

Jacki? Was that the woman he'd been talking about the night before? When Miller caught us kissing.

I gulped. If they only knew about Miller too.

"And don't forget the way Miller looks at you," she added.

I froze.

"It's okay." She winked. "It's our little secret. Though you have to tell me what the hell kind of perfume you have that attracts not one, but two men of that caliber."

"And have your brother come after me and bury my body?" I tried to lighten the mood as I grabbed my towel and went into the shower. Kinsey and her skinny ass followed me.

"Hah!" She turned both of our showers on while I hung up my towel. "Jax can't do shit, and he knows it. He's so focused on me not sleeping with anyone that he hasn't dated in years."

"Maybe we should set him up."

"Nobody will have him, trust me." She laughed and tossed her head back. "He pretends to be boring on purpose, especially with what he likes to call airheads . . . and then he leaves them with the check if they ask to come back to his place. His last date asked how much he made."

"That's horrible!"

"He's rich, which means he attracts the crazies."

"Hmm."

We finished showering in silence and walked out of the locker room only to find our bags gone.

Both of them.

"Oh no!" I gasped, nearly dropping my towel. The necklace was in my bag; it was more about that than my clothes.

"Those bitches!" Kinsey screamed. "Are we seriously in middle school right now?"

"What do we do? Drive home in our towels?"

"No," Kinsey growled. "We have to march over to the guys' locker room and find them."

My eyes widened. "What makes you think they put them in there?"

"Because two years ago I started the tradition of hazing the new girls and making them do the walk of shame to the guys' locker rooms. But don't worry. They're still practicing. It was more about them following leadership."

"Great, Kinsey," I said through clenched teeth. "And now the tables have turned."

"To be fair, you are a rookie."

"You're the captain."

She looked ready to fight someone. "And this captain's going to kick ass tomorrow morning, but for now, we need to grab our shit before the guys do."

"Deal."

Male voices sounded down the hall.

We shared looks of horror before running down the connecting hallway and across the room to the men's locker room.

And both of us tripped to a stop when Jax stood in front of us, a look of pure fury on his sexy face. "Kinsey," he snapped. "Emerson."

"We, uh . . ." I gulped. "The girls hid our bags."

"Then I suggest you grab them before the rest of the team barges in on you!" He opened the locker room door and shoved us inside.

I slid across the floor, nearly banging my body against one of the benches as my eyes searched for my blue bag and Kinsey's green one.

"Got mine!" Kinsey shouted from somewhere in the locker room.

"Looking for something?" Sanchez's deep voice caused a shiver to run down my spine.

"Classic, Emerson," Miller joined in.

I let out a groan of frustration and slowly turned to face them, each holding a strap of my bag, stupid grins on their gorgeous faces.

"It was a prank," I said defensively. "Now give me the bag."

They jerked it back. "I don't know, Sanchez." Miller shrugged. "I mean what are we going to get in return?"

"Gratitude?" I offered in a pleading voice as more male voices started sounding through the hall. I was running out of time, and I did not want the rest of the team to see me in only a towel!

"No." Sanchez licked his lips. "But Miller mentioned something about . . . What was it, Miller?"

"Cookies."

"Yes, cookies." Sanchez snapped his fingers.

"Moist," Miller said, knowing that I hated the word almost as much as I hated the scale. "Moist . . ." He just had to repeat it while Sanchez tried not to crack up. "Cookies."

"Yum." Sanchez licked his lips and then sucked on one finger. "I can almost taste the chocolate now."

"It melts . . ." Miller's eyes flashed. "All the way down to your—"

"Guys!" I threw one hand in the air. "Come on! Do you really want your teammates to see me in a towel?"

Sanchez scowled while Miller huffed out a "Fuck no."

"I'll make you cookies! Tonight, promise!"

"Nice doing business with you." Sanchez took the bag from Miller and handed it over to me. "Now run!"

The door opened. "Shit, she's not going to make it." Miller's voice sounded, and then he was yelling at Sanchez, "Distract them!"

"Don't come in!" Sanchez did a small circle. "I . . . um, I'm naked?"

"Dude, they see you naked all the time! Think of something better!"

"I'm trying! It's a lot of pressure!"

"Hurry!"

I was behind Miller waiting when Sanchez shouted, "I puked all over the floor! It's green!"

I burst out laughing while Sanchez sent me a glare that would have normally made me flinch.

"Go!" He motioned us out the other door.

Miller grabbed my hand and jerked me all the way across the hall and back into the girls' locker room in less than two minutes.

The lights were off.

Our chests were heaving.

And I could have sworn I heard my own heartbeat as the heat from his body spread into my space, wrapping itself around me.

"You okay?" His gruff question was like lighting a match in the darkness, making me lean into him when I knew I had no business doing it.

"Yeah," I croaked. "Thanks."

He ran a hand down my bare shoulder and then toyed with the front of my towel. I held my breath as his fingers tugged the material. "You don't want to know what I'm thinking right now."

He shuddered.

I gulped, too afraid to move.

His voice lowered. "You have no idea how badly I want to rip this off."

"It wouldn't matter. You can't see me in the dark."

"I have a very vivid memory."

I sucked in a breath.

He exhaled a curse and stepped away. "I'll see you tonight, Em."

"Okay." Disappointment slammed into me and then guilt. "Tonight."

"Bring my moist cookies, friend."

I laughed. "Say *moist* again, and I'm giving back that necklace."

"Deal."

I waited for him to leave. And in the darkness, closed my eyes and tried to calm my breathing before finally flipping on the switch.

Chapter Twenty-Three

MILLER

My fingers buzzed with a prickling sensation the rest of the day—from a damn towel. I tried to rein it in, only to lose it all over again when I went over to Sanchez's apartment, let myself in, and saw the most gorgeous ass in the air, directly in front of the oven.

It swayed back and forth as music pumped through the sound system, and the scent of cookies filled the air.

I almost had a heart attack when Emerson stood, oven mitts and all, and did another little shimmy before sliding the cookie tray onto the granite countertop.

"Enjoying the show?" she called over her shoulder.

I froze, pissed that I felt my cheeks heating. "You knew I was watching?"

"You walk loud."

"Bullshit. I'm a panther!"

"Sure." She still wasn't looking at me. "A two-hundred-and-fifty-pound panther with size fourteen shoes. It's amazing how you glide into the room." With a laugh, she started fanning the cookies with her hands. "You think you float into rooms. You stomp. Trust me. I could feel the vibrations through the floor."

I rolled my eyes and reached for a cookie. She smacked me with the spatula and glared, and pieces of her blonde hair fell across her flour-caked cheeks.

"What the hell, woman!" I rubbed my hand. It didn't hurt, but still.

"No." She thrust the spatula in my face. "Not until Sanchez gets back from the store. He only had enough for me to make one batch of cookies."

I tried sliding my hand near the cookie sheet again; my fingers almost came into contact with the chocolate before I earned another smack. "Shit, that stung!"

"Miller, I mean it!"

"We aren't monsters. It's not like we're going to eat one full batch."

Her eyebrows shot up. "Really? Because in high school I distinctly remember you eating two dozen by yourself and then hiding the rest of them in your pillow."

"Okay, first of all . . ." I leaned my hands on the counter. "I was a growing boy, and I needed protein."

"Totally not protein, but continue." She waved the spatula at me.

I jerked it from her hand and pointed it in her face. "Second, you know I used to get hungry in the middle of the night, and why walk all the way downstairs when my pillow had special places for hiding food?"

She shoved the spatula away from her face and put her hands on her gorgeous hips. "Miller! You had your mom sew a snack pouch in your pillow! That's not how they really make them!"

I grinned smugly. "Best idea I ever had."

"She was just tired of you waking everyone up with your loud walking up and down the stairs . . . up and down the stairs . . . whining, 'Mom, I'm hungry!'"

She did my voice perfect.

"You done yet?" I crossed my arms.

"'Ma! Where's my chicken!'" She giggled. "'Ma! We're out of milk again!'"

Slowly, Em backed away. She knew what was coming.

I eyed her and silently held up one finger, then two, then three.

She squealed.

And I chased.

I *always* chased.

With a roar, I had my arms wrapped around her body and was carrying her back into the kitchen, ready to do whatever necessary to get a taste.

Of the cookie.

Not her.

Oh hell, maybe both.

A very vivid image of Emerson covered in chocolate flashed through my brain as I set her on her feet and pinned her against the counter, "Cookie me"

"No." Her chest heaved.

"Yes."

"No."

"I can do this all day, Em."

"One." She held up a finger. "You can have ONE taste, but that's it, and don't tell Sanchez because I swore up and down that we'd wait for him. The poor guy sprinted down the hall, Miller. He nearly broke the button to the elevator."

"Man must love his cookies," I rasped.

"I never thought there'd be two guys so equally obsessed in existence," she said breathlessly.

"Are you just going to stare at me or taste?" Her smile fell as her eyes darted to my mouth and back again.

"Taste," I whispered, slowly grazing her ass as I reached around her body and grabbed a warm cookie. I lifted it to my lips and took a bite then held it to hers.

She shook her head. "I think I get more pleasure from watching you eat than actually eating them."

"Then watch away." I finished off the cookie and was licking my fingers, and then her thumb was brushing the side of my mouth.

My tongue met her thumb.

She didn't jerk back.

Even her skin tasted amazing.

"You, um, had chocolate." She gulped and looked away.

It took every ounce of control in my body to keep from kissing her, slamming my mouth against hers and giving her a real taste.

"If either of you ate cookies, you're dead to me!" Sanchez's voice boomed, before the door opened.

I destroyed all evidence by rearranging cookies on the sheet and winked at Em before Sanchez made his way into the kitchen.

He eyed the sheet, then me, then the sheet. "You moved one."

"I did." I gulped. "And then I was smacked with a spatula. Careful about this one." I jabbed a finger in Em's direction. "She's violent as hell."

"Aw, my woman got her panties in a bunch over one stolen cookie?" Sanchez teased, pulling her into his arms.

My chest cracked.

Stomach heaved.

I clenched my fists and tried to look away, but it was impossible. They were right in front of me. He touched her lips with his, then sighed against her body and proved to me yet again that she wasn't mine.

And the sick part was that I was pretty sure he wasn't doing it on purpose—he just couldn't help himself.

I knew the feeling, man. It haunted me every second of every day.

"Are we going to eat cookies, or do I need to leave you guys alone for a bit?" I teased.

"Cookies first. Sex second." Sanchez nodded.

Emerson gasped.

"A man with priorities." I nodded, trying to forget the sick feeling in my stomach. "I like it."

He held out his hand for a shake.

I took it.

And tried not to puke as I snatched another cookie and stuffed it in my mouth to keep myself busy. To keep myself sane.

It was either eat all the food—or do something stupid like stake my claim based on the fact that I had put more years in than he had.

But the present didn't account for the past.

Not anymore.

And we'd agreed to forget it.

And I knew I had two choices. I could avoid them like the plague and lose her forever.

I locked eyes with Em as she returned his bear hug.

Choices sucked.

Avoid.

Or live the lie?

I chose to live the lie.

Chapter Twenty-Four

EMERSON

My chest hurt.

I'd been able to down a half of a cookie with a gulp of milk, and that was it. We watched *Jason Bourne*. I sat between two of the hottest guys on the planet while they argued over cyber terrorism and threw cookies at the TV.

It was perfect.

And it was *hell*.

How was it possible to feel such conflicting emotions? Sanchez had put his arm around me and held me close, but a part of my thigh still touched Miller's, and I knew he knew it, because every once in a while he'd shift, and the torture would start all over again.

Whether it was feeling his muscled thigh through his jeans . . .

Or the graze of his fingers as he handed me the blanket . . .

But he stayed true to his word to be my friend; if anything, I was the one having a nervous breakdown, while he was having completely casual conversations with us while Sanchez held my hand and played with my hair.

And I'd be lying if I said having Sanchez's attention didn't feel good. It did. He wasn't what I expected. I mean he was cocky as hell, but after watching him play, and seeing the way he commanded a room, it made sense. There really wasn't a chance for him to be any other way.

And it worked.

It was endearing and, at least with me, I knew while he teased, there was still always a line he wasn't willing to cross, at least not yet.

If anything, it felt like he was proving to me, or maybe just himself, that he was capable of more than a one-night stand. I still hadn't asked him about Jacki, wasn't sure I even wanted to know, besides it wasn't my business right?

Once the movie ended, Miller gave Sanchez a fist bump and then gave me a high five because, in his book, I was too blonde to make a fist bump look cool.

Really, it was just because his hands were so big and mine were so small it hurt my knuckles! Which I, of course, said defensively, only to have both guys tease me for the next ten minutes while I stood there and took it.

The cleanup was minimal and took me only about thirty minutes. I was exhausted trying to keep my feelings in check and my focus on the guy that actually cared for me, the guy that didn't just want me because he'd had me first. I frowned. It was a potentially unfair assessment of Miller, but it's all I had.

"Emerson?" Sanchez padded down the hall in nothing but low-slung jeans and a smile reserved for the only other person left in the room: me. His muscled body was so thickly corded with golden muscles that I was afraid I was going to start hyperventilating.

He had a few tattoos wrapped around his right arm and one that stretched across his taut abs.

I licked my lips.

"Careful, Curves." His tone was warning. "If you lick it, you have to keep it."

"Who says I'm not keeping you?" I walked slowly toward him.

His eyes narrowed. "Some say I can't be tamed."

"Who said anything about taming?"

His gaze softened. "I don't deserve you."

"Don't say things like that, please." I had to look away so he didn't see the shame in my eyes. The shame I lived with. The guilt that crushed me. I wanted to be his. I wanted to jump into his arms and give him everything, but it would be a lie.

And I wondered if even he was perceptive enough to know that.

"Walk with me." He grabbed my hand and led me to the master bedroom then softly shoved me in.

Awareness washed over me as he gripped my hips from behind and pulled me against his clearly aroused body.

"I want you. In that bed." He whispered in my ear, then his teeth tugged my lobe while his tongue swirled in and out before he spoke again. "But I want you to come to me, alright? None of this bullshit seduction on my part. So hear me now, Curves. You walk into this room, that means you're mine. No sharing."

I nodded, not trusting my voice.

"No takebacks." He gripped my ass until pain mixed with pleasure as his fingers dug in, and then with his other hand, he pulled my pony-tail until my head was tilted back enough for him to press a punishing kiss to my mouth. "Got me?"

I whimpered against his kiss, and my tongue slid against his.

With a growl, he pulled back and swore.

I felt his hands imprinted on my body everywhere.

And in that moment, I did want more. I wanted to be that girl he was talking about, the one who could step over the threshold and freely give what he wanted.

I wasn't that girl. Not yet. I wanted to be. And maybe that was my first baby step toward finally being free of the past, of the damage done years ago when I had called Miller and his number had changed. I'd meant to tell him my suspicions were correct.

I was pregnant with his child.

Chapter Twenty-Five

MILLER

Game 1
Pilots vs. Bucks
Home Turf
Favored Team: Bellevue Bucks

"You got us?" Jax yelled in the middle of the circle.

He was talking to me. I knew it. The team knew it. The Pilots were the very first team that drafted me, but nothing could have prepared me for the brotherhood I felt with the Bucks. It was home. And I'd battle until the death. Incredible what good coaching and a hardworking team got you. I was excited to play my old team only because I knew that I was on the better team, not just because they had the money to buy good players, but because the players worked their asses off to stay the best, and didn't quit.

"You know I got you!" I yelled back.

"Bucks, Bucks, Bucks, Bucks!" We chanted as Sanchez stood in the middle of the huddle, tossing his helmet in the air one last time before we ended with a cry of "Buck you!"

Adrenaline pumped so hard through my system I was nearly dizzy with it as I followed my teammates onto the field.

The stadium was packed. Lights flashed from every direction, and to my right, a familiar face.

Emerson, dressed in the sexiest cheerleading outfit I'd ever seen. I looked away. I had to.

Because I had a quarterback to protect . . .

A crowd that I had to prove myself to . . .

And a game I needed to win.

"You nervous?" Sanchez jogged next to me and smacked me with his helmet.

We'd gotten to the stadium earlier that morning. I'd walked the field as usual with my music on, felt the grass between my fingers, and closed my eyes as I mentally rehearsed every damn play in the book.

I was ready.

"Our fans are breaking the sound barrier," I joked.

The Bucks fans were notorious for their loudness, causing so many visiting teams to go offside or have false starts it was almost comical. It hadn't been funny last year when it happened to us as the opposing team, but now I was thankful that my new home crowd felt it was their job to be a part of our game plan.

Like an extra player on the field.

That's how loyal they were.

And I was finally a part of that.

"Nah." I grinned at the screaming fans with their painted faces and colorful signs. "Not one bit."

"Good." Sanchez nodded his approval. "Because those preseason games were child's play compared to this." He closed his eyes and then opened them and a look of complete determination crossed his features. "Ready to war?"

"I've been ready for weeks."

And it was true.

I'd hung out with Emerson and Sanchez most days and every weekend during preseason. But ever since movie night with them, I'd done my best to keep my focus solely on football.

That was three weeks ago.

And it finally felt like I had control over some of my emotions.

When he kissed her, I didn't flinch.

When she hugged him, I didn't feel like throwing up or running him over with my car.

And at night, I only thought about her until I fell asleep, but I'd stopped dreaming about her. Progress?

It helped that Kinsey had started coming around with Em, but not enough to fully take the longing away. Don't get me wrong. Kinsey was hot, but she wasn't Em.

More than once I'd seen Sanchez and her arguing in the kitchen over something stupid like the salt, but I figured that was just Kinsey's way of lashing out—and getting him to notice her, despite the fact that he'd had two years to hook up with her and still had gone for her new friend.

I had to give it to her, though. Kinsey was tough as shit and kept her jealousy at bay; the only reason I even noticed it was because I was dealing with the same damn thing.

After the commercial break, artist Zane Andrews joined the field to sing the national anthem. It kicked ass, though I wouldn't admit to anyone that I actually liked the guy. He was too pretty for any male to ever acknowledge as being talented.

He finished to fireworks and F-16s flying over the field.

The applause was deafening.

A zap of adrenaline trickled down my spine. My nerves were nonexistent; if anything, I felt like I needed to run out onto the field and do a few laps before the game even started.

Our team won the coin flip and chose to return the ball first.

I put on my helmet, said a little prayer, thanking my mom for putting me in football to keep me out of trouble, and glanced across the field to Em.

She pulled out a necklace and kissed it then winked.

It had been a tradition before every game.

Warmth spread through my chest, mixing with the adrenaline, giving me a spike of energy as I did a few jumps in the air to keep my legs warm.

Things clicked into place.

My adrenaline focused into the right muscles, and my brain went on lockdown.

We were going to win.

Or die trying.

Special teams dominated a thirty-yard run, and it was time, time to take the field.

I inhaled a few times, sucking in the air between my teeth before exhaling and running out to the huddle.

Jax slammed his hands together. "Mellow Yellow, option two!"

Crazy freak named plays after soda.

At least it confused people.

As least he hadn't called Double Mountain Dew. That involved a hell of a lot of speed on my part, not that I wasn't good for it. I just didn't want it to be my first play in the first game.

"Hike!"

Sanchez ran a slant to the right, while I charged toward the defensive player who thought it was a good idea to try to blitz my quarterback. I took him down and turned around just in time to see Jax shake his head at Sanchez and then lock eyes with me.

Well shit. Double Mountain Dew, here I come.

I ran like hell as Jax threw a thirty-yarder. It sailed right into my hands. Sanchez knocked over the guy headed for me, and my old teammate made a choking noise.

Touchdown.

"That's right!" Sanchez roared. "Buck you!"

We jumped into the air and bumped chests while Jax ran toward us.

My heart was pounding so fast that it was hard to think straight. I hadn't been expecting Jax to trust me that much, being a new player to his team.

If Sanchez wasn't open or his other favorite wide receiver, Brandon, he typically ran it himself to get the first down.

"Good job, man." Jax slapped me on the back. "You hit your defender so hard that he fell ass-backward."

"Yeah well, I wanted to make a point." I shrugged.

"Instead you made six," Sanchez laughed.

"Let's make that seven," Jax yelled as our kicker, Jason Mills, walked out with a smug grin. The dude had been in the league for fifteen years and was still one of the highest paid kickers.

"One job," Sanchez muttered under his breath. "The dude has one job. Better make that point."

I shrugged. "He'll get it."

"He better." Sanchez rubbed his hands together. "Because while we were puking our guts out during training camp, he was hunting."

"Hunting?"

"Don't ask."

The commercial break ended.

And the rest of the game felt like a blur. Between my touchdown and then Sanchez and his one-handed catch that ended up making it look like he had magic gloves, it was a complete blowout.

Three touchdowns.

Two interceptions.

Sanchez was responsible for one of the three touchdowns after Jax threw a ball that should have been nearly impossible to catch; Sanchez decided he was going to try anyway.

I couldn't stop grinning as the game ended, and reporters flooded the field.

Sanchez groaned next to me.

"Part of the job," I said under my breath. "Besides, we won."

"Yeah, alright." He nodded and tensed as the first reporter ran up to him and grinned. She stood a little closer to him than necessary, and when she asked him questions, I could have sworn she touched his shoulder a few times. He kept backing away from her, which seemed strange since it was typically too loud to hear on the field, meaning you had to lean in.

He gave me an indifferent look and then glanced back where Em was standing with Kinsey. They were distracted for now, but still.

Jacki Jones wasn't my favorite correspondent—she thought she was God's gift to football for one, and second, she was notorious for using the sport as a personal platform to thrust herself into the spotlight.

She threw her head back and laughed, then touched Sanchez's forearm. He looked ready to strangle her.

I interrupted their interview.

I'd never done that before in my life.

"Oh, Miller Quinton! I'm so glad you came over here. How did it feel to get that first touchdown for your new team?"

"Probably about as good as it feels to touch Grant Sanchez's shoulder, am I right?" I was teasing, kind of.

Her eyes narrowed before she made a point to slowly pull her hand away from Sanchez. "We go way back, isn't that right?"

"How about that one-handed catch?" I nodded while Sanchez scooted toward me, his face pensive.

"Absolutely amazing!" Laughing, she faced the camera and then me. "Well, it looks like you two are working well together. You know it was rumored that there was a bit of bad blood between you two, how's that affecting your relationship on the field?"

"Rumors made up by power hungry social climbers." Sanchez wrapped a sweaty arm around me. "We're bros, that's all there is to it."

"So the move was good for you, Quinton, despite the fact that the Bucks didn't pick you first in the draft last year?" She shoved the microphone in my face. She left out the fact that I'd let them know I didn't want that team to begin with, but I bit my tongue.

"Best decision of my life," I said through clenched teeth.

"But it wasn't really your decision." She laughed again. The hell it was. But that wasn't her business.

I wanted to break the microphone in two.

Sanchez squeezed my body so hard I thought he was going to break me in half, and then he shrugged. "I think Coach is calling for us. A pleasure as always, Jacki." His tone was so mocking you'd have to be an idiot not to get the point that he had no respect for the woman.

He pulled me away before I could say something stupid.

"Thanks," I muttered. "And here I thought you were the one that was going to mouth off during an interview."

"Hah." He shoved me away from him and shrugged. "Just because I'm an aggressive asshole on the field—who may or may not threaten to screw players' moms to get in their heads—does not mean I can't be a gentleman during an interview, but when it comes to Jacki, let's just say there's a history there. After our relationship ended, she had no problem hitting on every other Buck team member and ever since she got a job with ESPN, she's been even a bigger pain in my ass. Good ol' Jacki Jones." He shook his head. "Just say no, man. No good can come from a woman whose smile looks that frozen."

I laughed as I followed him back toward the locker rooms. We both shook hands with the other team, I pulled my old teammates into giant bear hugs and laughed when they gave me shit for going to the dark side, even though we all knew I didn't have a choice. That was the great thing about football—for the most part we left everything on the field and were able to joke around once the clock ran out. Guys who didn't know how to do that never lasted long. And I was lucky that both teams I'd played for understood that concept.

"Shit." Sanchez swore. "Be right back, Thomas is getting out of control."

Out of the corner of my eye I saw Thomas shove one of the Pilots' backup quarterbacks, Jason Agrasi—the guy hadn't even played! I followed Sanchez, only to be stopped dead in my tracks when my eyes fell to Em.

She was walking in our direction. Across the field. Time stood still.

Sanchez shoved Thomas away from Jason then turned to her and crooked his finger.

She nervously chewed her lower lip before skipping toward him.

He lifted her into the air and slammed a kiss over her mouth, and a few cameras went off. Jacki Jones stopped dead in her tracks, her face twisted into an angry snarl before she stomped off.

I was a bit nervous about how people would react to a player dating a cheerleader, but nobody seemed to think anything of Sanchez gripping her ass and trying to see how long he could kiss her before she passed out from asphyxiation.

Jealousy attached itself to my legs like weights as I started walking past them.

And then Emerson's voice stopped me.

"Miller!" I got tackled from behind.

My body reacted so violently that I had to take a minute to rein it in before turning around in her arms and returning her bear hug.

"You killed it!" She pulled away and held up her hand for a high five.

"Oh, so you're doing high fives now?"

"Very funny." She waved it in my face. "Don't leave me hanging, yo."

I groaned. "Em, I can say *yo*. You can't."

"What? Why?"

I hit her hand and then gripped her shoulders. "You're too white to say *yo*. It would be like you trying to say *homie*."

"Yo, homie." The way she said it was so white I cringed.

"Never again," came Sanchez's voice. "Curves, just stick with *amazing*."

I burst out laughing. "Or *awesome*."

"So. Awesome," Sanchez said with a peppy voice. "OMG, Miller. Did you see that guy's ass? It was so—"

"Awesome." I sighed and batted my eyelashes.

"You guys suck!" Emerson stuck her hands on her hips, jutting them out, drawing my eyes, his, and, no doubt, anyone else's who could see. "And I really don't say *amazing* and *awesome* that much."

"Sure, little cheer girl, sure." Sanchez nodded smugly.

She glared.

"Celebrate with me tonight?" he countered.

She crossed her arms. "Maybe."

"That's a yes," he said confidently, nodding his head toward the locker rooms. "I'll text you later."

"'Kay." She grinned.

My gaze lingered on that smile a bit too long.

"Good job, guys." Her voice cracked a bit.

I stared at her mouth.

She licked her lips and quickly averted her eyes.

And when I turned around, it was to see Sanchez staring at me, not her, first with anger and then confusion.

"Sorry." I didn't know what else to say. Sorry? Old habits die hard? I still want her?

"There isn't anything to be sorry for . . ." He shrugged. "Yet."

"What the hell is that supposed to mean?" I jerked him back by his soaked Under Armour shirt.

He hung his head. "Don't worry about it."

But I did.

Because he was my friend.

And I felt like a dick that he had to even have that type of conversation with me, the whole stay-away-from-my-girl talk.

God, I was such a bastard.

"We good?" I forced him to look at me.

"Yeah, man." His eyes searched mine. "We are."

"Cool."

We walked in silence until Jax squeezed between us, putting an arm on each of our shoulders. "Is it just me, or is Jacki super handsy this year?"

"YES!" I shouted. "Thank you! She was all over Sanchez."

"She's always all over Sanchez." Jax shuddered. "Ever since the whole cheating scandal and broken engagement."

Sanchez groaned. "Really man?"

"It was her?" I was too stunned to say anything more. "Jacki Jones is the woman scorned?"

"Drop it," Sanchez said in a warning voice. "It's old news . . . besides, now I just feel dirty when she looks at me." His tone changed to teasing.

"Used," Jax added.

"Slutty?" I offered.

"Speak for yourself, Miller." Sanchez coughed out a laugh. "I think Jax is saving himself for someone special."

"I'm ignoring you." Jax didn't even seem fazed. "Just like you ignore all the girls you sleep with when they complain after five seconds of nothing."

"Five seconds?" I whistled.

Sanchez gave Jax a little shove. "Best five seconds of their lives!"

When we walked into the locker room, the rest of our team was bouncing off the walls with nervous energy—the energy that came after the first win of the season and the realization that we had giant targets on our backs now that we'd set the tone for the rest of the year.

"Hey." Sanchez elbowed me. "Can I ask you for a solid?"

"What's up?" I started taking off my gear.

"Do you have Emerson's address?"

I froze, my shoulder pads somewhere near the top of my forehead. "Uh . . ."

"You have it, right?" He leaned in closer. "Come on, man. Don't be a cockblock. It's not like that. I want to surprise her."

"Dude, you got her a car."

"On loan," he argued. "Come on, what's the big deal?"

The big deal was that I didn't want him making fun of her. I didn't want him seeing where she lived, and I didn't want him in her life—in mine.

And I had no choice.

Then again, if he rejected her based on her address, he didn't deserve her in the first place.

"I'll text it to you." I tossed down my shoulder pads and clenched my fists. "Now, go shower. You smell like shit."

"Stop smelling me, Miller." He grinned and walked off in that cocky way he always did, gaining high fives from most of the team before doing a little striptease in the middle of the floor and tossing his shirt into the air.

I rolled my eyes.

He was impossible not to like.

With shaking fingers, I texted him the directions to her apartment. And then texted her for her apartment number.

She answered right away with the number and a question mark.

Me: Not telling.
Emerson: I HATE SECRETS!
Me: Stop yelling at me!
Emerson: WHY DO YOU NEED MY ADDRESS?
Me: I can't talk to you when you're like this.

Emerson: I HATE it when you're calm.

Me: yawns

"Hey!" Sanchez looked over my shoulder. I jerked away so hard that I nearly stumbled backward over my chair. "You text it to me?"

I held my phone in the air, not showing him the screen. "Just did."

"Cool." He nodded. "Thanks, man."

"You still haven't showered," I pointed out.

"Dude . . ." He was shirtless, pointing to his body. "I was letting everyone look their fill before I soaped up."

I tugged off my own shirt and looked down. "Huh, imagine that. Another eight-pack. Color me not impressed."

"You need to work out your sex muscles."

"Stop staring at his sex muscles, man." Jax swatted Sanchez with a towel and then flung it back, causing a whip motion.

Sanchez turned around so fast that I almost missed him grabbing the towel from Jax's hands and twisting. "You better run!"

"Sanchez!" Jax shouted.

And I was left alone. With the phone burning in my hand, and the lie bitter on my tongue.

Chapter Twenty-Six

EMERSON

I'd wanted to tell Sanchez no.

I was exhausted, and I knew he had to be exhausted too, and yet, he wouldn't stop texting me about all the partying we were going to do.

And with those texts, pictures of movies and food . . .

The guy had enough energy and adrenaline for an entire football team, maybe that was why he was one of the captains.

Watching him on the field was unlike anything I'd ever experienced. I remembered all of the cheers and felt like my performance had been good, but honestly, my focus hadn't been on the cheers or crowd pleasing. It had been on him.

Sanchez.

The way he commanded the field.

The way he and Miller seemed to read each other's mind.

I'd always watched Miller play, even when I hated him, I'd watched. He was cold, calculating.

And Sanchez . . .

He was like a football professor out there—light on his feet, cracking jokes. When they'd been near our side of the field, the big screen had caught him grinning at the guy trying to block him and mouthing, *Watch this*. Only to outrun the defensive player, jump over another, and run into the end zone for a touchdown.

I'd about died when he took a bow in front of the goalpost, and Jax snapped a pretend picture while Miller jumped into the air and slammed his hand across his back.

Football.

God, I forgot how much I loved football.

My stomach clenched. Dad and I had watched all the games together. He'd loved college ball and I'd loved watching professional football. We'd always get into arguments about the purity of the sport. But since his decline, he'd been doing more sleeping than watching.

I shook it off.

Because today, regardless of my reality, was a really good day.

And an awesome game.

Ugh, maybe I did say *awesome* too much.

I wasn't sure if it was that I was finally cheering for the Bucks, or that Miller was out there, or that maybe, just maybe . . . things were starting to feel better.

When I thought of the past, it was painful, and it upset me, but I found myself more often thinking about the future.

And weirdly enough, it was Sanchez's face that I saw in that future, which scared me to death because it had always been Miller, even when I hated him, it had been Miller.

And now. Now I was confused. And tired.

And apparently being forced to hang out with the one guy I was having a hell of a time saying no to.

All bets were off if he offered a foot massage.

With a sigh, I pulled up to my apartment building and turned off the Honda, my eyes glancing around the parking lot and landing on a familiar car.

A car that had *Sanchez* on the license plate.

A loud car that did not belong next to broken windows and trash.

Panicked, I ran all the way up the three flights of stairs to my apartment and shoved the door open.

Only to see Sanchez playing checkers with my dad.

My. Dad.

"Damn it." Sanchez rubbed his hands. "Okay, your move, old man."

"Hah!" Dad clapped his hands and made a horrible move that should have lost him a checker.

Sanchez ignored it, which meant he'd lost his own checker.

I dropped my bag to the floor as my tear-filled eyes glanced around the bare apartment with its faded carpet and white walls.

Pictures lined the table near the family room.

Dishes were piled in the sink. Sometimes Dad couldn't get to them.

A smell I couldn't identify wafted from the kitchen, where Connie was busy making coffee and grabbing Dad's medication while trying to make herself scarce. She gave me a glance that said more than words would. Good day. Her smile lit up the room. I sagged in relief.

"How was the game, baby?" Dad asked without looking up from his checkerboard.

Thank God. He was at least lucid. "I, uh . . . well, we won, thanks to Sanchez and Miller."

Nervousness washed over me as Sanchez turned around and tilted his head toward me, a smug grin spread across his face. "You checked out my ass."

Dad coughed.

I felt my cheeks flame red. "What?"

"Honey!" Dad burst out laughing. "Is that appropriate for a football cheerleader?"

"No." Sanchez shook his head in disapproval. "And I'm sure she'll be punished, sir."

I scowled.

He winked.

"Good," Dad agreed. "Now, your move, Grant."

I waited for them to finish their game. They talked football, they talked about their love of steaks, and when my dad finally called it quits because he was tired, he stood and shook Sanchez's hand. "I'm glad she has a good friend like you." He frowned. "Her last friend who played football . . ." He shook his head. "That was bad. She cried a lot."

"Dad," I said in warning.

"What?" He released Sanchez's hand. "You did, after that loss and well, what followed."

The room felt thick with tension.

"Anyway, you deserve a good senior year."

I froze.

Sanchez didn't skip a beat. "I can't wait to take her to homecoming."

"Homecoming!" Dad yelled. "Of course! How silly of me. You just had the big game, honey. We didn't get him a corsage!"

"Dad—" My voice broke. "That isn't . . . necessary. He's allergic." It was a horrible lie.

Sanchez mouthed, *"It's okay."*

Tears spilled onto my cheeks.

Dad frowned. "Why are you crying, baby?"

"Um, sorry, I uh—" I didn't know what to say, how to make it better, how to get my dad to understand without causing him to get too upset, or how to get Sanchez to truly get that we were on shaky ground with my dad. Whenever he had episodes, he'd get emotional and seeing me cry was almost always a trigger.

"I just miss you, that's all." I settled for the truth. I did miss him. All of him. The dad who used to make me pancakes before every game, his version of carbing up. The guy who watched football every weekend with me. The brilliant professor who never let me settle. The man who promised to stay by my side when the only boy I'd ever loved broke my heart. That man was gone. And while I'd been grieving the loss of him for the last few years, it suddenly struck me.

I would never have that man back.

I choked back another sob and quickly pulled my dad into my arms. "I love you, you know that right?"

"Honey," Dad chuckled and hugged me right back. "It's just a dance, and I'll always be here, waiting."

Yes. Physically. He would.

Mentally . . .

Connie, with her ever-present good timing, swept into the room, ready to take him back to his chair where he was typically the most comfortable and able to sleep.

"Wait." Dad snapped his fingers and grabbed a ten-dollar bill out of his back pocket. "It's all the cash I have. You kids enjoy yourselves. Treat her right. She's all I have." Dad's eyes filled with tears. "I . . . sometimes, I get confused."

"Don't all men?" Sanchez shrugged. "Especially in front of a pretty girl?"

Dad's gaze softened. "She's beautiful like her mamma was."

"I bet." Sanchez didn't look away from me once. He reached out, grabbed my hand, and squeezed it so tight I felt myself start to tear up again.

"So, tonight." Dad looked between the two of us. "What was . . . tonight again?"

My heart clenched as a choking sensation wrapped around my neck. His good moments never really lasted that long anymore.

Please God, don't take him like you took everything else. I subconsciously touched my stomach, only to see Sanchez glance down at my hand, his eyes pensive.

I jerked my hand away quickly.

"Homecoming," Sanchez said smoothly. "I'll have her home on time. No worries."

"Great!" Dad clapped his hands. "And what about her dress?"

"At my place." Sanchez shrugged, the lie falling way too easily from his lips. "It was closer to the restaurant."

"That's right." Dad nodded a few times. "Well, love you, honey." He kissed my forehead and yawned, then walked back to the living room and sat while Connie brought him water and his pills.

Sanchez leaned in to whisper in my ear. "Grab some stuff, stay with me tonight, alright? No arguments."

"Give me a few minutes," I answered, quickly going to my room and packing a bag.

Connie walked in and closed the door behind her, leaving Sanchez alone with my dad in the living room. "He had a good afternoon, but things . . ." She swallowed. "Things are progressing pretty fast, I thought you should know."

"His doctor's appointment?" I asked. The one I couldn't take him to because of the practices. "How did it go?"

She was silent, and then, "I think we need to discuss possibly putting him in an adult care facility."

"Nursing home," I whispered. "We can't afford it."

"There are programs, state aid." She reached for my hand. "I'll help you for as long as I can, but it's aggressive, and I can only do so much."

"I know." I fought to keep the tears in. "Thank you, for everything."

"He's charming."

"Dad?" I asked confused.

"No. The tall good-looking football player currently filling up the living room with his muscles." Her blue eyes twinkled. "Go, have fun." Her grin grew as she made fake air quotes. "At homecoming."

I choked back a laugh. "Thanks."

"Seriously." She pulled me in for a side hug. "You deserve all the good things in this world. And that's exactly what your dad wants for you. I'll text you updates and call if I need you, alright? Go dance the night away."

"Okay." I tossed a few more things in my bag. "Maybe when I get back we can talk about . . . the nursing home."

"Live a little before then, alright?"

Live.

Is that what was happening with Sanchez? Is that why he was breaking down all my defenses? Because he was forcing me to forget the past? To live?

Within minutes we were outside in his car.

I was too embarrassed, too devastated, and too sad to say anything as he pulled out of the parking lot of my building and sped onto the freeway. I was worried about the future, about my dad's decline, and it suddenly struck me that part of the sick feeling in the pit of my stomach was because I was afraid that somehow, this would change the way Sanchez viewed me, and I hated it.

Which meant only one thing.

I was starting to really care for him.

In a way that made my heart clench in my chest.

But this was Sanchez.

His car cost more than my entire apartment building.

"I'm pretty sure that your dad loves me," he said triumphantly, breaking the tense silence with his smooth voice. "I mean what's not to love?"

I laughed, thankful for his sarcasm, and then a tear escaped, followed by five more; they were hot as they slid against my cheeks.

Sanchez jerked the car over to the shoulder and put it in park. "Are you okay?"

"No—" I hiccupped. "Yes—" I shuddered. "Maybe. I'm sorry you had to see that."

"Sorry?" he repeated in a confused voice. "Why the fuck would you be sorry?"

"Because it's hard to keep up with him sometimes. I love him so much but he's not that man anymore, he's like a shell of his former self, and you would have loved him, the guy who raised me. This person I live with, it's not him, and sometimes he knows it and I know it kills him just like it kills me. I feel like I'm constantly waiting for the good days that are fewer and fewer." I cried harder. "Add that to the fact that you had to suffer through the peeling paint, small apartment, and the weird smell." I shook my head.

"Curves, a weird smell? Really?" he asked gently.

"Like old hot dogs." I covered my face, only to have him pry my hands away.

"I like hot dogs." He tilted my chin toward him then swiped his thumb across my lower lip. "Know what else I like?"

"Football?" I sniffed. "Cookies?"

"I was going to say you," he whispered. His eyes were so pretty it hurt to look directly at him. "And I don't care if you live in a fucking tent by the river and have to use a fishing pole you made out of scraps in order to have a nice meal that isn't a hot dog, alright?"

I nodded.

"And I'm fully aware that the ten dollars your dad gave me has more meaning than any thousand-dollar dinner or bottle of wine I could ever buy you. That's not how a guy like me earns a girl like you."

"A girl like me?"

"A girl like you." His eyes, those gorgeous eyes, zeroed in on my mouth. "You better believe I'm going to take you to the best meal that ten dollars can buy, and you're going to eat it, and then later we're going to thank your dad for the best homecoming ever, alright?"

"Why?" I wiped my cheeks. "I thought all you wanted was sex? Why were you at my house?"

"Oh that." He grinned with a half-shrug. "I was going to wait for you naked in bed."

I gasped.

"Holy shit, I'm kidding. I just wanted to pick you up and take you on a real date. Don't get those panties in a twist, Curves. Not before I have a chance to peel them off."

"Moment gone." My stomach flipped as a million butterflies tried to escape and launch themselves in his general direction.

"No." He kissed me across the lips. "Moment not gone."

"You win," I said breathlessly as he sucked my tongue and then touched my forehead. "You kiss too good."

"You taste better than I kiss, trust me."

"Highly doubtful."

"I'm not a liar." He kissed me again, this time harder. His hands slid down the column of my neck as his fingertips danced along my pulse, and with one last tug on my lower lip, he pulled away and winked. "Hungry?"

Not for food.

"Sure." I gulped.

"I know that look." His grin was always so easy, so sexual, so predatory and yet exciting that I wasn't sure if I should look away or kiss him again.

"What look?" I folded my hands in my lap.

He threw his head back and laughed. "I can't wait for that day, Curves."

"What day?" I played with a piece of my hair as he pulled the car back into traffic and hit the accelerator.

I tried not to stare at him. I'd been trying not to stare at him ever since Miller came stomping back into my life all angry and accusing.

The minute my best friend had come back . . .

I'd been trying to ignore my feelings for this new friend.

Because I'd put him in the user category, and I refused to allow myself to be used again and then discarded as if I meant nothing.

I wasn't sure my heart could take it a second time.

So I'd pushed him away.

But Sanchez wasn't the type I could ignore for long.

And he'd just broken me down enough to gain my attention.

Because he'd accepted my dad, made him smile, and actually pursued me, waited for me, rather than just trying to sleep with me. Somehow it had turned into this lingering joke, and yet, he never pressured me.

It was like he truly wanted more.

It was enough.

Enough, to get my eyes to linger a little bit longer on the strong line of his chin . . . on the dimple on the right side of his cheek . . . the way his shoulders and neck were so huge that his shirt looked like it was in pain trying to stretch over his taut muscles.

His olive skin almost glowed with excitement.

And when he smiled, that easy side smile that made a girl choke on her tongue—I looked away.

"The day," he finally said, "when you can't take it anymore."

"Take what?"

"This." He slid his hand down my thigh. "The heat between us, the way it feels when we touch. Damn, just being near you drives me insane. And humans are only gifted with so much patience before they snap. I hope to God that I'm around when you do."

"You think I'm going to go crazy for you, huh?" My voice sounded way too excited about the idea, and my heart decided to skip a few beats while my body cheered *yes!*

Sanchez shrugged. "I admire self-control, Curves. After all, this isn't going to be a one-night stand, and I have a feeling that you're going to make me work for it in bed. But don't worry. I've been really focusing on my own self-control. I'll take care of you long before you have a chance to take care of me. So yeah, do I think you're going to go crazy? I'm counting on it. Betting on it. Praying for it."

"Be honest. Is that why I'm staying with you?"

"Hell yes." He laughed. "I'm not letting you lose your shit around Miller, proximity and all that. It's going to be me, all me."

"Selfish much?"

He took the exit and pulled up to the stoplight. His gaze burned into mine. "When it comes to you? Yes. I fucking am."

And that was it.

We drove in silence the rest of the way to wherever he was taking me.

My eyes nearly bugged out of my head when he pulled up to a McDonald's and, without asking what I wanted, ordered enough McNuggets to kill a person.

He spent all ten dollars on the dollar menu.

And when the smell of McDonald's filled the car, I felt a strange, eerie sense of déjà vu fill my consciousness.

I wasn't sure what I would have done had he parked and said we should eat. Instead he drove another mile and pulled into a parking lot in front of a giant playground.

"Rule number one, never eat a hot McNugget. That shit burns your tongue straight off." He opened the car door and glanced over his shoulder. "You coming?"

"Where are we?"

"Park. Slides. Keep up."

The door slammed.

I scrambled out my side and had to jog to keep up with him as he made his way toward a huge jungle gym and started climbing to the top.

"Wait!" I called after him, but he was too busy having, apparently, the time of his life. It was already starting to get dark, and okay, even though I was a cheerleader, I was never the flyer, meaning I didn't really appreciate heights and, like I said, the jungle gym was huge. "Stupid, Sanchez," I grumbled, slowly making my way up the metal bars.

When I finally got to the top, he gave me a disappointed look. "Curves, that took you at least six minutes."

"It's tall!" I argued.

He frowned and looked down. "Baby, did you need a boost?"

"Screw you!" I yelled, wanting to throw something at his face.

His head fell back as he laughed at my expense. "You're a cheerleader. Don't they fly?"

"That's like me saying, 'You're a football player. Can't you throw?'"

He frowned. "Honey, I hate to break it to you, but we can all throw."

I grumbled and tried to cross my arms, then nearly fell through the bars in my own sad attempt to protest.

"Come here." He reached for me.

"No. I'm safer here, thank you."

"You're safer out of my arms than in them?" He tilted his head. "You sure about that?"

"Stop that. Stop making sense."

His laugh was infectious as he made his way over and then straddled the bars in front of me. He leaned in for a short kiss before pulling back. Moonlight lit up his face enough for me to suck in a breath at his masculine beauty.

What was happening?

What was I doing?

This wasn't how the story was supposed to go.

"The McNuggets," I blurted. "They're probably getting cold."

"It's been eight minutes. Give the McNuggets a break."

"Stop defending them."

"Curves." His tone was serious. His eyes searched mine, like this was about more than nuggets, about more than a simple one-night stand—it was one of those moments where you know a serious talk is coming and you want to avoid it because you know it's going to be a defining moment, one where you have to make a choice, a choice I wasn't sure I was ready for.

"What?" I was snapping. I never snapped. But he was prying; even his body language was evidence of that. I wanted the Sanchez that teased about sex back.

At least that guy I could turn down. I could fight.

This guy?

I was defenseless.

Because every time I tried to erect a wall, he made me feel stupid for having one in the first place.

"You touched your stomach," Sanchez said in a low whisper. "Back at your dad's. You touched your stomach, not like it was growling, not like you were hungry." His forehead pressed against mine as he reached for one hand. "I want to know all of it."

"All of what?" I fought so hard to keep a smile on my face, the practiced smile that hurt like hell and made my lips twitch.

His face fell. "Alright . . . if that's how you wanna play it." He started climbing off the jungle gym.

"Wait, where are you going?"

He shrugged. "To eat some McNuggets."

"Sanchez."

He didn't turn around as I tried scrambling after him. But then my foot caught, and I squealed.

Suddenly, I was in his arms, my cheek against his chest.

His heartbeat was steady.

Firm.

Maybe if I kept listening to it, I wouldn't be so afraid of the next few words out of my mouth.

Maybe they wouldn't be real anymore.

Maybe this time it wouldn't hurt so bad.

"I was pregnant."

Nope.

Still hurt.

Like being stabbed in the chest.

I told him everything.

"Look at me." Sanchez wrapped his bulky arms around my body. "You were a kid, hell sometimes I think we're still kids. That was six years ago, Em. But just because it was a long time ago doesn't make it hurt any less. The past is a bitch, especially when we're having a weak moment in the present."

"What do you know about weak moments?"

His grip around my waist tightened. "I loved her."

"Who?"

"Jacki Jones, communications major, gorgeous, funny—and to top it all off, she seemed to actually like me, Grant Sanchez, and not the wide receiver in line for a number one draft pick."

I felt myself relax. "What happened?"

"The usual." His lips pressed into a thin line. "She tasted fame and got addicted. The first game I started in, I was so nervous I was in the bathroom puking before Jax came and told me to hold my shit together . . . I played well, really well, and when the game was over all I wanted to do was go to my apartment and sleep. Emotionally exhausted, I just wanted to decompress you know? She didn't. Threw a fit because I wouldn't introduce her to my team-mates, cried because she said I was ashamed of her, manipulative little witch. The minute I introduced her to my teammates, things shifted, and not for the better. She started hanging out with them without me, asking them to call in favors, basically she networked her way through every guy, using me as her in. Did I mention we were engaged?"

Tears gone, anger surged through me. "What a horrible person!"

"Yeah well, she was really good at manipulation." He shook his head. "She made it seem like she was doing everything for me, for us, and it's no secret that I grew up really poor. My parents busted their asses to put food on the table so I rarely saw them. She gave me attention that I never realized I craved until our relationship started to shift."

"What happened?" I was glad the focus was off me, but his expression, the anger was still burning beneath the surface right along with the hurt.

"She was cheating, with Thomas."

I gasped, "How are you guys even friends?"

"He denied it." Sanchez shrugged. "And I had to choose between letting it affect the way we play or forgetting it for the betterment of the team. I broke up with her and decided I was better on my own."

"I'm sorry." My voice cracked. "You don't deserve that."

"I think a lot of people would disagree with you. Haven't you heard? I'm a man whore." His smile was sad.

"You want them to believe that."

"Or, I'm just really, really manipulative."

"No, you're not." I said it so fast that I surprised myself. "Don't cheapen our friendship."

His smile lit up my world. "I knew you'd finally give in."

"Trickery."

"The best." His lips grazed my ear. "Curves, know this." His breath was hot on my neck. "If you need to cry, I'll hold you until you're done. Sometimes the only way to get over things is to walk through them, but that doesn't mean you have to do it on your own."

My breath hitched in my chest. "Does that mean you're going to walk with me?"

"That's all I've wanted since meeting you." He pulled back and gripped my hand. "You know, other than sex."

I laughed. "You're ridiculous, you know that right?"

"But, I did just make you laugh, when minutes ago you were crying. I hate those tears, Curves. Never want to be the cause of them, ever."

"Don't make promises you can't keep."

"I'm not." He said it so sternly that I sucked in a breath.

"I think I need to use that hand now . . . maybe on your chest, possibly that shirt."

"Let it go." He squeezed my hand. "Like in *Frozen*, but without the singing."

I nodded, and after a shaky exhale, unlocked that little box in my head with the memories of a baby I lost—along with the best friend I ever had.

"I lost my best friend and my father all within the span of a year." My voice was hoarse. "And then a baby I never got the chance to meet."

"Come here." He held me while I cried and when I felt exhaustion set in, when I imagined he'd pull away, bored with my tears, I looked down at our joined hands.

And when I was done crying, when I was done sobbing all over his chest and apologizing and basically telling him that I wasn't the girl for him, he'd kissed me and told me we needed to eat.

Right. Because food was going to solve things.

And oddly enough, once I had salt and some nasty-tasting soda in my system, I felt better.

He'd turned on the heat in the car and held my greasy McDonald's hand. And kissed my knuckles.

"You need to tell him," he whispered.

"I can't."

"Not now, Em. But soon. He needs to know."

"I know."

"Em?"

"Yeah?" I was afraid to look directly at him, but his gaze was like a tractor beam, pulling me toward him even when I was too afraid to look into his eyes.

"I'm so fucking sorry." He gripped my hands tightly. "It wasn't your fault the baby died, and it wasn't his—it was life, nature. And it's okay to still be sad about it, even years from now, but it will still be okay. Loss is loss, allow yourself to feel it so you can deal with it."

I never realized I needed permission to mourn, permission to feel sad, but I did.

Just. Like. That.

I felt released of the guilt and the shame.

That was it.

Released.

But even after saying all the words—I still had that heaviness in my heart because Miller deserved to know—everything. By putting the past in the past—we weren't really ever able to move on toward our future. We both deserved that peace.

Chapter Twenty-Seven

MILLER

It was the postgame party—which meant I basically had to go even though I wasn't one to party. Sanchez and Em still weren't at the bar and I didn't want to leave without at least saying good-bye.

Right. I was that big of a loser that I was waiting to say good-bye to two people who probably couldn't care less about the fact that I even waited in the first place.

"You gonna drink that or just stare longingly into it like you want to make it your bitch, but the nice kind?" Kinsey's voice sounded from behind me, and then her hand patted my shoulder. "If it makes you feel better, all love sucks."

"Wow, thanks," I said with fake enthusiasm. "I really needed that pep talk after scoring my first touchdown."

She plopped down in the seat next to me and grinned. "You're welcome."

Jax glared at me over her head.

"Ah, your brother's giving me the warning stare."

"Just stay the agreed upon five feet away from me at all times, and he won't rip your face off."

"I can't imagine Jax being violent," I admitted, finally taking a sip of my beer.

"Jax?" She burst out laughing. "My brother? You clearly don't know him very well. Then again, I don't think anyone does. He's . . . reserved, calculated, and yes, it takes a lot to piss him off, but push him too far and yeah . . ." She made an exploding motion with her hands. "It's not pretty."

"Huh." I stared at the guy who looked like he would be more likely to coach a high school football team after retirement and volunteer at a children's hospital. "If you say so."

"I know so." She rolled her eyes. "Care to test it out?"

"What? You mean like sitting at the four-foot parameter instead of the five? Living dangerously, hmm?"

"That's me." Her shoulders slumped. "Dangerous."

I eyed her drink. "Is that a Shirley Temple?"

With a scowl, she plucked the cherry between her two teeth and shrugged. "I like a clear head."

"Cheers to that." I put down my beer, picked up my water, and clinked glasses with her.

"It's really too bad." Her blue eyes examined me from head to toe like she was taking stock of every single muscle that coated my body.

"What is?"

"You." She pointed her straw at me. "You're hung up on Emerson, which, don't get me wrong, I get it. She's beautiful, genuinely kind, hilarious, besides she's got an ass." Her shoulders slumped even more. "Which is probably why most of the good guys look at me and pass right on over the backside."

"Wait, back up? Why are you so depressed about asses?"

"I want one."

"Emerson's ass?" I asked, confused.

"Just an ass." She threw her hands in the air. "And not the kind that you're thinking. You know, controlling boyfriend-types. I want an actual ass." She stood and slapped her own backside. "You know? Like look, there's nothing here to grab!"

I started choking on my water as she wiggled her ass in front of me; my eyes found it really damn hard to look away with each movement.

And then Jax was marching over to us, his fists clenched.

"So, what do you think, Jax?" I said smoothly. "Your sister said she wants an ass."

Jax's mouth opened then closed then opened again. "Say what?"

"You should feed her more so she can have one. That's what good brothers do."

"I think I'm confused." Jax's eyes narrowed. "Weren't you just checking out her ass?"

"Nothing to check out." Kinsey sighed and sat back in her stool. "But thanks for proving my other point. Even if I had one, no guy would touch it because every time anyone breathes in my direction, you come sprinting over. Maybe I'll switch teams? Find myself a nice girl. Or a cat. Maybe both?"

"Enough." Jax's voice had a hard edge to it. "I wish I drank during the season."

I handed him my water.

He glared. "Wow, thanks so much. I'll be sure to drown my freaking sorrows."

"Oh, you're right. I think I see part of that temper." I looked around him to Kinsey.

She winked. "Told ya."

"I'm too exhausted for you both to be ganging up on me. Have you seen Sanchez yet? I wanna talk to him before I head out."

"About what?" I asked, curious.

"Ah, you know." He set my water down. "The stupid bet the new guys make about the cheerleaders in preseason. They bag them and then win a trophy, or whatever the hell it is now. I know he likes Emerson, but none of the players have ever taken it into the season. He's doing a hell of a lot for just sex and as much as I love the guy, Thomas has been talking shit behind his back about how he's turned into a pussy and we don't need that sort of drama during the season."

Kinsey frowned down at the table. "Jax, I think whatever is going on between them it's more than just getting laid. And you guys still do the whole bet thing?"

I shifted uncomfortably.

Jax's eyebrows shot up. "No shit. Anyone can see he likes her, that's not the point. I just want to know for sure, so it doesn't mess up his game. No offense, but if she's toying with him—"

"Stop." I stood, chest to chest with my leader, my brother. "She's not like that, alright? So just stop."

Jax held up his hands. "Dude, I wasn't trying to insult her or Sanchez."

"Really?" I snorted. "Because that's what it sounds like."

"Let him fight his own battles, man, and let her fight hers." Jax's voice had a serious edge to it. "God knows she isn't yours to protect anymore."

I wanted to punch him for saying that.

But it was the truth.

And I hated it.

It was my new reality.

The one where I watched the couple walk off into the sunset.

The one where I wasn't included in any future plans.

Just then, Emerson and Sanchez walked in the bar, his arm was around her protectively like—like she needed protection.

And when they walked toward us, he basically pulled her into his side to where I couldn't even see her face.

The hell?

And that's when it occurred to me.

Sanchez wasn't protecting her from the stares of other guys.

He was protecting her from me.

I just wished I knew why.

And why the look on his face was so disgusted you'd think I'd just committed murder.

"We need to talk." His voice was hollow, gruff.

"No." Jax stood between us. "We all need to talk." He jerked both of us away from the girls and shoved us outside.

"Heads in the game, ladies," Jax hissed. "I don't know what the hell is going on with you guys and Emerson, but you keep it off the field, alright? Don't let drama destroy a good thing."

"I won't," Sanchez said in an honest voice. "Swear."

"Yeah." I let out a rough exhale. "Me either."

"And Sanchez?" Jax shoved his hands in his pockets. "This thing with Emerson—it's not about getting laid is it?"

"Hell no!" he roared. "Are you serious right now?"

"Whoa." Jax held up his hands, backing into me and nearly running us backward into a parked car. "You know I had to ask."

"It's not your place to ask about my personal life, Captain," Sanchez sneered, his eyes finding mine before he slowly shook his head. "I know you may find this hard to believe, but I like her. I want to protect her from all this shit." He waved his hand around before it basically pointed at me. "You guys know how bad the press can be. The last thing we need is for them to think I'm dating her because of a bet, especially with Jacki all over my ass after the game."

"She saw you guys kiss," I mumbled.

"Everyone saw them kiss, it was trending on Twitter," Jax added, rubbing his hands over his face. "Look, you know that the coaching staff won't care as long as you perform and we keep winning, but the minute this turns into a distraction, your ass is going to get called into that office." He swore. "We have the day off tomorrow before practice Tuesday, let's all just get some rest. You guys killed it out there today, but we have the rest of the season left and we need wins, not losses."

"Agreed," Sanchez answered.

Jax nodded and walked off.

Leaving me and Sanchez together.

He didn't say anything.

"What's up?" I crossed my arms. "You look like I just ran over your brand-new puppy."

He cursed and kicked the side of the wall with his shoe. "Nothing. Maybe I'm just having a temper tantrum."

"That's not like you."

"Come again?" He jerked his head up, his eyes flashing. "How do you know me so well?"

"I hated you all last year." I swallowed the dryness in my throat. "Because you were good, and you were cocky—still are." He rolled his eyes. "But now, this year, now that I have reason to hate you more, for taking something I thought was mine, I can't."

"Why's that?" He moved until we were chest to chest.

"Because maybe that's how it was always supposed to be."

Guilt flashed across his face, so quick I almost missed it. "I wouldn't be so sure this was the plan, man."

"What the hell is that supposed to mean?"

"Look, we all need sleep. Emerson had a rough night. Her dad—"

The guilt was back.

"Her dad, what?" I was greedy for information, and I had no idea why.

"He's not well. I talked with the nurse before Emerson came home and when she refused to tell me anything I snooped while she was in the bathroom. He has really aggressive Alzheimer's, and it's only a matter of time before he has to be put in a home. As much as I'd like to think I have a lot of shit on my plate, she has more. I saw paperwork, it didn't look good." He scratched the back of his head and cursed again. "Was he sick when you two were in high school?"

"No." My voice sounded hollow. "Not even a little bit. They had a really nice house by the lake, he was a professor—"

203

"Guys?" Kinsey poked her head out of the bar. "Emerson looks dead on her feet and she's been here a grand total of ten minutes."

"I'll take her home." Sanchez started walking away, and I realized he meant his home, not hers.

Kinsey let Sanchez step past her and then crossed her arms as she took in my pathetic state. "Did I miss a bro fight?"

I snorted. "No."

"Good."

"Good?"

"Brothers that war together stick together. Don't let this"—she lifted her hands in the air—"destroy the good. And you, Miller Quinton, are good."

"At football?"

"Yes." She smiled. "Football, and from what I'm seeing with this little love triangle drama, you're a damn good friend."

"Doesn't feel like it sometimes."

"Of course it doesn't. Because sometimes, being good hurts way more than being bad."

At that I laughed. "So true, Flat-ass. So true."

Her eyes bulged. "Did you just call me Flat-ass?"

"If the panties fit . . ." I made a run for it only to have her jump on my back and start pounding her little fists into my muscles. "And a massage? You're the best!"

She slid off my back and glared, her chest heaving. "I have no more energy."

"Food." I pointed to the bar. "Go on. Work on that ass."

She swallowed and looked down. "I kinda don't want to eat by myself. The rest of the cheer team is being sort of . . ."

"Like the girls in *Bring It On* when everyone was against Torrance for using a choreographer that pimped the same routine to every cheer squad in California, and they start hating on her? Are they being like that?"

Her eyes widened. "Who are you?"

"Apparently, your new dinner buddy." I opened the door for Kinsey and whispered in her ear. "Flat-ass rule number one, eat the fries."

"With ketchup." She rubbed her hands together.

Sanchez and Emerson walked by us.

Time slowed.

And although it felt wrong . . .

A part of me wondered if that was why it was right.

Chapter Twenty-Eight

EMERSON

We were in bed.

It wasn't weird.

It should have been weird.

But ever since confessing to him about finding out I was pregnant in high school two months after Miller left, I felt—free.

I'd confessed to the wrong guy—and felt better, exhausted but better.

"You know . . ." Sanchez was flipping through channels on the TV, shirtless, wearing a pair of low-slung black sweats that hugged him in all the places I really shouldn't be looking if I was going to keep my promise not to sleep with him.

"What?" I yawned behind my hand and fluffed my pillow about ten times before he finally sighed and jerked it away from me, then pounded it with his giant fist, only to chuck it off the bed and pat his chest instead. I gulped. He repeated the motion. And because I was exhausted, I gave in.

His body was warm against my cheek, and then I found my hand drawing circles down the rivets of his perfect abs.

And somehow my legs inched themselves closer to his until I was both tangled and pressed up against him like a freaking sticky pretzel.

"Is it my heat or my body?" he said with a warm laugh.

"Both?" I snuggled closer. He felt so good. Both safe and dangerous, and just . . . right.

Great. Now I was quoting *Goldilocks and the Three Bears.*

"Were you saying something?"

"I wouldn't have left."

"What?"

"You," he whispered as he started playing with my hair, twisting it between his fingers like he did when he was thinking. "If you asked me to leave you now, I wouldn't. I can't imagine us being friends in high school. You know, because I was the shit, and you sounded like a total loser."

I punched him in the stomach. He clenched his abs so the blow wouldn't hurt—the bastard—and kept laughing.

"But . . ." His hand found mine, probably to protect other parts of his body. "Had we been friends, had I slept with you, tasted you, been with you, I wouldn't have gone through with it."

"He had no choice." I sighed. "His dad was moving."

"Em . . ." He wasn't calling me Curves anymore.

I wasn't sure what that meant.

"You always have a choice."

"Not in high school. You don't understand. You—"

"No, you don't understand." He sat up and gripped my face with both of his hands. "You love someone, you stay. There is literally no choice beyond that. All I'm saying is I would have fought. I would have emancipated from my own parent if that's what it took. I would have gone with my dad and then hitchhiked my way back, and every single time I was caught, I would go to sleep, wake up, and do it again. Hell, I would have transformed the shit out of some car and driven myself. There is no choice, Em. There isn't. Not when you love someone. Love doesn't need a justification for its actions. It's a free pass. And I would have taken that free pass and run—back toward you. That's . . ." He released my face. "That's all."

He leaned back against the bed and switched the channel again.

The shadows from the TV danced along the walls . . . and down his sculpted lips and face.

And I seriously stopped breathing.

Because in six years . . .

It had never occurred to me that neither of us had fought it.

I'd cried.

He'd cried.

It had been horrible.

But neither of us had fought it beyond that; we'd just freaking accepted it, like it was law, like there hadn't been alternatives.

We'd accepted it and tried to move on.

"I can hear you thinking." Sanchez's lips twitched as he kept flipping through channels as if it was a hobby.

And suddenly, all I wanted was to stop thinking—to kiss him, to thank him, to be with him.

Him.

I wasn't sure who moved first, he or I, but suddenly the remote was launched into the air and, in a tangled mess of arms and legs, we were kissing with me on top and him on bottom, his hands gripping my ass so tight there were going to be bruises.

The spiral was slippery.

The fall—easy.

I let myself.

I closed my eyes and just allowed it, allowed his hands to roam across my body like he owned me.

It was like diving into dark water not knowing what was beneath, not knowing if you would ever breathe air again, but not caring if those few seconds of bliss were all you'd ever experience.

That was Grant Sanchez.

He pulled away from me. His eyes were at a complete half-mast as he inspected my lips. "Yeah, Em." He licked his lips then tucked my hair behind my ears with shaky hands. "I would have fucking run back to you."

All the air left my lungs in a whoosh as I sagged against him, my hands reaching for his neck as our mouths met in an open-mouthed kiss, lips parting. His hot breath ran down the side of my cheek as he pressed kiss after kiss down my neck.

Body trembling, I tried to tell my heart to stop beating so loud.

But it was too excited.

Racing toward him.

Toward someone who I'd always seen as the wrong guy.

Who quite possibly could end up being the right one.

Because no matter how damaged your heart may be, it never loses its ability to choose again, to try again, to want love even after loss.

How could something so wrong feel so right?

He cupped my breasts through my shirt and then, in a fit of cursing, tugged it over my head, nearly taking off one of my ears. He tossed it to the ground and looked his fill.

"Sprinted." He pressed a hungry kiss to my mouth. "Sprinted and prayed for wings the entire way." Another kiss and another, I was counting them, storing them for later, just in case.

Because I was still afraid, afraid that this was a dream, that this feeling—this thing we had between us—wasn't real.

And I needed it so badly to be real.

For something this good to stay this good.

He groaned as he lowered his head. His rough hands tugged off my bra and tossed it with the shirt, and that same tongue, the one my mouth mourned to lose, was swirling around one nipple then the other.

I arched against him.

The feeling wasn't something I was used to.

A guy taking his time.

My only experience had been a few horny, rushed times in high school with my best friend. Powerful, but different than this, so much different. Liquid heat spread until it was impossible to sit still.

"Shhh, I'm having a moment with your breasts." With the strength of the football player he was, he flipped me—ME—onto my back and pinned my hands above my head. "I may need to have several moments. They have a lot to say." He moaned, pressing his ear to my chest. "Uh-huh, what was that? You want to stay? In my bed?"

My laughter broke through the nervousness of him seeing me naked, a guy who was the new face of Armani, the same guy who made girls forget their names, the same guy who within five seconds of meeting me declared us best friends.

Each touch of his tongue was painful; I was on sensory overload and was pinned down by over two hundred and fifty pounds of Bellevue Buck wide receiver.

He made me feel powerful—sexy.

I writhed beneath him. "Are you done talking? Because I'm kind of dying here."

He pressed that same ear higher. "Your heart's just fine, see? Beating's a little erratic. I may need to give you a sedative later. Hope wine's okay."

"Sanchez."

"Grant," he whispered. "Say my name."

"Grant."

He hissed out a breath before his mouth met mine again. His giant body hovered over me protectively as if he was afraid the ceiling was going to see me shirtless or something.

"Tell me you're staying here."

"Where else would I go?"

His eyes searched, and I knew exactly what for.

I held my breath.

And then he was kissing me again.

His hands tugged down my shorts until the heel of his palm was between my thighs. Between his mouth and his one hand, I was ready to die a blissful death.

"Stop squirming." He chuckled in my ear.

"I'm not. I don't do these . . . this . . . . things . . . like this."

He pulled back, his eyes serious. "Good."

And then the rest of my clothes were gone.

And I was completely naked. With him.

I gulped.

He placed both hands on top of my thighs and grinned. "Let me."

"Let you what?"

"Let me taste you."

He was asking permission. Who was this guy? This so-called womanizer? The one who asked permission and made me lock my door at night?

With a playful smile, he waited, his head nearly resting between my thighs, his fingertips drumming across my skin as if he had all the time in the world.

"No sex, but I do want to lick you, make you scream," he finally said. "Final offer before I lock that door and let you cry yourself to sleep like you know you will if you turn me down, because—and here's where I really seal the deal—I'll cuddle."

"What?" I leaned up on my elbows. "Did you just say the C-word?"

His grin went from playful to downright lethal. "Which one was that again?"

"I walked right into that."

"And I'm about to lick that." He winked. "Plus, you know what they say. You lick it, it's yours. And you, Emerson, you're in my room. You're mine."

I nodded.

But I didn't say it.

Not yet.

The only thing he didn't own was my heart—at least not yet—and I knew that if I said it, if I confessed, my heart would follow. Then Miller—everything about him—would be gone forever, and although I was moving on, I needed at least to tell him first, about everything.

It must have shown on my face, my indecision, because Sanchez waited.

"Yes." I breathed. "But you have to cuddle and stop, if I need you to stop."

"Deal, but here's a little secret. When a guy knows what he's doing, a girl won't want him to."

"Oh."

Anxiety mixed with excitement as he lowered his head, and then cool air hit between my thighs, causing me to flinch and then spread them.

"Neat trick." I gritted my teeth.

"I'm full of them." I could still see his eyes flashing before he let out a hoarse moan. "And now I feast."

I was about to protest. To say he was being ridiculous, scold him—who knows? It was Grant Sanchez!

And then all logical thought flew out the window.

And my body pulsed with Grant Sanchez.

And the way his tongue slid places I didn't even know existed, applying pressure, sucking, licking, making me feel like a wanton little slut.

But so good.

So—free.

I clutched the sheets between my fingers as sweat pooled in the palms of my hands. His tongue thrust, only to retreat just when I needed it more.

He groaned between strokes.

And with each movement, little spasms hit me, until he gripped my thighs with his hands and whispered against my skin, "Patience, Em."

I almost kicked him when his hands joined team Try to Make Emerson Die in a Professional Football Player's Bed.

And then absolute magic.

An explosive shudder ran through my body as I shamelessly climaxed against his mouth, my body nearly launching off the bed and throwing itself off the balcony in triumph.

Only to have a second tremor follow.

And a third.

My eyes were still closed when I felt his lips on my neck and then covers sliding over my body. And that same man, the one I promised myself I'd stay away from, pulled me against his body.

His aroused body.

One that said, *I may not sleep tonight because I'm so hard I could pound nails.*

He whispered in my ear. "Thank you."

I went completely still.

"But."

"Em." He slid his hands down my bare arms. "This. This is all I want from you. Not all the sex, not all the foreplay, though that's great. Right now, I want to take care of you. Just you. And then I want to hold you, in my bed. And not sleep a room away from you, wondering if the last man you think about is the same one I have to get along with for the next sixteen games without ripping his head off or wondering if he misses your taste the way I would. If he thinks about you naked like I'm going to. I can't do that now. Not after tonight. Probably not ever. So don't analyze this, don't make this about you. Let it be about me, this man sharing a bed with you, and his jealousy over a past he was never a part of—and the fear he has over the fact that the past could still unfairly dictate his future."

I finally exhaled the breath I'd been holding. "You say really poetic things for a dumb football player." Tears filled my eyes. *Please, God let it be real.*

Don't take him away too.

"Graduated summa cum laude, Curves. Told ya."

"Grant . . ." I flipped around to face him. He was so pretty, so ridiculously good-looking with his chocolate-brown hair and heart-stopping smile. "Why?"

"Why did I graduate?"

"No, why me?"

He peeked under the sheet. "You for real right now, Curves? Look at you!"

"Serious." I swallowed past the lump in my throat. "Why me?"

He sobered and cupped my chin. "That's easy." He pressed a kiss to my mouth. "You refused to be my friend. And everyone wants to be my friend, for whatever reasons they may have. But you pushed, which meant you were one of the good ones. And when you looked at me, it wasn't about what I had. It was what I was lacking."

"You like me because I find your faults?"

"Hell no." He laughed. "I like you because you make me want to fix them."

Chapter Twenty-Nine

MILLER

I lay in bed and imagined them watching movies like we used to. I let the memories of me and Em wash over me until I was sick with them. Because no matter how damn bad I wanted to be the guy sharing her present, I'd lost that opportunity the minute I walked away in her past.

Part of me wondered if I had given up too easily because I'd been hurt.

Because, deep down inside, I didn't expect a girl that incredible to want to stay with me, and when I'd driven away from her, I'd had a sinking feeling it wouldn't end well.

Not because I didn't love her.

But because I wasn't sure how to love her so far away, not with our relationship being so new. Not with my dad breathing down my neck about football and college scholarships.

It was as if the further away I drove from her the more issues popped up, making it impossible to even see her waving figure anymore.

I turned over on my back and stared up at the ceiling.

Football.

Winning games.

Focusing on the positive.

I needed to do all of those things and stop acting like such an emotional wreck over things I had no control over—like how she felt about Sanchez.

As if I needed another reason to slam my face into the pillow and hold my breath, I heard laughter next door and then his name.

Not Sanchez.

Grant.

She yelled *Grant.*

Pain sliced through my chest. I waited for it. The hurt. More pain.

And then the strangest thing happened: it kept beating, the world didn't end, and everything continued on like I didn't just hear what I thought I'd heard.

My mind toyed with me; it made me want to believe they were playing tag, when really I knew there were less clothes involved and a hell of a lot more tongue.

I groaned again and set my clock for an early wakeup call so I could go for a run.

"Wake up!" A loud male voice yelled, and then my mattress was moving. "Earthquake!"

"What the hell!" I roared. In a tangled mess of sheets, I fell to the ground and finally opened my eyes to see Sanchez towering over me with nothing but a grin on his face and gray Armani sweatpants.

"Morning sunshine." His grin widened. "I was afraid you slept naked, which is why Emerson is hiding in the safety of my kitchen. Then again, she's cooking so . . ."

"Cooking?" My stomach rumbled.

"Uh-huh. That's what I thought." Sanchez yawned. "Figured you'd want some food after yesterday's win, and what better way to celebrate than with friends?"

Right. Friends.

"Kinsey's coming over too, with Jax and Thomas."

"Even better." I stood.

Sanchez shook his head. "And to think she missed out on such a nice show. Put on some clothes before you scare someone."

"I only care about scaring the dudes." I yawned and shoved past him toward the bathroom. "Give me ten minutes."

"Cool." He walked off, and my front door slammed. Had I left it open? Did the psycho have a key or something?

I shook my head and quickly took a shower and got ready. The smell of bacon was already filling the hall by the time I knocked on Sanchez's door and let myself in.

Jax and Kinsey were both drinking orange juice while Sanchez opened a bottle of champagne.

"Mimosas?" Em scrunched up her nose.

"Don't worry. I'm giving you more champagne than juice. Less sugar." He eyed Kinsey. "It's in the manual."

"Stop memorizing our shit." Kinsey rolled her eyes.

"That's what you do when you sleep with all the cheerleaders," Thomas said out loud, like the dumbass he was, clearly not thinking *Oh hey, Emerson's a cheerleader, and she's been with Sanchez for a few weeks now.*

"Apologize." Sanchez slammed his glass onto the granite, sending orange juice flying all over the pristine wood floor.

Thomas's eyes flashed briefly before he shrugged at Em, nothing about his body language said apology. "Sorry, I wasn't thinking, Emerson. I know it's not like that with you guys. I mean if it is that's cool— What I mean is that . . . he's like that with other cheerleaders and—"

Jax smacked him on the back of the head. "Stop talking already."

Thomas shut up but didn't stop glaring at Sanchez, or Em for that matter.

"It's fine." Emerson's smile was fake. "Should we all eat?"

"Food!" Jax shouted a little too energetically while Kinsey started grabbing plates.

Nobody noticed Emerson sneak off down the hall.

Except me and Sanchez.

I nodded to him.

Only to have Jax grab him by the arm. "I was thinking about that trick play and . . ."

"I got this," I mouthed.

His relief was tangible as I quickly headed down a hall that mirrored my own and found her in his bedroom. And a part of me wondered if he actually trusted me alone with her—or just wanted her to be comforted no matter who did the comforting.

I expected to feel rage.

Jealousy beyond belief.

Instead, all I could conjure up was a hell of a lot of sadness at where we both were in our friendship, and disappointment that I didn't know how to get it back. Because, before I kissed her six years ago, she'd been everything to me. My rock. My best friend. And I would kill to have that feeling back, that solidarity we used to share. Yes, I'd always been attracted to her. I'd always wanted her, loved her, but not as much as I needed her by my side. That would always win out, and I figured it was time I stopped moping and actually acted on that shit. She deserved at least that much—and more.

"Hey." I knocked on the open door. "Sanchez was headed in, but Jax stopped him about some play, so today you get second string."

"You've never been second string a day in your life." She snorted.

"Until now," I answered honestly. "Gotta say it's not one of my favorite things, Em."

She wiped her cheeks and flashed me a smile. "Second string is still important, you know."

"Hah." Damn it. Her tears were killing me. "Are you giving me a pep talk? Isn't that why I came in here?"

"Say your quarterback gets hurt, the backup better be just as good, or the team's chances of hitting the playoffs are slim to none."

"True, true." I nodded. "And the quarterback has to have balls of steel but still be able to calm the storm."

"Right." She folded her hands in her lap. "And I mean your position—the tight end—you need to be big, tall, fearless. You have the opportunity to score, but you also have to protect the quarterback. You can't just be the best tight end in the league one day and a sucky one the next. Some may even argue that third string is important—they pay them like they are. Look at the Pilots. They're on one of their third-string wide receivers right now!"

She was animated as she threw her hands in the air and huffed.

"You love football." I grinned, sitting on the bed.

"I love football," she agreed. "So, what do you think? About second string?"

I glanced around the room, the room that smelled like *them*, the room that she was currently staying in, if the clothes on the bed were any indication.

"I'd say it sucks balls, but I'm willing to take even that."

"Why are you talking about sucking my balls, Miller?" Sanchez was leaning against the door, his bulky arms crossed.

I flipped him off.

"Ouch, and to think I thought we were going to be best friends." His voice dripped with sarcasm.

I was completely out of my comfort zone, unsure if hugging her was wrong, if touching her hand in comfort was off-limits, so I scooted away.

Sanchez shook his head. "I'm not saying this because I've ever stunk so bad that I've been put on second string . . ." He took a seat on the other side of Emerson. "But I guess it's all in how you look at it."

"Yeah?" I stared straight ahead, voice cracking, showing my weakness. "And how's that?"

"Well, at least you're still in the game."

I sucked in a breath.

And looked at him, like really looked at him.

And damn if that wasn't a man I could respect.

"Isn't that the most important thing?" he asked.

"Yeah." My voice cleared. "It is."

"Guys?" Emerson looked between us. "Are we still talking about a game or about what Thomas said?"

"Thomas is a jackass," Sanchez growled. "I'm surprised he's still on the team after all the shit he's pulled in the past."

I wasn't sure how much Em knew about Thomas and Sanchez's past, but it wasn't my place to say anything. I was just as shocked that he was still playing for the Bucks, especially since they were known for their stance on drama between players. Guys had been kicked off the team for less, but Thomas was damn good at what he did. Part of me wondered if Sanchez's reaction was the only reason Thomas was able to stay on the team. And again, my respect for the man grew especially since there was so much bad blood between them.

"An immature piece of shit that I'm going to forget to protect during practice tomorrow," I added, as I gave a serious nod. Sanchez gave me a high five over Emerson's head.

"You guys are like your own version of the mafia."

"Football mafia." I grinned. "Kind of has a ring to it."

"I need you to do me a favor," Sanchez said in perfect *Godfather* voice with his jaw jutting out.

"This? This is what we're waiting on? You guys playing *Godfather* in the bedroom while poor Em has to wonder if she's going to get forced to play the horse?" Kinsey appeared in the doorway.

"You are disrespecting the family," I joined in, pointing at Kinsey.

"Yeah, I'm out." Emerson laughed and then turned around. "Thanks guys. Both of you."

They left us alone.

It was awkward as hell for a few minutes, and then it wasn't.

"Regardless of what happened in the past or whose fault it was . . ." Sanchez stood. "You left."

I licked my lips and swore. "Yeah. I know."

"The difference between you and me." His eyes flashed. "I never would."

I hesitated, searching his eyes for any sort of bullshitting and found nothing but honesty, so with a shake of my head, I muttered out in disbelief, "The hardest part of all of this? I actually believe you."

"Guys!" Kinsey yelled. "FOOD!"

"Better go before she burns your apartment down," I muttered, walking past him, feeling like maybe the past was defining our future—just in a way neither of us could have imagined.

Or planned for.

Or prepared for.

Chapter Thirty

EMERSON

My body was still buzzing from last night. I felt good, so good, until I locked eyes with Miller, and the guilt was back. Normally, other feelings accompanied it, feelings that made me feel guilty about everything going on with Sanchez, feelings that told my body that maybe I wasn't over Miller, but the butterflies weren't back full force and I wasn't looking at him with longing anymore.

Instead, I was feeling guilty more than anything.

"Hey." Sanchez grabbed me from behind, then twirled me in his arms and kissed the side of my neck. "Did you drink all your mimosa like a good girl?"

"Every last drop." I grinned like a lunatic. "Thanks."

He pressed another kiss to my neck and tugged me against his body. I loved the way he felt. The world faded away. All of it. It was like the more time I spent with him, the more my past disconnected, leaving me no choice but to cling to my future—to cling to him.

So while the past strings were cut . . .

The future strings were attached.

To him.

"So, today's a free day." Sanchez pulled away. "I thought we could all do something fun?"

"I'm out." Thomas yawned. "Coach has to talk to me about some stupid shit that most likely has to do with why I've been playing even shittier than normal."

Sanchez's expression was tense. "Sorry, man. Hope it's not bad news." The look he gave was anything but sorry, but I didn't say anything.

Thomas shrugged and grabbed his keys. "See ya." He nodded to the guys and reached for Kinsey. She put her hands in the air and took a giant step back.

"What, no hug?"

"Not if you want the quarterback to throw to you."

"One night. May change your life, Kins."

"Eh, I've heard of your life-changing seconds. I think I'll pass."

His expression hardened. "Suit yourself."

"Uh-huh." She started putting the food away, completely ignoring him as he stomped out of the apartment.

"What was that?" Miller asked the room.

Yeah, I was wondering the same thing.

Kinsey answered before Sanchez could. "He's been playing like shit. Jax can't create a miracle, and Thomas . . . well, at this point he needs a miracle. He was undrafted last year, and Coach wanted to take a chance on him." She put the lid on a dish and shoved it into the fridge, her long dark hair swaying down her back with the movement. "But here's the thing, you have to want the dream, and at first, he did, he really did. You could see the excitement in his eyes. The awe. And then, the fame came, right along with Jacki and look how that turned out? Not everyone can handle it. Thomas is apparently one of those people."

The kitchen fell silent.

She kept talking.

"I mean he's on the freaking defensive line! All he has to do is blitz and stop crazy shit from happening. Instead, he's focused on getting an interception. Dude, you aren't a corner, you know?"

My eyebrows shot up.

Miller's mouth opened, closed, and then, "Another cheerleader who likes football?"

She stared down at the counter. "I wanted to play when I was little, but they didn't let girls on the team, so I cheered instead. It's no big deal. Hey, anyone gonna finish this champagne?" She didn't wait for anyone to answer, just grabbed the bottle and tossed back the last few inches.

"You wanted to play?" I smiled. "I'd be terrified of you. You seem—"

"Ballsy," Miller finished. "And a bit scrappy. Yeah, I think I'd be scared too."

"Says the guy who's nearly six foot six." She grinned. "But thanks. Anyway, what are we doing today?"

With the subject officially changed, I looked up at Sanchez, but he was busy looking between Miller and Kinsey.

I elbowed him.

His face slowly molded into a knowing grin. "I say we go to the stadium and play a little . . . football."

"Football," we all said in unison.

"The hell, man?" Miller glared. "Isn't this our day off?"

"Can't be the best if you don't practice every damn day." Sanchez rubbed his hands together. "Plus, I really want to chase Emerson. Tell you guys what, we'll let the girls be quarterbacks, and we'll recruit some of the practice squad, who you know are already there working, to help us. Whatever team wins has to cook tonight. Deal?"

"Deal," Kins and I said at the same time.

"But . . ." I shoved away from Sanchez. "Kinsey and I are on the same team. Boys against girls."

"Aw . . ." Sanchez put a hand across his heart. "Aren't you adorable. Miller, my girl thinks she has a chance."

"I'm really good at kicking ass," I snapped back.

Miller took a step toward Sanchez. "Dude, I don't know if you want to do this. She made a guy ugly cry in high school. He literally ran off the field and called his mom."

"Please." Sanchez snorted. "What could she possibly do?"

Miller gulped.

He had a right to be a bit fearful, because yeah, maybe what I'd done that day on the field had been a bit illegal. After all, it was flag football not tackle. But how had it been my fault that Jack tripped over my body?

"This is going to be fun." I rubbed my hands together. "Get ready to lose, boys."

"She does realize we're two of the highest paid players in the league, right?" Sanchez asked Miller. "Or is she just that delusional?"

Miller shuddered. "I was her powder puff coach."

Sanchez lost his smile. "Well shit."

"Taught her everything I know."

"You think that information wouldn't have been freaking helpful about four minutes ago?" Sanchez playfully shoved him.

"Whatever." Miller shook it off. "We're giants compared to them. We'll be totally fine."

I gave Kinsey a knowing look.

We may not be as big.

But we played dirty.

"Game on." I crossed my arms.

"Clean that O-line up now!" Sanchez roared. "Jones, you get your ass back for extra coverage!"

Jones limped over to his spot on the field.

"Bunch of pussies!" Miller yelled. "You're professional athletes. Act like it!"

Kinsey and I nodded to each other as we adjusted our flags. We'd been playing for the past forty minutes and had already scored two touchdowns.

We were tied.

Fourteen to fourteen.

The other team, Iron Men, had a constant fear of hurting us, because you know, we were girls. So, each time they approached us, they were worried about either getting their asses kicked for touching boob or butt, or they were worried about hurting us. Meaning, it really wasn't fair.

The worst was that everyone always gave Kinsey a wide berth.

Meaning, our first touchdown had basically been given to us.

I highly doubted the guys took that into consideration.

The minute she'd texted Jax to let him know about our pickup game, he'd come down to the practice stadium and stared daggers at everyone, and nobody wanted to piss off the quarterback. He'd left breakfast early and I hadn't seen him since.

"Let's go!" Sanchez roared. He hated losing. And I loved that every time I had the ball he attacked me like I was his equal. I truly didn't think he would even blink an eye if he had to run me over to win. He'd just say, *Hey, you wanted to play.*

I loved that about him.

I wasn't weak to him.

I was just . . . Emerson.

Miller, on the other hand, looked ready to murder his own team right along with Sanchez.

They were both covered in sweat and dirt. So much for a day off, right?

"One, two, hike!" Sanchez dropped back and looked for an open receiver.

I was covering Jones on the side and saw Sanchez look to Miller. This was my chance. I charged through the opening and blitzed the hell out of Sanchez, knocking him completely on his ass and scratching for the football.

"Seriously?" He heaved, looking up at me. "Who are you?"

"Why . . ." I batted my eyelashes. "I'm a professional athlete. And you?"

He smirked and smacked me on the ass. "Way too turned on to be around people right now."

I helped him to his feet, only to have him whisper in my ear. "Please tell me you'll do that to me in bed sometime. I love a good . . . tackle."

He swatted my ass again and walked off with the ball, ready to set up.

And I was frozen in place, my breathing erratic, my heart wild.

"Focus!" Kinsey screamed at me.

"Sorry!" I yelled back, getting into position as they went for the third down.

Sanchez threw a spiral to Miller, who caught the ball then ran straight into Kinsey, knocking her tiny body to the ground.

"Oh shit!" Miller yelled.

Jax yelled for her.

I ran over.

She was on her back with tears of laughter pouring down her face. "See, this is why I need an ass, guys! I need something to land on." She blinked up at Miller. "Did I stop you?"

A stunned expression crossed his features before he shook his head and helped her up. "I was too busy not killing you to notice."

"Oh." She frowned. "Shoot, a yard short. That's okay. Maybe next time, champ." She slapped him on the back and walked off.

Leaving him standing there with a familiar expression on his face.

I crossed my arms and smirked.

"Don't." Miller pointed the ball at me. "I know that look. Don't even go there."

I shrugged.

"Stop that!" His frown turned into a smile. "I know what you're thinking."

"Oh?"

"Yes." His eyes heated, and then he burst out laughing. "God, I missed you."

"You too, big guy." I winked as he put an arm around me and shoved me back toward my team.

When I glanced up at Sanchez, he was smiling at me. A real smile, not a jealous, I'm-going-to-kick-his-ass smile, but something that told me he knew who I was going home to.

And it wasn't the guy who kissed me six years ago, slept with me, and walked away.

It was the guy who asked me for sex and was relentless in his pursuit. It was the guy who told me we were friends before he ever knew my name.

It was Grant.

"You okay?" he mouthed.

"Of course," I mouthed back.

A whistle blew, and then Jax was running onto the field. "You guys are both playing like absolute shit." He shook his head in frustration. "I can't believe I'm related to this." He was pointing at Kinsey, who Miller had to hold back by the shirt to keep from charging toward her brother.

"Now . . ." Jax rubbed his hands together. "Next touchdown wins. Clearly, you need a referee."

"Ah, Jax isn't good enough to join, so he has to judge?" Kinsey shouted.

"Fifth grade." Jax pointed at her. "She taught me how to throw."

All the guys looked at Kinsey.

Her cheeks reddened. "Hells yes, I did!"

"So no, probably not good enough to be on your team, Kins." He grinned and then blew the whistle again. "Alright, Sanchez, Miller, for the love of God, stop embarrassing yourselves and score, okay?"

"It's bullshit!" Sanchez yelled. "They cheat!"

I gasped. "We do NOT cheat!"

"She grabbed my ass!" Sanchez pointed an accusing finger at me.

"You liked it!" I fired back.

The guys on both sides laughed.

"Next touchdown," Jax said again as he set the ball on the line of scrimmage. "Let's go, Sanchez."

Chapter Thirty-One

EMERSON

"I'm really looking forward to you in an apron and nothing else." Sanchez gripped me by the hips and held me close to his body as we both walked toward the locker room. "In fact, I think you should let me help you shower—just in case you have grass and dirt in places that need inspection."

"Very funny." I shoved him away and ran. I was pissed. I liked winning.

"Aw, baby." He chased after me and then tackled me to the ground right before I ran off the field.

He held his weight above me by bracing his arms on either side of my body. "I like you."

"Is that your way of apologizing for winning?"

"You shouldn't have blitzed again." He grinned. "I read it."

"Bullshit!" I shoved his rock-hard, totally sexy chest. "I wasn't even looking at you!"

"Yeah, but I *felt* you." He licked his lips. "And I know how competitive you are. You were thinking about stopping me—stopping the play—not about the actual play headed in your direction or the fact that I'd do a quarterback fake."

I scrunched up my nose and sighed. "I thought you were going to throw it."

"Uh-huh, and I ran instead."

"You hadn't run at all the entire game."

"Which is why I ran." He nodded slowly. "Is my girl really this competitive? Because I gotta tell you, it's hot as hell." His lips found my neck.

I didn't shove him away; instead, my treacherous body met him halfway in a searing kiss. His mouth moved across mine with such tenderness that I wanted to cry. His fingers dug into my shoulders, and then when he pulled back, his green eyes didn't leave mine. "We should hit the showers."

"Don't think I didn't notice that you said *we*."

"Don't think I didn't notice that my kiss made you breathless," he countered.

I gulped, eyeing his mouth again. "Maybe."

His eyebrows rose as he smirked and then slowly stood to his feet and offered his hand.

We walked hand in hand down the hall toward the two locker rooms. Someone was shouting.

Miller was in the process of shoving Kinsey behind him.

"This is bullshit!" Thomas rounded the corner, slamming a chair against one of the hallway walls as the practice squad stood in silence around him. Then some squad members trickled out of the guys' locker rooms while others still leaned against the walls, expressions stunned. "It's because of you!" He jabbed a finger at Miller. "What? YOU think you're big shit because you have a huge contract?"

Miller said nothing.

"Man . . ." Sanchez took a step forward just as Jax grabbed my arm and pulled me against the wall. I wasn't sure why he was putting me out of sight, but I didn't argue. "You guys aren't even close to being the same position."

"I'm getting cut!" Thomas kicked the chair he'd just thrown. "And since when do you ever take Miller's side? What, you guys friends now?" he sneered.

"Teammates are *family*." A muscle in Sanchez's jaw twitched. "After all the shit that went down between us, you of all people should know that."

"That's bullshit! You're *my* friend. You're supposed to defend me. You've always defended me! You've known him for less than two months!"

"Thomas . . ." Sanchez put his hands out in front of him. "You're upset. I see that. Let's just go somewhere and talk out options, yeah. You're super talented. It's not that bad, right?"

"Options?" Thomas repeated with a snarl. "I have no fucking options, Grant! You know that! And what's worse is Coach said he'd talked to the captains about this, meaning you knew it was a possibility, and you didn't say shit!"

"Sanchez didn't know." Jax stepped around me. "But I did."

Sanchez hung his head and cursed.

"And based on this little outburst, I helped Coach make the right decision."

Thomas lunged for Jax, but Sanchez grabbed him by the shirt and then shoved him against the wall. "Shake it off, man."

"This," Thomas said in a harsh whisper. "Before that stupid bet, you would have never been like this. You choosing girls over me too, Grant? Because we all know the only reason you're cozying up to Coach and pretending to be Mr. Perfect all the time is because you bet you could fuck the cheerleader and she's yet to put out. Who's going to care then? When you mess up like you messed up with Jacki! That's what you do, you screw with girls, then leave them!"

I gasped and covered my mouth.

Jax wasn't standing in front of me anymore, so all eyes turned to me.

Sanchez punched Thomas in the face twice before Miller could pull him away. "That's bullshit, and you know it!"

"Is it?" Thomas snarled before he disappeared into the guys' locker room and came back with something in his hand. It looked like a trophy. "Every year, the players pick a girl to screw. Last year, I won, then again that was after your cheating fiancé made a pass at me."

He walked toward me; my back was glued to the wall. I wasn't sure what to do except breathe in and out while everyone watched with wide eyes.

"This year, Sanchez picked *you*." Thomas shoved the trophy into my hands and towered over me.

"Don't fucking touch her!" Sanchez yelled.

Miller let him go and followed Sanchez down the hall.

I felt it first, the metal on my fingertips.

It looked like something you'd get in middle school. It had a football player posing on top and an inscription on the bottom that read *Player of the Year.*

"Some captain." Thomas scowled and shoved through players to leave the hall while I kept staring at the trophy.

My heart told me it wasn't true.

Not after everything we'd shared.

But logic . . .

Kinsey's words . . .

Everyone's warnings . . .

And then the silence I was met with when I looked up into Grant's eyes and waited for him to deny it.

Instead, his next words were basically the opposite. "Let me explain."

It was almost worse than hearing the damning words of guilt.

Because that sentence made it seem like he had justification for what he'd done, for making me think that he wanted more than to screw a cheerleader.

And the stupidest part?

I'd walked right into it. He'd never lied about wanting to have sex with me.

The trophy fell from my fingers and made a loud clang on the floor as a buzzing erupted in my ears.

Miller clutched me by the arm. "Let him explain. It's not what it looks like."

I jerked away from him as fresh pain washed over me. "You knew?"

Miller's nostrils flared.

"So, I had one guy trying to sleep with me for a bet, and my ex-best-friend . . . what? Just wanted to hurt me as bad as he thought I hurt him?"

Miller swore. "You have it all wrong. That's not—"

"Let her go." Sanchez grabbed Miller. "Kinsey, can you make sure she gets home?"

Tears filled my eyes. "That's it? You're just going to let me leave?"

"Yeah."

I'd never seen Sanchez look so sad in my entire life.

"Because regardless of what this turned into, it started out exactly how you think. And that's not fair to you. I like you. I never lied about that. I want to have sex with you. I never lied about that either. I want you to be mine. Another truth. I never lied to you. I just never told you about the bet because it stopped mattering the minute I met you." He shrugged. "Those are the things I want you to believe, but you're too angry to hear it, and right now . . . I'm too pissed to talk rationally."

"But—"

"Go." His voice was hoarse as he turned his back on me, marched down the hall, and literally broke a chair in two as he slammed it against the wall.

"There goes our season," someone muttered.

"So much for another championship." Another player eyed me with irritation and shuffled toward the locker room.

Someone must have restrained Sanchez because I heard fighting.

And then I was getting walked down the hall, outside to my car—Sanchez's car. I didn't even realize it was Miller instead of Kinsey until he wrapped an arm around me briefly before jerking it away.

Miller didn't say anything; he just started the car for me and cursed as I tried to get my seatbelt on. He leaned in, buckled it, and cursed again as more tears ran down my cheeks.

"You know . . ." He knelt right outside my door. "I know you. This isn't you. I don't recognize this broken person." He sighed. "When I first came here, I wanted nothing to do with you. Obviously that lasted a whole week before I realized I still . . . had feelings for you." He exhaled. "I knew about that stupid childish bet a lot of the players participate in. What you don't know is that the minute Sanchez saw you, I knew I never stood a fucking chance. God, I can still see the look on his face, this complete awestruck wonder. So, before you start blaming him and getting angry at me, think about the fact that he never lied—and that he's probably hurting just as much as you are."

"How can you say that?" I whispered. "I was used."

"Did he ever tell you it was more than what it was?"

"No, but—"

"Sanchez doesn't date. And yet, you've been going out with him for two months. Did he ever try sleeping with you? Pressuring you without your consent?"

"No," I whispered.

"Did he ever lie to get you into bed?"

"No."

"No man is that patient, especially when it comes to you, Em. Just think about it, alright?"

"Why aren't you cheering?" I gulped, addressing the elephant between us, the one neither of us talked about. "You're competitive, even if it comes to just the friendship between us."

"I want you, and yeah I want to be more than friends, I want to get that piece back, but not like this. And if I'm being honest, you never looked at me the way you look at him."

I glanced up with tear-filled eyes. "That's not true!"

His smile was sad. "Em, go home, get some rest, but talk to him, okay?"

I nodded and, fifteen minutes later, crawled into my bed, and cried myself to sleep.

Chapter Thirty-Two

MILLER

What a day from hell.

And we still had practice that next day, which meant that we were all supposed to get along as if nothing had happened with Thomas.

I got there early, hoping to talk to Sanchez, since, when he got home the night before, he'd said he just wanted to crash.

But he was already suited up and on the practice field. His back was to me as I approached him. He was watching the cheerleaders practice.

I didn't blame him.

"Remember that time you said that you would have never walked away? And that's what made us different?" I stood a foot away from him, not taking my eyes off the field as I clutched my helmet in my right hand.

"Yeah." He sighed.

"You're doing it by not going after her now, by not explaining yourself."

"It's called self-destructive behavior." Sanchez turned to me. "Trust me, I know what I'm doing. I just don't know how to make her listen, make her understand. And the sick part is that I know I don't really deserve her." He paused. "Neither of us do."

The girls were doing a dance routine, and Emerson was helping one of the girls with her moves. That's the thing about her. Screw her over, make fun of her, tell her she can't do something and she would always be the bigger person by helping out even if that same person was the one who took her clothes a few weeks ago and stashed them in the guys' locker room. It was something I had conveniently forgotten six years before, when I'd assumed she'd left me. "You got that right."

"But I want to be good enough for her. It wasn't even about sex. I mean at first it was, but now? Now, I just . . . I don't know, man. I think I'd die a happy man if she'd just hold my hand."

I swallowed the lump in my throat. "I know what messing up feels like. Don't be that guy, Sanchez. Six years ago, she had no second string—" I bumped him with my helmet. "And now she does. And like you said, it's about being in the game, so know this. I won't hesitate like I did then, not after all this shit."

"Are you challenging me right now?" The bastard was smiling.

"Well . . ." I shrugged. "If you aren't gonna man up, someone will."

He hung his head. "I fucked up."

"So don't take six years to make it right."

When he looked back at me, it wasn't with anger, but guilt—a hell of a lot of guilt. "She hasn't told you yet, has she?"

Chills spread down my arms. "Told me what?"

"The reason she called that day."

He knew?

Of course. He wasn't just the guy she was with. She'd replaced me with him, completely, in every way. She told him things.

"No. Part of me thinks the past needs to stay there."

"Agreed." This time his eyes flashed with anger. "Let's get this practice over with and figure out Sunday's game before I start turning into a chick and asking for more advice from the only guy who's ever slept with the girl I love."

The minute the words left his mouth, I stopped walking.

He froze, as if he couldn't believe the words that he had just blurted, and then shoved past me.

Love. He loved her.

Of course he did.

And then like a punch to the gut the rest of what he said registered like a neon sign.

The only guy she'd ever slept with—was me?

That wasn't right.

Six years?

Did I do that to her? Was it my fault? Had she been waiting? And did that mean they'd never slept together?

My respect for Sanchez grew.

And I wanted so badly to hate the little shit for it.

Instead, more respect happened.

Because he'd had her for two months—I'd seen the way she looked at him and the way he devoured her with his eyes. For sixty days, he hadn't slept with her.

And yet, when I knew I was leaving her, and we'd been only eighteen . . .

I'd taken that from her, granted, she could have said no. But I was grieving and it was Em—I took her virginity regardless of the situation, I was the one who initiated the sex.

I took her heart with me.

And selfishly had never given it back.

I stood there—I don't know how long   seconds, minutes. I stood and hated myself.

Because it really was clearer than I wanted it to be.

I'd been the stand-in.

Until Sanchez, the better man.

"Get your ass over here, Miller!" Jax yelled at me. "Champions don't stare at cheerleaders all day!"

"Or do they?" Sanchez asked the group, cracking the tension with ease.

I glanced one last time at Emerson across the field, only to see Kinsey staring back at us.

Back at me.

Glaring.

I jerked my head away as if I was in high school and then rolled my eyes at myself. *Good one, Miller.*

She didn't belong to me, not anymore. And for some reason, a part of me felt . . . better because of it. All this time I'd been thinking about myself, about wanting her because of the way we left things in the past, needing her, because I didn't know how to live without her and be happy. And selfishly thinking that Sanchez was a playboy man whore who didn't know what type of woman she was.

It was painful.

The realization that he'd been there for two months, sharing his life, earning her trust, gaining her love. And I'd been so worried about winning her that I hadn't even asked if her dad was okay.

Or why they were living in the apartment in the first place.

Because it had all been about me.

He was the better man.

She deserved a man like that.

I smiled through practice even though I got the shit beat out of me.

And when it was time to shower, it felt like a part of the past was finally righting itself. I just hoped nothing more happened. I wasn't sure I could live with more drama.

Chapter Thirty-Three

I felt his stare all through practice.

I needed to talk to him and stop being that girl who just ran off without letting the guy explain. Because everything Miller said was true, and I refused to let history replay itself. I wouldn't just ignore what my heart was saying in order to protect it from getting hurt again.

So after our night practice—where I made leaps and bounds with a few of the girls on the squad by offering to help with the new routine, I drove over to Sanchez's place.

And, like a total coward, I sat in the car for a good ten minutes before I finally walked to the elevator, pressed the penthouse button, and made my way to the top.

Loud music sounded from his apartment.

Yelling followed.

I knocked then let myself in.

Players were everywhere, none of them drinking, and a lot of the party girls I'd seen over the past few weekends were hanging on them, stars and dollar signs in their eyes.

Jax was in the kitchen staring at everyone like he normally did, like someone had elected him Dad and security at the same time.

"Hey, Jax." I bit my bottom lip. "Is Sanchez around?"

Jax looked guilty. "He's in his room, sleeping. It was my idea to have a party so the guys could let loose after everything yesterday. I promised him nobody would break shit."

"Ah . . ." I pointed at his glass. "That explains the water."

"We rarely drink during the season, you know that." He shrugged. "And for the record, Emerson, he's a really good guy. I have a little sister. I'm too protective to let you walk those few feet to his bedroom if I thought otherwise."

I swallowed the dryness in my throat. "Thanks, Jax."

"Anytime." He winked.

I made my way down the hall, palms sweaty. By the time I reached for the door to Sanchez's bedroom, I was ready to throw up from nerves. How could I ever have thought that he wasn't already part of my heart?

"Come on, Grant." A woman's voice sounded from his room. "Nobody has to know. We can just kiss, whatever."

"Go away." He didn't sound like himself. "Seriously."

"Aw, c'mon, you're too drunk to say no."

"Lily . . ."

I knocked then shoved the door open. Sanchez was lying in bed shirtless, and the one cheerleader that had turned him down before was smothering him with her boobs, sans shirt.

"Am I interrupting?" My voice cracked, I was ready to break her in half and then smack him in the face with her body.

Sanchez glanced up, but his vision looked off. He glanced between Lily and me and stumbled out of bed. At least he had pants on. "S-s not what this looks like."

"Or is it?" Lily laughed and wrapped her arms around his waist. "Come on, Grant, you can tell her all about us."

My waist. That was my waist she was hugging.

Tears threatened to fall.

"Aw, the fat girl's going to cry." Lily laughed. "Why would he ever want you when he could have this?"

I snorted. "At least I don't have to get him drunk to get him into bed, Lily."

She glared, her cheeks burned bright red.

"Get off me!" Sanchez stumbled even further from her. "Em, I swear . . ." He pinched the bridge of his nose and shook his head.

"Swear all you want honey," Lily stood on her feet, still topless. "You asked for it and I gave it."

I nodded as Sanchez lowered his head, like he was guilty, like he was ashamed. "You know what? Have at it." I stumbled backward, colliding with the door, and then started to run.

Sanchez called my name.

I ran out of his apartment and plowed right into Miller in the middle of the hall.

His door was open, so I made a quick decision and barged through the opening, slamming the door behind me.

I could hear yelling in the hall.

"Whoa!" Miller shouted. "What the hell, Sanchez? Are you drunk?"

"Nothing happened!" It sounded like they were fighting. "I swear!"

"Sleep it off, man." Miller's voice was harsh. "I was just on my way over. Get whatever skanks you have in that apartment the hell out and sleep it off. I'll talk to her."

"I love her."

I gasped, covering my face with my hands as fresh tears fell. Now? He had to choose this time in our lives to say he loved me?

"I know, man. I know." Miller's voice was closer.

And then Jax's voice joined in as the sound of footsteps neared.

I waited for Miller's door to open, and when it did, I started sobbing.

He caught me before I hit the ground, then picked me up like I weighed nothing and set me on the couch. He rocked me back and forth until all of my tears were dry. Until I wasn't sure I could cry anymore.

"What happened?" Miller finally asked.

I shuddered in his arms, the arms I would have killed to be in for the past six years—the ones that suddenly felt so wrong. So foreign.

Not the arms I wanted.

Not anymore.

"Lily was in his room. I mean I know he was drunk. He said no, I heard him, but she had her top off and then—" I cringed as fresh tears found their way down my cheeks. "She said—she said—" My stomach plummeted as a heavy weight pressed down on my chest. "—She said, *Is the fat girl gonna cry? Why would he be with you when he could be with me?*"

I sobbed harder, so angry at myself for letting some naked teammate I'd only known for a few months, who was notorious for trying to sleep with the players, get through my armor!

"Aw, baby girl." Miller hugged me and then gently pushed me away. "Do you really think a guy like Sanchez wants a skinny bitch with small tits who doesn't even know how to bake cookies?"

"Yes!" I sobbed. "No!" I was hurt, and not thinking clearly, and letting old insecurities attack. "Because it makes no sense. Just like *we* made no sense. It makes no sense! And at the same time, I know I should go kick her ass!"

"Yeah, you said *sense* already, and it's probably unfair to kick her ass if she's drunk and you're sober, plus I taught you how to fight," he teased, wiping my cheeks with his thumbs. "Look, she's just jealous because you're the only girl he's ever paid attention to, and everyone knows it. And . . ." He shifted uncomfortably. "I guess it's really no secret—our past—Jax knows, Kinsey knows, Thomas even found out after that first party. News like that spreads fast. There's a giant red target on your back, and that's on us. Not you."

I sniffed. "But—"

"Nope." He stood. "I'm not listening. You're beautiful. You've always been beautiful. Inside and out." He licked his lips. "And I'm glad that I'm not the only guy smart enough to realize that the inside and outside are that perfect. Even if he's an idiot at least half the time."

"Seventy-five percent." I laughed through my tears. "At least that much."

"Well, we are talking about Grant Sanchez."

"Such an idiot," I whispered. "I was going to talk with him, give him a chance to explain."

Miller swore. "Look, he's drunk off his ass. In fact, I've never seen him that drunk before. The guy could barely stand up. He never drinks during the season, which tells me one thing."

I swallowed my tears and looked away. "Oh yeah, what?"

"He's sad." Miller grabbed my chin and forced me to look at him. "Care to guess why?"

"Because . . ." I tried to look down.

Miller held my head firm. "Because?"

"Of me?" I guessed.

"Bingo." He released my face. "God knows I'd be drunk too if I lost you— Oh wait." His smile was warm, but sad. "I don't wish that on anyone, Em. I really don't."

"It was my fault too." I sighed. "I was angry. You may have moved, but the minute you didn't answer, the minute I believed your dad and the things he said, I accepted them because I was angry with you for leaving. And because, I think—well, obviously, I know—I was too insecure to believe that I had anything to offer you, other than—"

Miller froze. "What? Other than what?"

"I didn't want to be that girl," I whispered, and finally looked him in the eyes. He stood and paced in front of me. "The girl who got knocked up by her high school boyfriend, the one meant for greatness. I didn't want to be that girl, Miller."

Miller swayed on his feet and then grabbed the edge of the couch. "What are you saying, Em?"

We were having a stare down, both of our chests heaving with the effort to breathe.

I took a deep breath. "I was pregnant."

He closed his eyes. Then shook his head. Then collapsed onto the couch, hanging his head between his knees like he was going to pass out.

I kept talking, afraid that if I didn't blurt it all out, I never would.

"I found out eight weeks after you left. I thought I was just stressed, and then . . . then my dad took me to a doctor. I was sick, so sick, and it wasn't going away, you know? I took some tests. And I called you once I saw they were positive. I was in the parking lot. Your dad answered. You know the rest. The minute he hung up, I flung my phone out of the car, and it shattered. Just like my heart. I blamed you. I was so angry that my best friend was gone, that I was going to have to fight without you, but mainly upset that you broke your promise, Miller. You broke it." I realized I wasn't crying. And I wasn't sure why.

But Miller?

He was.

Silent tears ran down his face before he quickly rubbed them away and stalked toward me. "You should have done everything in your power to tell me, Em. My child? You were pregnant. You were—"

"I lost our baby," I whispered, "the next day."

He froze as more tears welled in his eyes.

"Maybe it was stress. Maybe I was too young. Maybe the baby just wasn't healthy. I don't know. By then, I knew you had your life, and I wasn't a part of it, not anymore."

"Em—" Miller's voice cracked. "I would have moved mountains for you and our child. You understand that, right?" He wiped his face and turned around. "How can you miss a life you never knew?"

"I wasn't sure if it was a boy or a girl, but it felt like a girl, you know? So, after everything happened, I gave her a name, and my dad and I set balloons free with her name on them in her memory."

"What's her name?" He didn't turn around. I could tell he was crying again.

"Adera." Saying the name didn't hurt as bad as it used to. But it still hurt.

When Miller's shoulders hunched, I wrapped my arms around him from behind and rested my head against his back as my tears slid onto his shirt.

"My mom's middle name." He sniffed.

"Yeah."

"She would have been beautiful."

"Like her dad."

"I'm so fucking sorry." He turned around and pulled me against him. "I had no idea. You went through that and your dad's illness all by yourself."

I froze. "Who told you?"

"Sanchez. We are friends, you know."

I sighed against his chest. "Yeah, I know. And yeah, I did."

"You have every right to hate me."

"No, I don't." I shook my head. "Miller, we were young. So damn young. We're still young." God, we were both only twenty-four!

"I know." He pressed the hair away from my face, tilted my chin up with his finger, and softly kissed my mouth. Then he pulled away.

"Good-bye," I whispered. "That was the goodbye kiss you never gave me."

"I was too afraid to." He nodded. "And maybe a bit of a selfish prick about taking everything from you and being too hurt not to look back."

"I'm sorry too." I felt hot from crying. "About everything. Not telling you . . ." I sniffled. "Sanchez . . ."

Miller smiled the first real smile since I'd launched myself into his apartment. "And yet, it feels right, doesn't it?"

"I want to lie. I want to cling to safety, Miller. You're my safe place. You've always been my safe place."

"Baby girl . . ." Miller cupped my face again. "I don't want to be your safe place. I want to be your adventure. I want to be your risk, not the fallback. I deserve that, and so do you."

My smile was watery. "He scares me."

"Love always should." He kissed the top of my forehead and separated us. "Em?"

"Yeah?" I looked up.

"Best friends again?"

Tears filled my eyes for a completely different reason as I launched myself into his arms and hugged him as tight as I could.

I was home.

"Yeah, Miller. Best friends."

"Love you."

"I love you too."

Chapter Thirty-Four

Sanchez

I woke up with a splitting headache. My mouth was dry as hell, and water was the only thing on my mind.

When I stumbled out to the kitchen, I noticed the entire place had been cleaned up from the party. I remembered having had one drink, which led to two, and then I'd started thinking about Emerson, which meant I'd grabbed a third, fourth— Hell, when had it even stopped?

I found a glass and filled it up with water to the brim, then chugged at least three glasses before I finally leaned against the countertop and tried to conjure up memories from the night before.

I'd stumbled to bed.

Jax had sent me there, the bastard.

I'd held my phone like a freaking child, waiting for Emerson to call.

Hating the weakness I had for her.

Almost as much as hating how much I loved her, because it made me feel weak, helpless—two words I rarely associated myself with.

I'd been in bed . . .

Lily.

I froze.

Lily had been in my room.

Lily wanted to have sex . . . I think. I'd denied her, pissed, and then . . .

"Shit!" I grabbed a pair of sweats, threw them on, and jerked open my door only to see Emerson standing there, hand poised to knock.

"You're here," I choked out.

"I'm here." Her eyes were red, cheeks puffy. And she was wearing a giant sweatshirt that sure as hell was not mine, if the name Miller stamped across it was any indication. "To be fair, I was next door."

Rage overtook me, but before I was able to do something else stupid and add to my stellar record for the last twenty-four hours, Miller opened his door, took one look at me, and said, "Don't be a jackass," before sending me a knowing smirk and hitting the elevator button. After he stepped in, he turned and nodded at Emerson and said, "You don't walk away from the girl, remember? Don't be that idiot. He sucks."

I was the guy who stayed.

I nodded jerkily at him as the doors closed and then stole a glance at Em.

She slowly wrapped her arms around me and then pulled back and held up a grocery bag.

I breathed her in with a shaky breath, my hands pressed against her shoulders, holding her there for a few seconds so my brain was able to actually tell my heart that it wasn't a figment of my imagination. She truly was standing in my doorway.

"I'm making breakfast. Go shower. You smell like whiskey and bad choices."

"You'll be here?" I found myself saying, like an insecure dick. "When I get out?"

"Yeah." She smiled. "I'm not going anywhere."

I backed up then stole another glance at her. Then like an idiot, did it again before finally walking into the restroom.

I got as far as brushing my teeth and making sure that I didn't look like shit, before I gripped the sink, huffed out a breath, then charged back into the kitchen.

"Grant—"

I devoured every word she was going to say.

Any sentence that would come next.

But I silenced her with my kiss.

My hands dug into her ass as I lifted Emerson onto the table and deepened the kiss. I wrapped her legs around me so I could get closer, because with Em, I was never close enough—and sometimes I wondered if I ever would be.

Tears collided with my lips.

I'd made that happen.

I'd hurt her.

I broke off the kiss. "Never again."

"Never again?" she repeated in confusion.

"I never want to make you cry again. But I know I will, because I'm a selfish jackass who has a fucking poster of his own face in his living room."

Her lips twitched.

"And I know I'm going to mess up. I don't want to, but narcissists tend to be fully aware of their own flaws."

"You aren't a narcissist."

"In high school, I referred to myself in the third person."

Her eyebrows shot up. "Yeah, I would have kicked your ass in high school."

"I would have deserved it." I cupped her face. "I deserve it now. I deserve a good ass kicking every day. It's why I'm a wide receiver." I grinned. "Em, I need you."

"I need you too."

"I won't be that guy." I kissed her again then pulled back. "The one that walks away, the one who gives you up to be the bigger person.

I will never be the bigger person, I'm too selfish for that. I know . . ." My voice cracked. Damn, this speech wasn't going how I wanted it to. "I know you guys have a past. But can you leave it there? So I can be your future?"

"Grant Sanchez, did you just propose to me?"

"You're such a smartass," I grumbled.

She threw her head back and laughed through her tears. "Come here." She hopped off the counter and grabbed my hand. I was afraid to speak as she continued tugging me toward my bedroom, and then, very slowly, stepped over the threshold. "You said I wasn't allowed in your bed—not until he was gone, right?"

"Right." My voice cracked again, revealing my weakness—her.

"Then . . ." She turned and faced me. "Here I am. What are you going to do?"

I fell to my knees in front of her as she ran her hands through my buzzed hair. "I'm going to love you."

"I thought you didn't make love? What's all this bad-boy talk about sex? Hmm?"

"I deserve that."

"Yup."

"Stop me before I make a bigger ass out of myself and cry, Em, because I want you so bad it hurts to breathe."

"Who knew you were so romantic?"

"I hide it well." I smirked up at her. "I believe you, about Miller, but just to make sure he's really out of here . . ." I stood and placed a hand on her chest and then tapped the side of her head. "And here . . ." I slowly tugged the sweatshirt off her body and tossed it in the corner. "I'm going to make sure you forget everything but my name."

"Oh yeah?" Her grin was huge, and her cheeks—damn those gorgeous cheeks—went pink for me like she was nervous about me touching her. And honestly, I was the one who was nervous. She was everything . . . and she was mine.

Em was wearing a simple black sports bra. I'd never seen anything so sexy in my entire life, because it was on her. Well that, and even though I loved her ass, her breasts were a close second, heavy for me, perfect for my hands.

"Grant?"

"You're saying my name." I grinned triumphantly.

Her eyes narrowed. "I'm not sure I like that smirk."

"What smirk?" I smiled harder. "This one? Right here? On my face? The one that says I'm going to have the best morning of my life and give you multiple orgasms while we wake up the neighbors? Don't worry about that smirk. It's kind of my thing."

I stalked toward her.

She backed up slowly.

"Making me chase my meal?" I tilted my head. "You know I'll catch you."

"So now I'm your meal?"

I licked my lips. "Every fucking inch of you."

"You swear a lot."

"You inspire it," I fired back. "Now . . ." I leaned toward her until she fell backward onto the bed. "I'm going to make you mine."

"I think . . ." She grabbed my sweatpants and tugged. "That I've always been yours. I just didn't realize it." Her face softened.

God, I loved this girl.

"You love me?" she whispered.

"Did I say that out loud?" I wondered.

"Yeah."

Her awe-stricken eyes filled with tears again, but this time they were the good kind—the only kind I wanted to cause, ones brought on by happiness, not idiocy and me being a dick, again.

She tugged my pants.

I shoved them to the floor and pressed a rough kiss to her mouth, followed by another and another. My mouth was desperate for hers, my body hungry to be inside her. I'd been hard for her for months, and now that I had her, I just wanted to consume her. But unfortunately I'd grown a conscience, and a heart.

And because it freaking pounded for her . . .

I backed away . . .

Took a deep breath and slowed down.

"What's wrong?" Em's eyes searched mine.

"Want you so bad," I whispered against her mouth, "that all I can think about is feeling you clench around me." I slid my hands down and gripped her thighs. "These spread for me, wide open, only to wrap around me so tight I forget my own name." I pressed my hands against her hips and drew in a deep breath as I kissed her again, my tongue invading her mouth, imagining what it would be like to finally pump into her—make her mine. Her fevered skin only amped the anticipation. I reached for her bra and tugged it over her head. "I want to suck you until you're spent, worship you until you're so exhausted you can't think straight, and then I want to do it over again." My rough hands cupped her breasts as I leaned over and sucked each nipple until she was panting my name.

I grasped her by the knees and eased them apart. My hand found her core. "You're already ready for me, hmm, Curves?"

"What can I say? You're good with your mouth," she teased.

"Compliments get you more orgasms."

"I think you have the sexiest mouth I've ever seen." Em leaned down and grabbed the back of my neck with her hand, pulling me until I was on top of her, my length pressed hard against her stomach, ready for her, already pulsing with anticipation.

She crushed a possessive kiss to my mouth then grabbed my head with both hands and parted her lips; her tongue snaked around mine like she was trying to hypnotize me with her mouth. I fought for dominance, and she fought right back.

My girl would fight back.

I slapped her on the ass when she stopped kissing.

And invaded her mouth over and over again.

The last time I'd kissed this much before sex was high school.

But with Em, if the kissing was this good, I was willing to wait for the sex, though my body was screaming at me.

Em gripped my length and pumped her hand twice.

With a growl, I shoved her hand away. "Baby, as good as that feels, the last thing we need is the guys somehow finding out that I couldn't make it all the way."

"Oh." There went those pink cheeks again.

"Love the way you blush for me." I jerked away the rest of her clothing and reached into my nightstand.

Her eyes widened a bit when I slid the condom on.

I waited.

Waited for her to panic.

Waited for her to say it was a mistake.

That I was a mistake.

That the past was more powerful than the future.

Instead, she leaned up on her knees and reached for me, wrapping her arms around my neck before pulling me down on top of her. She kissed me, drowning me with her scent and the way her mouth drugged me into submission, a guy who typically screwed and walked.

Her lips quivered beneath mine.

I kissed her harder.

I kissed away her memories.

I kissed away the hurt.

And I swore that I'd take all that pain—the pain she'd been carrying alone—and carry it for her.

My jaw clenched when I nudged into her and stopped, again waiting, waiting for something. Because girls like her weren't girls you pounded into and gave a high five afterward with a bottle of water and a signed T-shirt.

She was—everything.

"You okay?" I gritted my teeth as sweat slid down my cheek and onto her naked chest. I leaned down and licked across her breast.

She arched beneath me, pulling me farther in.

Making it harder for me to go slow.

Making it harder for me to not lose my mind.

I ached. I'd never been so tight—so hard, so ready.

"Grant."

I didn't realize I was closing my eyes until she said my name. I glanced down at her.

"I'm yours." She hooked her feet behind me and jerked me toward her.

I died.

I almost died in that bed.

Would have died, but my body had other plans as I gripped the headboard and tried not to pass out over the most gorgeous woman I'd ever met, with curves made for me.

With each thrust, a surge of ecstasy crossed her features.

"Grant!" She threw her head back against the pillow as I invaded more, beginning to move at a faster pace before suddenly remembering to slow down because I didn't want it to be over. It had to last forever.

I wanted to be fucking buried in that bed.

Still balls deep inside her.

She stretched for me, every slick movement better than the last as she gripped my biceps and cried out.

Panting, I started moving again, circling my hips, finding every spot she never knew existed. It was never like this. It had never been like this.

With a shudder, she locked eyes with me and bit down on her lip so hard it turned white.

"Get there, baby," I panted as another wave of pleasure hit me, making it impossible to hold back anymore.

Her mouth dropped open, and with a piercing scream, she fell back against the bed, her face completely blissed out. I followed with a climax so swift I couldn't help but add to the loudness factor. With one last slam into her, the bed smacked the wall, and I was kissing her again, my fingers grasping her hair, tugging pieces as I rode out the last of my orgasm still inside her.

Tongues fought, teeth knocked, and then she was rolling on top of me. I had more in me. I wanted more.

"One hour," I promised. "Give me one hour, same place, no clothes allowed." My chest heaved, and her hair splayed across my chest as she stared down at me and laughed.

"I think we put a hole in the wall." She pointed to the headboard.

"I'll buy a new wall." Yeah, I was still not in my right mind. She was naked, on top of me, and her breasts just wouldn't quit staring me down. So, I did what any sane man would do.

I licked them.

Sucked some more.

And went on to give my girl two more orgasms before my body was ready for round two.

"So . . ." I said a few hours later, noticing the bedroom looked like it had been hit by a hurricane, and we were the only survivors. "Are you going to move in or what?"

"That—" She slapped me on the chest so hard I coughed. "Was a horrible way to ask!"

"I'm a guy!" I said defensively.

She arched her eyebrow, crossed her arms over her chest, and then tugged a sheet across her naked body.

"No! Shit, don't do that. No clothes! No sheets, baby. We talked about this, come on . . ." She flung a pillow at my face, and I dodged it. "Hah! Missed—" The second one clipped my ear. Damn girl should have played baseball. "Em."

"Yes?" She tilted her head, arm raised with a third pillow. "What would you like to know, Sanchez?"

"Wow." I whistled. "So, my last name's somehow turned into a curse word. Nice." I took a deep breath. "Will you please . . ." She smirked. "Move into my apartment and share this amazingly comfortable ten-thousand-dollar bed with me?"

"Ten grand?"

"Is that a yes or a no?"

"For a bed?"

"Em?"

"But why?"

"Because I need sleep. Really, can we divert our attention back to the answer to the question?"

"But—"

"Em—" I growled. "Killing me, Curves."

She lifted her shoulder. "Yeah sure. Whatever. That works."

"Seriously!" I yelled.

Em tossed the pillow lightly in my face then dropped the sheet and put her hands on her hips. "Yes? Maybe?" Guilt washed over her face. "I have my dad to think about, I can talk to Connie and maybe figure something out, she can stay later, he does text well and—"

"Curves." I whispered her name. "You realize when I asked you to move in with me, it's with full knowledge that together we're going to figure out how to get your dad the best care he needs right?"

Tears filled her eyes. "That's not your job, you don't have to—"

"I know I don't. This is pure want. Besides, I've been doing research and, the point is . . . I want to take care of you. Let me."

She nodded. And then whispered. "Yes."

"I'm sorry. I was too busy thinking about all of the things I was going to do to you since the minute I stopped talking and your chest started heaving. Did you say yes? And does that mean I can make you scream again? Because I think it's a good thing Miller's not home right now."

"Probably why he left." She nodded.

It was silent.

Shit. I shouldn't have said his name.

"I'll always be friends with him." She crawled over and then straddled me with those gorgeous thighs. "But this bed, this ten-thousand-dollar bed— Crap, that's so much money—"

"Baby, focus."

She huffed. "This bed . . . is the one I'm going to be in. These arms . . ." She gripped my biceps. "These huge, golden, amazing arms . . . are the ones I'm going to be held in—"

I didn't let her finish.

I kissed her so hard I was afraid I was going to hurt her.

"Love you so much." I gripped her head and then laid her down next to me and started to show her again, just how much.

Chapter Thirty-Five

MILLER

I went to practice earlier than necessary. Mainly because I knew that once Sanchez and Em talked things out, I wouldn't want to be within a one-mile radius of whatever the hell sort of bedroom gymnastics they were going to be a part of.

I ran a few laps around the stadium and started to stretch, when some of the cheerleaders made their way onto the separate section of practice turf they typically took over either right before our practices or sometimes during.

Em wasn't there yet.

For months I'd been trying not to love her, trying not to want her, and now that I knew the truth about our friendship and about the way she felt for Sanchez, it just seemed so . . . normal.

The world hadn't ended.

The sky hadn't fallen.

My life wasn't over.

But the crack in my heart . . . it was still there, just not as painful since I'd talked with her, since we'd made our peace and I'd watched her walk away.

But it was there.

And it made me wonder if sometimes the greatest loss you ever feel is something that nobody will see when they look at you.

Because when your heart breaks, somehow it keeps beating.

Mine felt broken, but I knew it wasn't. I knew I was just feeling sorry for myself that while I had been her past . . .

He was her future.

We both deserved to move on.

I just didn't know how.

Because it sucked to finally realize I never had. I'd just lived in a constant state of anger and limbo when it came to Em, and now that I was released from all that shit, I didn't know what to do.

"Hey, stranger." Kinsey put her hands on her hips and stood by my side. "What exactly are we looking at?"

"Grass."

"Grass," she repeated. "How very interesting. And is there something about this grass that intrigues you? Or are you just having a moment?"

I smirked and ducked my head. "I'm having one of those moments guys get when they realize they're selfish tools."

"Don't worry." She patted my arm. "Jax has those every day."

"Well he's a guy so . . ."

"Right." Her bright-blue eyes blinked up at me with amusement. "Well, are you gonna cry now?"

"Hell no," I barked, and then I whispered. "Already did that last night."

She burst out laughing. "Ah, Miller, you win some . . . you lose some. I'm guessing this is one of those losing scenarios?"

"Honestly, Em's with the better man. I'm glad I got my best friend back, but sad we had to go through so much shit to get there."

She slapped me on the shoulder. "Think of it this way, Miller. There's more fish in the sea. I mean I'm not saying that from experience because a certain shark named Jax seems to be really talented at scaring them all away and I'm probably destined for a nunnery or a life with multiple cats, but yeah, Miller, loads of fish—tanks of fish. Besides, we live in Bellevue. Ocean's just over the ridge."

I stared down at her. "No fish at all?"

"Not even a minnow."

"Damn Jax."

"You have no idea. I have a plan to get him laid so that he'll stop locking me in my room."

"Wait." I frowned. "Back up. You live with him?"

"See?" She shrugged. "Hell. I live in hell, but he has a ninety-inch flat screen that I get to watch all the away games on so . . . I'm easy, what can I say?"

I nodded appreciatively. "Tough trade-off though."

"Know any single girls who can steal his virginity?"

I choked on my spit. "I'm sorry did you say—"

She made a face. "I mean I'm not sure, but he's so freaked out over people wanting him for his money and fame that he rarely lets them get close."

Jax took that unlucky moment to walk onto the field.

"Maybe even just foreplay." I shrugged. "Couldn't hurt."

"Even a boob, like one flash, maybe two."

"Three flashes. Always go for three, Kins."

Jax stopped stretching and stared at us. His eyes narrowed, and then it was as if the dude had discovered a cure for cancer, he grinned, rubbed his hands together triumphantly, and walked off.

"That look, right there. He had that look when he locked me in my room so my prom date couldn't find me."

"Dude does a lot of locking."

"I think he's under the impression that it will break my spirit."

I laughed. I couldn't help it.

It felt nice.

To know that I could still laugh and actually mean it, to know I could have an entire conversation and not once think about Em.

"I'll help," I found myself saying.

She grabbed my arm. "Shut up! Are you serious?"

I shrugged. "Eh, why not? I mean the guy's good-looking, rich, famous, and actually a legitimate human being. We'll find a fish for him, then find you something bigger than a minnow."

"Hah!" She elbowed me and looked up. I'd never noticed how pretty her eyes were, how crystal clear the blue was. "I tend to like bigger . . . fish." She swallowed and quickly looked away.

I stared at her like an idiot, with a grin probably twice as wide as necessary.

"Big fish, huh?"

"Just . . ." She waved me off, laughing. "Shut up."

"Hey, it's okay. I like big fish too, Kins!" She walked off and saluted me with her middle finger.

"Glad we're friends!" I called back.

She did a little twirl and blew me a kiss.

I dodged it and pointed at Jax.

She burst out laughing and skipped over to her brother and planted a giant kiss on his cheek, then pinched it.

He rolled his eyes.

And suddenly, as I stretched my hands over my head and continued doing my warm-ups, things didn't feel so bad.

Chapter Thirty-Six

Sanchez

I couldn't wipe the grin from my face. I hated that guy. The one who smugly puffed out his chest like he was the shit after a banging round of sex.

I clenched my fists; the leather of my gloves made a tightening noise as I rounded the corner and made my way onto the field. Em had already run the opposite direction after I'd slammed my mouth against hers in front of at least half my team. Staking my claim. Daring any of them to say shit against me for fraternizing with one of the sexiest cheerleaders I'd ever met. Mine, she was mine, and I sure as hell wasn't going to let anyone stand in the way of that—not even Miller.

I clenched my fists harder.

And worried that the look on his face would break me.

Because I knew that it could have easily been me, the guy whose fucking heart was split in two because he hadn't gotten the girl.

I took a deep breath and made my way toward Miller. Jax eyed me cautiously, but he didn't tell me to stop.

"So . . ." Miller didn't even need to look up to talk to me. What? He could smell her on me, or what? And why the hell did that make me so damn happy? "Are you going to wear that smug grin the entire practice, or are you at least going to let me punch you in the face and dirty you up a bit?"

I smirked harder. "You can try."

He glanced up, his eyes pensive. "You treat her good."

"She deserves better than my best, man."

He sighed, shoulders slumping. "God, you're so hard to hate when you say shit like that."

"I'm a very likeable guy. Ask anyone." I shrugged. "We good?"

"Is she crying anymore?" he asked.

"No." My expression went from smug to serious. "If she were crying, I'd ask you to punch me in the nuts and run me over with your SUV."

He laughed. "That idea really does have merit, but yeah, I think I'll pass on touching your nuts, man."

"How disappointing." I held out my hand.

He took it and stood.

Chest to chest.

Man to man.

The field was quiet.

And then Miller patted me twice on the back and gave me the most awkward hug I'd ever received in my entire life, before rolling his eyes and shoving me back so hard I nearly tripped over my own feet. "Don't fuck up."

"Not planning on it."

"Good."

"Hey, did we just have a moment?"

"Go to hell, Sanchez." He grinned.

I fell into step beside him as we walked toward Jax, who finally let out the breath he'd apparently been holding in.

"You girls done talking?"

"Yup," we said in agreement.

"Ready to get the shit beat out of you?"

"I better not." I pointed my helmet at Miller. "Come on, don't let me get hit, Miller. My face is too pretty for that."

"Not my job!" He put on his helmet.

Practice started with a hell of a hit midair as I caught one of Jax's insane torpedo passes.

"I think you bruised my spleen, asshole," I huffed when Xander helped me up and grinned.

"Yeah, well, I wanted to do a solid for Miller."

"Huh." I made a face. "So, nobody's Team Sanchez?"

"Did you just refer to yourself in the third person?" Miller frowned.

I burst out laughing.

Earning shocked looks from the O-line like I'd just grown two heads, but all I kept thinking about was Em's face and how she'd said she would have kicked my ass in high school. Yeah, I think my ass deserved kicking.

"What?" I glared at all the guys. "Can a dude not laugh up in here?"

"Two months ago, a dude laughed during practice, and you literally told him you were going to rip his head from his body if he didn't get his shit together," Elliot said in a calm voice. "So, you tell me."

"Is this what happens when you get laid, Sanchez?" This was from Jax.

I gave him a murderous look.

One shared by Miller.

"Oh hell!" Jax yelled. "Joking! I was joking!"

I grabbed Elliot. "Blitz his ass."

"Um, he's our QB."

"And I'm one of your captains. Blitz."

The play was called, but the bastard knew it was coming. He slid before he could get hit and then flipped me off from the ground. "Bastard!"

The entire team laughed.

Including Miller.

And that's how the rest of the practice went. Play after play, we worked our asses off and laughed our asses off.

It was the best practice I'd ever had.

Miller was on his game too.

Things felt right.

They felt good.

And that's when I panicked.

Because nothing in my life had ever felt that good before, which meant one thing. The other shoe was about to drop. I hoped to God it was on Jax's head and not mine.

Chapter Thirty-Seven

EMERSON

"Wow." Kinsey crossed her arms. "You didn't stop smiling the entire practice, even when Coach Kay did a surprise weigh-in at the end of all that conditioning." She paused. "Must have been . . . magical?"

I scowled to try to hide my smile and failed. "It was . . ." I sighed, trying to find the words. "Unexpected."

"Whoa there." She jogged to catch up with my stride as we made our way through the parking lot. "What do you mean unexpected? This is Grant Sanchez. One should expect greatness from that guy. I mean look at him."

Amazing timing as always. The guy was supermodel-gorgeous as he strode through the parking lot with Miller. Both of them were wearing sunglasses. Miller had a tight T-shirt on while Sanchez was wearing a leather jacket that hugged every part of his body in all the right places.

And his jeans . . .

Ripped in all the right places. They were probably illegal in most states, not that I cared. He was mine.

Mine.

"Stop sighing," Kins whispered under her breath. She tilted her head. "Then again . . ." She whistled. "Damn, those two together are completely lethal. I wonder if they'd be okay with a little ménage moment, nothing crazy, just, you know—"

I cupped my hand over her mouth.

She nodded as if to say, *Yup, I deserved that. Sorry.*

"Curves." Grant stopped in front of me and then scooped me into his arms and pressed a hard kiss to my mouth before setting me back down. "Afternoon."

"Well . . ." Kins fanned herself. "Where's my kiss, Miller? I think it's only fair every football player greet his cheerleaders with such adoration."

She was teasing, but something in Miller's face changed. I looked between the two of them, then elbowed Sanchez.

"Shit." He heaved. "Sorry, got hit a lot today. What? Why are you elbowing me?"

I slammed a hand over his mouth.

Kinsey yawned. "Alright, kiddos, we officially have one more day until game three of the season against—wait for it—" Sanchez did a midair drumroll. "The hated Pirates."

"Boo." Miller gave everyone a huge thumbs-down. "Patrick Hennesey can kiss my ass."

Sanchez gave him a high five. "If that kid buys one more exotic animal and tweets about it, I'm going to set him on fire."

"Graphic." Kins frowned. "Even for you, Sanchez."

"He has a tiger and a python he named after his dick. Kid needs to be taken down a few notches."

"Weird, I feel like there's someone in this group who has a picture of his naked body on—"

Sanchez silenced me with a kiss. "What was that?" he whispered.

"Nothing, totally . . . nothing."

"Sanchez, Miller!" Jax ran out into the parking lot. "Coach wants to see you both."

Grant froze next to me, while Miller gave him a worried look.

"It's fine," Kinsey said loudly. "Guys, you're adults. It's fine. I'm sure it's just about the game on Sunday."

"Right . . ." Sanchez repeated. "The game." He turned and kissed me on the head. "See you at home?"

"Yeah." I frowned. "Let me know if—"

"It's going to be fine," he assured me, but his look said he was worried, which in turn, had me worried enough to look to Miller for some sort of comfort.

Instead, he was pale, like they were going to get cut from the team or something, even though I knew that was completely ridiculous.

"Let's go." Kinsey locked arms with me. "I rode with Jax. Take me to your sex kingdom before he locks me in my castle again."

Sanchez frowned and pointed between us. "Sex kingdom?"

"Yeah, apparently, you don't suck in bed. Well done, Sanchez. Maybe one day they'll have trophies for that sort of thing, but for right now, I'm just going to give you a solid high five. Off you go!" She shoved him toward Miller, who was laughing behind his hand.

"It's going to be fine, right?" I watched them walk away, my stomach filled with dread with each step they took.

"I'm ninety-nine percent sure it's about game stuff." Kinsey frowned.

"And that one percent?"

She gulped and whispered. "You."

Chapter Thirty-Eight

MILLER

General Manager Jackson Mills was in Coach's office.

"Shit," Sanchez hissed beside me. "That's not a good sign."

"It could be nothing," I lied. I knew it was something. You didn't just pull in the GM for nothing. I knew we were too good to cut, so that meant they were pissed about something.

"Gentlemen . . ." Jackson pointed to the chairs. "Have a seat. This won't take long." The man was a silver fox, could make money in his sleep, and had five kids by way of his equally attractive Southern belle of a wife. I liked him—a lot. But from far away, not up close; it felt like I was getting called into the principal's office, only a hundred times worse.

Coach eyed us both and frowned. "You two getting along alright?"

"Yup." We both answered quickly and then chuckled.

"He's the best tight end in the league." Sanchez shrugged. "What the hell isn't there to like?"

"Oh . . ." Coach nodded. "So you're gonna play it that way, hmm, Sanchez? How about the fact that you're supposedly dating his ex-girlfriend—someone who also happens to cheer on the Bucks Squad."

Sanchez gulped.

I felt myself completely pale as I raised a shaky hand to my face and swiped my chin.

Jackson noticed my reaction. "This affecting the team, Miller? Because according to a disgruntled player, you guys have been at each other's throats for the past two months. We don't want a repeat of what happened last time you decided to get serious with a woman, do we?"

"Us?" Sanchez pointed between him and me, not missing a beat. "With all due respect, sir, we're professional athletes. Whatever shit was between us was not only handled off the field, but completely taken care of. I think my track record has proved that, I mean we have back-to-back championships." He leaned forward. "I'm assuming Thomas is the little shit that said something, which should tell you everything you need to know. He's pissed and trying to put the blame on drama that doesn't even exist, drama that a few years ago he helped initiate by sleeping with my fiancé. And yet I'm the one getting called in here, seems a little . . . dramatic, wouldn't you say, Miller?"

"Very." My voice was hollow, my heart thudded angrily against my chest. Sanchez didn't deserve this type of shit.

"Happy to hear it." Coach rubbed his hands together. "You satisfied?"

Jackson nodded. "For now."

"Great." I stood, thanking God that it hadn't gone worse, and had just made it out the door with Sanchez when Jackson called out.

"One more thing."

Sanchez gulped, lowering his head and cursing before turning around and flashing a smile. "Yeah?"

"The policy still stands." Jackson's eyebrows rose. "You play like shit, and the first thing to go is going to be the excess baggage."

Rage tore through me. I knew exactly what baggage he was talking about. I was seconds away from losing it when I saw a shift in Sanchez. He went from calm to completely murderous, like he was seconds away from charging both men and doing something that couldn't be undone.

I grabbed his arm, digging my fingers into his tense biceps. God, I could feel the rage pounding through his body because it matched mine perfectly. That son of a bitch!

It was a tie between which one of us was going to slip and rip the asshole's face off first, and I wanted dibs.

"Understood?" Jackson crossed his arms.

A muscle twitched in Sanchez's jaw. "Not really. No." He gritted his teeth. "I don't understand how my relationship with a girl I love off the field has anything to do with this team."

I sucked in a breath.

His nostrils flared as he continued. "Guess that means we better not suck—since it's my love life on the chopping block, yeah? I wonder how the media would react to that sob story. I'd hate to slip. God, can you imagine what Jacki would do if I gave her an exclusive?

Damn, the guy had balls of steel. I wasn't sure if I wanted to stand by his side or let him go up in flames on his own.

But hell, the respect I felt for him in that moment . . .

"Watch yourself." Jackson's eyes narrowed.

Sanchez visibly relaxed though I was still using every ounce of strength in my right hand to keep him from lunging forward and doing something that would get him kicked off the team. "I'm just saying . . ." He grinned toward Coach. "It was a good practice today. I think I smell another championship."

And just like that, the subject changed.

And we were back on even ground.

Jackson ran a hand through his silver hair. "You boys have done a good job so far."

"Just wait until Sunday." Sanchez nodded.

I let out a sigh. "Thanks for the talk, guys."

"Miller . . ." Jackson just wouldn't quit, would he? "You sure you want to take Sanchez's side on this? I'd hate to see something so unnecessary cause trouble with your spot on this team."

I laughed. I couldn't help it. "Really?"

It was his turn to look pissed.

"Maybe you don't get this because you aren't a player, but he's my brother. I bleed for him. I war for him. I die for him." I never realized how true my words were until they were out of my mouth. "So, hell yeah I'm standing by him. I'd be a bad team member if I didn't. Just like Jax is going to stand by him, and Elliot by Jax. That's what a team does. We win together. We lose together. Now . . ." I clenched my teeth. "Will that be all?"

Jackson's expression did a complete 180. "Good to hear it, Miller." His smile was wide, friendly. "That's the answer I was looking for."

"This is bullshit," Sanchez said under his breath. I could feel his arm sweating. Either that or it was my fingers.

"You're both dismissed." Jackson grinned wider.

When we made it out into the parking lot, Sanchez shook his head and glanced back at the building. "What the hell kind of Jedi mind training did we just get put through? Because if he refers to Em as excess baggage one more time, I'm going to prison."

"Honestly, I'm surprised you didn't jump over the desk and smash his face in," I admitted.

"I would have . . ." Sanchez shook his hands and snatched his keys out of his pocket. "Except some dick wouldn't let me."

"Hah." I rolled my eyes. "Next time I'll just let you kill your career, cool?"

"Did you mean all that shit?" He stared down at the keys in his hand then looked back up at me. "About bleeding? Warring?"

"Sanchez, if you hug me, I swear, I really will kill you."

He threw his head back and laughed and then did something completely unexpected.

The dick actually hugged me.

And I hugged him back.

"Now that . . ." He slapped me on the ass and ran. "Was a moment, Miller!"

"You little shit!"

He unlocked his car, jumped in and started it, then rolled down the window. "Seriously, though, thanks for helping me keep a cool head."

"Yeah well, I think we have a mutual girl who's counting on you."

His face softened. "Yeah, we do."

"Get out of here before you start crying, man," I teased.

He flipped me off and rolled up his window, and I smiled the entire way to my car.

Chapter Thirty-Nine

EMERSON

I ran to my house to grab more clothes and check on my dad. I also needed to grab my laptop so I could catch up on some schoolwork. Dad said he was doing well, but I felt guilty the minute his eyes lit up when he saw me.

I'd been spending almost all of my time either at practice, working, or with Sanchez. I'd been checking in on my dad every day, but I knew it wasn't as much as I normally did. The texts from Connie helped and Dad always texted me with updates on what he was doing, even if the texts were jumbled and didn't make sense.

I'd opened my mouth to apologize, but Dad spoke first. "I've been thinking."

"Oh?" I was almost out the door. "About what?"

"Maybe it's time you found your own place." He smiled, it was one of his old smiles, the ones that he used to give me before his illness.

And I wanted to cry.

He was having one of his good days. Which meant he knew how old I was, and that I lived with him because I couldn't bear for him to be on his own.

"I'll think about it," I lied. I was afraid it would upset him, set him back if I moved in with Sanchez. And as it was, he barely noticed I was gone during his episodes.

"Emerson." He full-named me. Shoot.

I turned on my heel and faced him. "Yes, Dad?"

"I'm proud of you. You realize that, right?"

"Dad." My throat closed. I could only nod and whisper. "Thank you."

"He treat you well?" he asked. "The guy that let me beat him at checkers?"

"He does." I smiled sheepishly. "He really does." My thoughts went into dangerous territory—love territory—a territory that Grant dominated in every way, amongst several others.

"I can see that." Dad kissed my forehead. "I want you to be happy, baby girl. And I think he makes you happy, I haven't seen you smile since . . ." His own smile fell. "Since, Miller Quinton."

For the first time in years, when my dad said his name—there was no ache. No longing. No anger. No pain at the loss of my best friend and my unborn baby. The memory of those feelings was there, but both Miller and Sanchez had helped me put back together all of the pieces that had once been burned, and breathed new life into them. Sanchez with his love and Miller with his friendship, something that I knew I would treasure the rest of my life.

"Miller and I are actually friends again." I don't know why it felt necessary to tell my dad things that I knew within minutes or hours he'd most likely forget, but he was such an important part of what happened with Miller that I felt it was unfair not to give him closure. "He's playing for the Bucks."

"The hell he is!" Dad grinned. "And things are good? Tell me everything!" And just like that, Dad's entire demeanor changed. "Does he start for the team? What are his stats?"

Ten minutes.

I was given ten minutes with the dad I knew.

The old dad.

The one who memorized football facts and beat me at fantasy football every year.

The dad who loved football almost as much as I did.

The dad who'd held me when I'd lost my baby.

The dad who told me that eventually things would be okay, that life would go on.

"I'm so damn proud," Dad finally said, "that you've fixed things between you . . ." A funny look flashed across his features. "You know, I like that Grant Sanchez though . . ."

I burst out laughing. "Yeah, me too, Dad, me too."

He chuckled and kissed my forehead then walked back to his recliner, grabbed a seat, and pressed power on the remote.

"Oh, and honey?" Dad called. "Don't stay out too late, remember you still have a curfew!"

And just like that the moment was gone.

But I didn't care.

Because I'd been given a gift.

Not only closure with Miller.

But closure for my dad, even if he never realized it, I had to believe that he needed it, that it made a difference, even if just for ten minutes of his life.

By the time I made it to the apartment, Sanchez's car was parked in its usual spot. I smiled to myself and made my way up the elevator. I'd just reached for the door when it jerked open, and I was lifted into the air by his massive hands and slammed against the nearest wall, his mouth silencing any protest I may have had.

Would it always be like this? So explosive? So perfect?

He grinded against me, already aroused, already ready.

I broke away from the kiss on a moan as he trailed more hot, wet kisses down the side of my neck, only to release my body just enough so I could slide down the wall.

"So perfect." He kissed my nose, then my forehead, before grabbing my T-shirt and pulling it over my head. The minute I tried to suck in a breath, his mouth was there again, teasing, plundering, making sure that every inch his tongue hit was fully explored, almost as if he was afraid he was going to miss out on some golden opportunity each time his mouth slanted over mine.

I hated how good he always tasted.

Because it was impossible not to respond to him.

And something told me that his meeting hadn't gone well, maybe it was in the rushed kissing, or the way his hands kept peeling off my clothes until I was standing in front of him almost completely naked.

He picked me up, tossed me over his shoulder, and walked into the living room. When he set me down, he was already making quick work of his own clothes before picking me up again and setting me on the piano.

My eyebrows shot up. "You play?"

"Hell yes, I play." He ducked his head.

I groaned. "So not what I meant."

"I'm gifted in all areas," he said gruffly. "Don't you think?"

I spread my legs for more of him.

With a hoarse curse he found my mouth again, and then he was tugging me to the very edge, until I was ready to fall off the expensive piece.

Instead, I fell onto him.

Or he fell into me.

Maybe, we just fell into each other.

With quick thrusts, he was already driving me crazy.

"Needed you, baby." His dizzying kisses made it impossible to keep up as his mouth met mine again and again. I couldn't think straight. Every inch of my body was on fire for him, holding him close, begging him to never stop.

Or maybe that was just my yelling. "Don't stop! Don't ever stop!"

"Not planning on it." He swallowed my cry and filled me to the hilt, staying there for a brief moment before moving again, and then cold air hit my butt as he walked us from the piano to the couch. He sat back, his eyes at half-mast as he shook his head and muttered, "Damn."

"What?"

I could feel him pulsing inside of me, and yet he didn't move. He was straining to, every muscle taut.

"What's that look?"

"Smug satisfaction." He stole another kiss before cupping my hips and forcing me to move on top of him. I'd never been secure being this naked—not even by myself, not really.

The lights were on.

And I was basically having the ride of my life.

On Grant Sanchez.

I wasn't sure if I should be horrified with my own behavior.

Or thankful that I felt his love so strongly that I didn't once think about the fat at my sides or the cellulite on my legs. Because he looked at me the way every girl deserves to be looked at.

Like he was the lucky one.

I fell in love a little bit more, not even realizing it was possible as I moved on top of him, giving him everything I had as his eyes rolled to the back of his head.

He clenched his jaw. "Killing me, baby."

I leaned over until the tip of my breasts grazed his chest. "Good."

"You'll pay for that, tease." He gripped my ass and drove into me so hard I saw stars—and felt my body explode on impact.

Chest heaving, he grinned. "Told ya."

"Cocky piece of work," I said lamely after laying my head against his warm bare chest.

"That's why you love me," he said confidently. "You'll always know where I stand because I don't have the censor to keep from talking good or bad. You'll always know, Curves."

I gulped. "So, does that mean the meeting went bad?"

He froze and then rubbed his hands down my arms. "Not exactly sure. All I know is this." He gripped my chin between his thumb and finger. "You're it for me. I know it's been two months. But I know. I just know. And I don't give a shit if the whole world knows too. I just . . . I guess I need to know if you're on the same page."

I slammed my mouth against his and then punched him in the arm.

"What?" He groaned. "Why? You know I got beat up today!"

"Oh, I'm sorry. Were the boys on the playground rude to you?" I teased.

"Sarcastic little—"

I covered his mouth with mine again then pulled back. "I'm here. With you." I wrapped my arms around his neck. "Grant Sanchez, I've got you." I sighed and placed a hand on his head. "Not just here, you dumb football player . . ."

He grinned.

"But here." I grabbed his hand and placed it on my heart. "Now any more stupid questions, or can I bake you cookies?"

He groaned. "Cookies then more sex?"

"You can't just have sex during all of your free time."

He pouted. "Who the hell says?"

"People who need sleep!" I crawled off him only to have him swat me in the ass.

"I love that ass," he whispered reverently. "Bend over for me?"

My cheeks burned bright red.

He laughed. "Ah, there it is. I needed that today, Curves. That blush that I know is only for me. Thanks for that."

"Sometimes I hate you." I crossed my arms over my body.

"Aw, Em, don't cover them up. What did I tell you? It causes cancer!"

"It does not!" The guy was unbelievable.

"I read it online." He nodded his head. "Bras bad. No bras, good."

"You're impossible."

"You love me." He stood. His body was so ripped I sucked in a breath and felt my cheeks heating again. "I know that look."

Without saying anything else, he turned me around and pushed me onto the ottoman. "And that, folks, is a view I'd kill for."

I opened my mouth to say something snappy but shut up the minute I felt the tip of him again. Ready for me, yearning.

I arched my back and glanced over my shoulder. "You were saying?"

His chest rose and fell so fast that I wondered if he was going to hyperventilate. "You're perfect for me. Made for me." He ran his hands down my back, then the back of his knuckles skimmed across the skin of my thighs before he locked eyes with me and said, "This okay?"

"More than okay."

"Thank God, because I don't know what I'd do if you denied me right now."

"Nothing to cry about, Sanchez." I winked.

And then couldn't help but shyly watch as he pressed into me and did what he did best. Love.

Chapter Forty

Sanchez

Game 3
Pirates vs. Bucks
Home Turf
Favored Team: Bellevue Bucks

I needed my mind in the right place, and Em had this uncanny ability to focus me where nobody else could. She was my center, my gravity. I worked through my warm-up routine and shoved jackass Jackson's words out of my head.

Focus, focus, focus.

I counted to ten.

Jumped twenty times.

Walked the field and listened to some Mozart—my secret, and one I knew I'd eventually confess to Em just because I didn't want anything between us. I knelt and felt the grass between my fingers, then the dirt. I counted the distance from the fifty-yard line to the goal on both sides.

And I envisioned every single catch I'd make.

Rachel Van Dyken

I thought about the Pirates' weaknesses and how to expose them and went through every route I knew Jax would call.

I was ready.

A half hour later, I was walking with Jax toward the middle of the field for the coin toss.

"Home team, Bucks. What's your call?"

"Tails." Jax always called tails. The last time he called heads we lost. It was his thing.

"Tails." The ref blew his whistle. "Kick or receive?"

"Receive," Jax said in a bored voice as we shook hands with the Pirates' captains. I could have sworn Hennesey had gotten a spray tan. Either that, or he'd been traveling and spending his millions like an idiot—again.

When we walked back, Jax mumbled under his breath. "Did that douche get a spray tan?"

"Exactly," I responded.

Special teams went out and did their thing. Johnson ran a good thirty-yard return, which always made me breathe a bit easier since Jax hated starting the game with a pass. He liked to pound the defense so they got tired before we started throwing. It was his way to avoid interceptions. He was paranoid, and even though people knew how he worked—how our team worked—they still had trouble beating us, so until it failed, we did it our way every time.

The first play was a fake to Miller. Jax ran in for a first down and slid before he got his head taken off by one of the lineman.

"Pussy!" someone from the Pirates yelled. Yeah, he's a pussy alright for not wanting to break his leg? Sometimes I hated football because of those guys, the ones who were too stupid to make sense.

"Coke Zero flag on two!" Jax clapped.

Basically, that meant I was up.

Once the ball was hiked, I ran like hell straight down the field, faked to a hard right, and waved for the pass.

284

I felt the defensive player coming for me, so it was either bail, or catch and tighten up.

I caught the ball and turned.

Right into another defensive player.

Slammed between two of them midair before I crumpled to the ground and saw spots.

I blinked, tried to stand up, then collapsed.

Miller was at my side immediately. "You okay?"

"Yeah." I shook my head. "Just a hard hit. I was a fucking cheese sandwich. I hate being the cheese."

Miller snorted out a laugh. "Don't we all?"

"Cheese smells," Jax added once he knew I was okay and not concussed. "Besides, I'd rather be—"

"Lettuce," Miller and I said in unison. "We know."

I stayed on the field for the next play, thankful that Jax was going to run it, but by the time we got to the third down, we'd only gone another fifteen yards.

We needed this point to set ourselves up.

Back in the huddle, Jax listened to his earpiece.

"Double Mountain Dew times two." He grinned up at Miller.

"Well shit." Miller sighed. "Let's do this."

The minute the play was called, I ran up to block while Jax threw a side pass to Miller and then made a run for it for the goal.

Miller threw the spiral so hard I winced when Jax caught it in the end zone.

Naturally, Miller was taken out by one of the defensive ends, but he was a big enough dude I knew he'd be okay.

"Touchdown Bucks!" the announcer called as the fake sound of fireworks and music erupted over the stadium.

We had it. I knew we had it.

I looked over to Em and winked.

It was a mistake to break concentration.

It was a mistake because suddenly I remembered I was playing a game.

It was a mistake because the minute I glanced back, one of the cameras panned to Emerson and put her on the big screen.

Yeah, I'd just put a giant target on her.

And I knew the media were going to be relentless afterward.

Especially Jacki.

Shit.

Chapter Forty-One

EMERSON

They won the next five straight games.

And even after I was shown on the big screen, nobody asked Sanchez questions about his love life.

It seemed like everything was finally settling.

The only thing I hated was his away games. It's not that I didn't trust him; it was just that I knew what went on when guys got together. And I knew that there were plenty of girls who wanted nothing more than to seduce the crap out of someone like Sanchez.

Visions of Lily always popped up then.

So, I'd have Kinsey over, we'd laugh about it, and I'd shake it off.

We were at Jax's place watching the guys annihilate the Jacksonville Tigers when I had a bad feeling. I couldn't explain it, other than when I talked to him on the phone, I'd felt like I was losing it. I just . . . I didn't want him to play. What kind of girlfriend was I? I even texted Miller to make sure that he watched out for Sanchez.

I knew the next play; Grant and I had kind of teased one another about how he knew my playbook so well it was about damn time I learned his. So I did, mostly because it turned him on, and I liked the dirty football talk it provided. Miller was supposed to get the ball, but there was double protection, and Sanchez was open.

Jax threw a prayer. It was a long shot.

Sanchez, being Sanchez, caught it, but not before getting hit so hard that his helmet flew off.

I screamed, covering my face with my hands.

He wasn't moving.

"He's not moving." I couldn't stop shaking. "Kinsey, he's not moving!"

"Calm down." She grabbed one of my hands. "Sometimes they tell the players not to move, especially if they're worried about a head injury."

"Okay." Tears filled my eyes. "He's okay, right? He's going to be okay?"

She was quiet. Too quiet.

Her face went from green to pale.

Something was wrong.

The camera zoomed in. He was blinking, swallowing. The other team was on one knee, and Miller and Jax were hovered over him.

I started to hyperventilate.

"No, no, just breathe, in and out. There you go." Kinsey rubbed my arm while we waited for information from the announcer.

"Folks . . ." He sighed. "I'm getting news from downstairs that Grant Sanchez is being taken to the hospital for a possible spine injury."

It would be the end of his career.

The end of his life.

The end of everything.

"Please God, no," I whispered. "Please, no."

They cut to commercial. I was already grabbing my laptop and booking a ticket when my phone rang.

It was Miller.

"Get your ass down here now." He didn't sound like himself. "Em, I'm so fucking sorry. I didn't—I should have been open. I'm so—"

"No." I heaved out a sob. "It's not your fault, Miller. It's not, okay?"

"My agent's going to call you with all the details of your flight. I'm taking care of it. Bring Kins with you. They're sending the jet."

The phone fell out of my hands.

Kinsey's face went pale. "Did he say—"

"They're sending the jet," I whispered.

"Oh, Em." Tears filled her eyes as she wrapped her arms around me and held me while I cried.

It was like moving through sand. I tried to pack but couldn't even focus on what socks to bring. He could be dying, and all I could think about were stupid socks and if they matched and . . .

I broke down too many times to function.

I always wondered what could be worse. After losing Miller, losing our unborn child. What could possibly be worse? How could the human heart handle any more pain?

I finally knew.

I really did.

This. This was worse. Knowing that the love of your life is hundreds of miles away without you—possibly breathing his last breath—and there wasn't a damn thing you could do about it but pray.

It was worse.

So much worse.

"The car's here, Em." Kinsey grabbed my arm. "Let's go."

Miller texted me updates throughout our flight. The guys won the game, and I couldn't care less. I just wanted to feel Grant's arms around me. I wanted to hear his laugh. I wanted to walk into that room and see him sitting up with a stupid grin on his cocky face.

I wanted more than I deserved.

It hurt so bad that I thought I was going to be sick.

After the car picked us up from the airport, the entire ride was tense, and Kinsey never let go of my hand. When I got to the actual lobby of the hospital, Bucks players were littered everywhere, most of them pale, dirty from the game, still in uniform.

Miller breathed a sigh of relief when he saw me. "Em!"

I ran into his arms and sobbed uncontrollably while he rubbed my back.

"Shhh . . ." He held me tight. His uniform rubbed against my skin. "It's going to be okay. I know it."

"How—" I cried. "How do you know?"

"Because . . ." He kissed the top of my head. "He's a cocky bastard. He wouldn't let a hit get him down, right?"

He was trying to make me feel better. But I knew there was only one reason they would send the jet for me.

One reason.

It was in all of their contracts when they were in a relationship.

If there was a chance they could die, they sent the jet.

If they were already dead, they sent the jet.

If they were breathing their last breath, they sent the jet.

I couldn't stop thinking about it. I was afraid to even say it out loud, so I waited, sandwiched between Miller and Kinsey, waited for something—anything.

No news was good news. I had to believe it. Right?

From what Miller said they were worried about damage to his spinal cord, possibly paralyzed from the neck down, broken neck, or a coma.

All bad things, very bad things.

"It could be a sprain too," Kinsey piped up. "I studied sports medicine, and I know I'm not a doctor, but sprains can shock the body that way. I'm just . . . Don't give up hope, okay, guys?"

I nodded.

The doctor walked in, his expression grim.

I don't even remember falling to my knees, only that Miller caught me before I passed out onto the floor.

Chapter Forty-Two

MILLER

If I could take his place, I would. And I meant it.

To see my best friend utterly destroyed . . .

I would rather die.

I would rather be dead.

I held her tight. I made him promises I knew I would die to keep. And I prayed . . .

To a God who never listened when I asked for my mom to come back.

To a God who never listened when my dad turned into an alcoholic.

To a God who ignored me when I cried over losing Em.

You owe me, I thought angrily.

And I could have sworn I heard a voice say, "Trust me."

Chapter Forty-Three

SANCHEZ

I dreamt of her lips—they were hot, then cold against my burning skin. Each time I saw her face, I tried reaching for her but couldn't feel anything, not even her mouth when she touched mine. It was torture. And then the dream would end and blackness would consume me again.

It was either the worst nightmare ever . . .

Or I was dead.

I think I'd choose death over constantly dreaming of a woman I couldn't touch, couldn't kiss, couldn't taste.

"Grant?" her voice called to me.

I opened my mouth.

Parted my lips.

"Grant!" The voice was stronger. God, I wanted to reach out and touch the voice. "Open your eyes."

I was trying.

I felt my wrist move and then my fingers.

"He's moving!" Miller yelled.

Why the hell was Miller in my dream? Stay the hell out, man! I was having a moment with my girl! Could have sworn she was going to take off her shirt.

I smirked.

"Why is that bastard smiling?" Miller said out loud. "Swear, if he's faking this, I'm going to punch him in the dick."

I tried to laugh.

It came out like a muffled mewling sound that sure as hell wasn't coming from me, was it?

"Grant." I smelled her, my girl, my Curves, and then she touched my hands, my face. "Please, baby, open your eyes."

Come on, man, easy! Just open! I concentrated so hard I felt like I was getting a headache and then, suddenly, they popped open.

Miller jumped backward. "Seriously? Could you not do that a bit slower as to not scare the shit out of me?"

"I don't do things slow," I rasped. "Only fast."

He looked like hell, still in uniform. More dirt was on him than on the field. I was sure of it. "You look like shit."

His eyebrows shot up. "You clearly haven't seen yourself."

I winced. "What happened?"

Em burst into tears and didn't stop crying for at least ten minutes.

My heart shattered into a million pieces as I reached for her and held her as close as I could with all the monitors and cords hooked up to me.

"You thought it would be super fun to play football without a helmet," Miller said. "And someone literally nearly took your head off."

"Severe sprain." A man in blue scrubs walked in. "Which is odd, since I was ready to pronounce you dead the minute you were rolled in here."

"Fuck! Can I please have a doctor with a better bedside manner?" I growled.

"It's true." Em sniffled. "I mean I didn't know it until the nurse came running out to tell the doctor you were moving, but—"

"Basically . . ." The doctor interrupted softly. "You're either very lucky, or the Big Man upstairs doesn't want your arrogant ass taking up space in heaven, at least not yet."

"Aw, he said I was going to heaven." I grinned. "See? That's better, Doc."

Em punched me in the shoulder. "Of course you would! You're, you're—" She shook her head as more tears ran down her face.

"Baby, I was kidding. I'm sorry." I held her cheeks between my hands and pressed a kiss to her forehead.

Miller stared at us in wonderment.

"You okay, man?" I asked.

"Yeah." He frowned then scratched his head. "Never mind. I just . . ." He grinned down at the floor then looked up at the ceiling, tears filling his eyes. "I think I had one of those moments."

"By yourself?" I asked.

"Kind of," he said, vague as hell. "Try not to die next time you get hit, alright, man? I'm going to give you some time alone."

My annoying doctor kept writing shit on a clipboard. I stared him down; he stared right back.

With a sigh, I waited.

"You can't move too much, and we need to run more tests, but it looks like you'll make a full recovery. Clearly, you won't be in the play-offs this year, but if you look good after three weeks . . ." He shrugged. "And if your team beats ours . . ." Another grin. "You may be able to play in the championship."

"Thanks, Doc." I was just happy I wasn't dead like he seemed to hope, the bastard.

"Anytime." He nodded. "I'll give you two a minute alone."

Em sniffled and then pressed her face against my chest. "They sent the jet."

"Fuck." Tears filled my eyes. I tried to keep them back, but they fell anyway. "I'm so damn sorry, baby. I'm so sorry." I held her so tight my knuckles turned white. "So sorry."

"I thought you were dead," she whispered. "I can't . . ." She gripped my face with both hands. "You suck so bad!" She smacked me lightly with one of her hands then kissed me. "You made me love you so much, and now . . . now I can't, Grant. I can't live without you. I can't. I wouldn't be able to do it."

"I don't want you to have to, but you'd be fine," I said soothingly. "You're strong."

"You make me stronger." She sniffed. "Braver." She kissed my cheek. "You make me all the things I wish I was. You complete me, you cocky jerk, and I wish I could walk away because it does hurt, so damn much, but I'm not that girl either."

"What girl?" I asked as something huge lodged in my throat, making it impossible to breathe.

"I'm not the type of girl who walks away," she said softly. "I'm the girl that stays."

Yeah, those tears were suckers from hell, but they just kept filling up my eyes like they belonged there, dirty bastards.

"So even though it hurts, I'm staying. Even though I'm afraid, I'm staying, because you make me brave. And I love you so much that I can't breathe without you."

I was too choked up to say anything other than what my heart was screaming for. "Marry me."

She blinked and then shook her head. "What?"

"Me. Marry me." I kissed her roughly across the mouth. "Not now, I have to look badass, and Grant Sanchez does not look badass in a hospital gown."

She smacked my stomach. "You third-personed yourself in your marriage proposal, you asshole!"

"I wanted you to laugh," I said honestly. "Marry me, Curves. I've always wanted to marry my best friend."

"You forced that friendship, and you know it."

"You needed it, and you know it."

She nodded as more tears fell across her cheeks. "I hate it when you're right. You're impossible to live with, you know."

"Baby, it's because I have all the answers."

She rolled her eyes.

"Is that a yes?"

"On one condition." She pressed a finger to my lips. "I want my ring to cost more than that stupid bed . . ."

I sucked her finger into my mouth and swirled my tongue around it. "Done."

"And the piano."

I sighed. "Baby, I'm not made of money."

She tilted her head. She knew my net worth. It's not like I hid shit from my girl.

"Yeah okay, I'm made of money." I shrugged. "That better not be why you've been letting me take you on the kitchen counter and eat off—"

Someone coughed.

Poor Kinsey was standing there with red ears and cheeks.

"Sorry." She waved. "I was afraid of the end of that sentence."

"I think we all were," Miller said next to her, his arms crossed. "Sanchez, why do you gotta be such a crude little shit?"

"It's in my blood," I answered honestly. "And my girl likes it."

Miller rolled his eyes. "Kins wanted to make sure you were breathing, but I think I speak for all of us when I say I'm going to escort her out of here before you two start ripping each other's clothes off." He saluted us and wrapped an arm around Kinsey before shutting the door behind them.

"What do you say? A little hospital memory?" I wasn't above begging.

"The doctor said— "

"The doctor thought I was dead. Do we really trust this doctor?" I moved a hand to her right breast and squeezed.

She shivered. "Just . . . okay, fine, but just . . . you need to be still."

"Holy shit, I think I'm in heaven. Are you just going to pleasure me until I pass out? I'm down for it, just let me hydrate first."

She pointed to the IV bag and shrugged. "You're good to go. Now, where do I go first?"

I put my hands behind my head and sighed. "Everywhere."

"Slave driver."

"Remind me to get rope later, a bit of masking tape—"

She silenced me with her mouth, nearly sending me bucking off the bed. I was done laughing and though I couldn't move much—

Yeah, I was in heaven.

Epilogue

MILLER

Post-Championship Party
Las Vegas Aria Penthouse
3:00 a.m.

I woke up to a pounding between my eyes that felt like someone had taken a jackhammer to my nose and pounded for hours. Wincing, I tried to move and felt so nauseous that I froze.

I never partied during the season.

Which meant, since we'd won the championship, the guys and I along with all of our friends had decided we needed to go big.

Party in Vegas!

We took flights down the night after the win and had been drinking ever since.

Emerson warned us.

Kinsey warned us.

Hey, guys, they'd said in those irritating voices. *Remember, you haven't been drinking, so you can't drink as much and not get hungover.*

Yeah, that hadn't gone over well.

We drank more to prove them wrong.

Though, Sanchez had stopped because he wanted to be able to perform sexually. But when he said *sexually*, I could have sworn he'd added in a few extra x's and nearly stumbled into the wall.

The room finally stopped spinning. I reached for the bottle of water on my nightstand and made the slow progression of getting up to go get some Advil. Our penthouse had three bedrooms, but poor Kinsey got the couch, since Jax was paying for her, and he'd taken one of the rooms for himself.

I quietly walked out to the living room so I wouldn't wake her, dug around for some ibuprofen, popped five, then tripped over a trash can.

I winced; now my head and my foot hurt.

But no movement from the couch.

The hell?

She wasn't even on the couch.

Oh hell, Jax wasn't going to like that. I should at least text her to get her ass back to the room so she didn't get locked somewhere again.

I walked back to my nightstand and grabbed my phone, only to see movement in the bed.

What.

The.

Hell.

A feminine arm poked out from underneath the duvet, and then the woman turned on her side.

I couldn't make out her features.

Who the hell had I slept with?

Panicked, I switched on the flashlight on my phone.

And locked eyes with Kinsey.

"Are you seriously pointing a flashlight at me right now?" She hissed, "Turn that shit off, Miller! I'm trying to—" She clutched the sheet and jerked to attention, grabbing her head and then the sheet before it fell down. "No. Nope. No. No. NO!"

I slammed a hand over her mouth. "Do you want to wake up Jax?"

She shook her head.

I looked down.

Yup. Naked.

I licked my lips while she ducked her head under the sheet, cursing so loudly I almost shushed her again, and then she took a deep breath. "What happened?"

"Seriously?" I threw my hands in the air. "Don't you think I'd look a little less panicked if I knew?"

Her eyes fell to my cock.

"That . . ." I pointed. "Is because— Stop staring, Kins, seriously."

"Did that thing—"

"And don't call it a thing! Shit, you don't do that to a guy!"

"But—"

I slammed a pillow over her face. "Better?"

She nodded.

"Ready to talk with your inside voice?"

Another nod.

"Let's just . . . go back to sleep and deal with it in the morning."

"Okay." She breathed a sigh of relief and slid back under the covers.

"What the hell are you doing?"

She flopped on her side. "You said to sleep on it!"

"You sleep on the couch. I sleep here."

"Oh hell no." She smacked my arm. "The couch hurts my back!"

"I'm literally four times your size!" I snapped.

"Guys!" Emerson made her way into my room. "Why is there so much yell—"

Her grin was so wide I wanted to suffocate her with a pillow.

"So . . ." She put her hands on her hips. "This is fun."

"Swear on your life, Em—"

"Baby, where's the Advil— Oh hello." Sanchez leaned against the wall while Kinsey covered her head with a sheet. "A little midnight rendezvous?"

"I hate football players," Kinsey said underneath the sheet.

"And yet, it seems you let one touch your special place," Sanchez just had to say, the ass. "Imagine that. Should I get Jax?"

"Don't you dare!" Emerson smacked him in the stomach. "He'd kill Miller! We need him next season!'

"Thanks, Em." I nodded. "Glad that's your only reason. See if I ever get you a Christmas present again."

"What?" She shrugged.

Sanchez let out a moan. "Oh, by the way, since I was too drunk to perform, I have a bet that you didn't either, my man, so I wouldn't worry about it, but I am curious how little Kinsey ended up making her way into your room after we all got back."

Kinsey didn't say anything.

"Alright then." Em grabbed Sanchez. "Water, go. Leave them to argue it out . . ."

"I'm tired," I said once they were gone and the light was off again.

"Me too." I could hear her yawn.

"Just . . ." I stacked pillows between us. "Stay on your side."

"Okay, middle school." She snorted. "Wouldn't want to get cooties."

"God, you're annoying right now." I tossed the pillows to the ground and smacked the one under my arm, fluffing it.

"That's not how you fluff." She turned around so fast her face smacked into my chest, and then she was fluffing my pillow and lying back down, only this time she was facing me.

"It would have been a mistake, you know," I whispered.

"Yeah." Her voice was barely a whisper. "Huge mistake."

"Giant."

"Enormous," I agreed.

And then I was kissing her, my friend's little sister. I knew what might happen next, but once I had a taste . . .

There was no going back.

One choice . . .

That I had no idea would affect my life forever.

One girl.

Let that be a lesson. Where one door closes, a freaking garage door opens.

"Our secret," she whispered between kisses.

"Our secret," I agreed.

I lied.

Her eyes said the same.

Acknowledgments

I'm so thankful to God that I'm able to wake up every morning and live this incredible dream—my road started with being a children's counselor to somehow writing romance and I wouldn't change a thing. If anything, I've learned that the road always leads, you just have to follow it, and sometimes that's a really scary thing. Thank you to my savior Jesus Christ for so many things that it would take years to list.

My husband and Thor (the totally awesome toddler who's more like his daddy every day—especially with that whole fruit snack situation). You are my BOYS and I love you dearly. It's like wearing my heart on the outside of my body and then trying to protect it while said heart runs into walls and jumps off cliffs . . . I'm probably already gray, I just don't know about it because my hair stylist keeps letting me dye my hair purple, which brings me to my hair stylist, Jake, thanks dude, for always lying to me about the true color of my hair and constantly giving me a thumbs-up when I ask if blonde is my natural color.

Beta readers! Kristin (best sister ever), Liza, Jill, I even had Jen and Jessica in on this one and it was so much fun to have all of your feedback. You do realize I only listen to the positive right? HAH kidding, I feel like I listen to negative more than anything because I know it helps me get better, so thank you for your honesty when things didn't work and for letting me know when a certain scene rocked it! I swear I only went through ten bottles of wine the ENTIRE TIME, just kidding ;)

It was twelve.

Moving on . . .

Jill, you kept me sane, like actually sane, through this release and through the past few ones where I was ready to lose my mind. Thank you for slapping me that one time when I got out of line, kidding. Really though, you treat your authors like gold and do such a great job!

Rockin' Readers (best fan group ever because let's be honest it's more like family), you guys are so incredible, thank you for your constant support and encouragement.

Rock Stars of Romance, Lisa, thank you for yet another great tour and release day blitz, I love working with you guys! To other blogs on this tour, ones who messaged me, signed up, who actually read the book and liked it (even those who didn't), thank you for taking time to actually do it, I know how time consuming it can be and how demanding. I so appreciate it and am so blessed by you guys!

If you want to stay in contact follow me on Insta @RachVD or you can join my totally awesome group on Facebook, Rachel's New Rockin' Readers. To be kept up to date on future releases and all the stuff in between just text MAFIA to 66866 to be added to my newsletter!

HUGS!

RVD

About the Author

Photo © 2014 Lauren Watson Perry, Perrywinkle Photography

Whether they're Regency romance or sexy New Adult fiction, Rachel Van Dyken's novels have appeared on national bestseller lists, including the *New York Times*, the *Wall Street Journal*, and *USA Today*. She writes—a *lot*—but makes sure she takes time to enjoy the finer things in life, like strong coffee, watching *The Bachelor*, and dreaming up hot new hunks.

Rachel may get way too excited about the little things, but she loves the important things in life too—like living in Idaho with her husband, son, and two boxers. Follow her writing journey at www.RachelVanDykenAuthor.com and www.facebook.com/rachelvandyken.